THE KNIGHT PROPER

THE KNIGHT PROPER

Adam Greven & Matt Deller

This is a work of fiction. Names, characters, organizations, places, events, and incidents are either products of the authors' imaginations or are used fictitiously.

Published by Quill, an imprint of Inkshares, Inc.,
San Francisco, California
www.inkshares.com

Cover design by Sinisa Poznanovic
Cover art by Brian Garabrant

ISBN: 9781942645269
e-ISBN: 9781942645276
Library of Congress Control Number: 2016940279

First edition

Printed in the United States of America

To my family: Paul, Lynn, Ian, and Caralie
To Evelyn, Matthew, and Elizabeth,
for the inspiration you give me each and every day

PROLOGUE

Sit closer, my friends and, yes, please do have another drink, won't you? Let me twist your thoughts for a moment or two, for I've a tale to tell . . .

The night was old.

Burdened with the weight of all the silent hours just before sunrise, its heavy black air hung over a cemetery road tarnished by a thousand thunderstorms. A great bolt of lightning ushered yet another tempest in, a rumbling boom of thunder following in its wake. And as white heat split the air, shadows took shape and form, revealing a small tribe of women running for their very lives. Hidden under heavy grey patchworks of frayed cloth with dark locks of hair sliding out from under their hoods.

A tale of the Trauergast . . .

Up the winding cemetery road they ran, chased by a score of hulking knights, their banging steel and angry shouts ringing out over the storm's thunderous din.

. . . and their relentless adversaries, the Konig Protectorate.

As the cloaked figures pushed through the stiff mud, a towering archway of rusted iron and weathered stone loomed before them . . . the entrance to the vast graveyard that lay just beyond. They seemed emboldened by this, a surge of energy in their desperate steps, while their pursuers momentarily blanched with fear before continuing the chase.

A tale of a witch . . . and her knight in tarnished armor.

Amid the steady downpour, the hood of one witch was thrown back by the rush of her flight, revealing exotic, slender features—a dark beauty in every sense of the word. Her eyes, normally given to warmth and comfort, were now seized with panic and despair. A steel-plated glove came down on her shoulder—one of the armored brutes had finally caught up to her, but Evelina's anxiety eased when she realized who it was.

Young and bold, his face split with cuts and burdened with bruises, the knight known as Edwin gave her a quick nod of assurance. She offered a hopeless smile in return as they both looked down to the precocious little girl holding tightly to Edwin's mailed hand. Clutching likewise at a tattered doll dressed in grey rags, little Mela was the mirror image of Evelina, sharing the same complexion and wistful locks of long dark hair. But she also had Edwin's steely grey eyes, a gaze that spoke of an inner strength, of a resolve before her time.

***

Just ahead, two witches finally reached the towering gate of the cemetery and stumbled across its threshold. One bore the hard lines of old age, wrinkles cutting deeply across her flesh as she looked back to see the knights still in pursuit. The other witch was just shy of womanhood, relief upon her face as she nearly threw herself atop the cemetery's ragged soil.

In haste, the two of them closed their eyes and breathed in the decrepit tombstones, the leafless, dead trees, holding their hands out as if they were basking in the warmth of an open fire. A sliver of fog rose from the ground and pooled around their feet, circling up and around their bodies, until it engulfed them in a column of milky-white mist laced with faint blue sparks. Without warning, it imploded with a sudden pop . . . and then they were gone.

Their powers, drawn from cemeteries and graveyards, absorbed the sadness, the melancholy of such places, the bleak thoughts and the spent tears, wielding it to their own mysterious ends. Yet they were peaceful beings, wishing only to be left alone in their crypts, their burial grounds . . . forever tending to the dead for a coin or two.

***

Another graveyard, this one choked with wild grass and not a cloud in sight. Silver moonlight illuminated a freshly dug grave that waited to receive the linen-wrapped body lying just beside it. Gently tending to the body were more witches, garbed in their grey cloaks, crowned with their telltale locks of dark hair. A young family stood nearby, dabbing their red teary eyes, grateful for the benediction their loved one was receiving.

The witches methodically toiled away, dusting the linen free of dirt, chanting softly over the shroud, until a faint crackle of eldritch power captured their attention. They stood, surprised to see dual shafts of fog spiraling upward in the distance . . . finally revealing the old woman and her counterpart. The two women immediately embraced each other, a deluge of tears streaming down their cheeks as they acknowledged their narrow escape.

***

More witches straggled past the threshold of the cemetery's vaunted gates, finally able to call upon their powers. Multiple columns of fog rushed up from the ground to then implode into nothingness. One witch struggled to keep pace with the sisters ahead of her, gasping for breath; a crossbow bolt slammed into her shoulder. The impact rent flesh and crushed bone, sending her tumbling forward, as a second bolt quickly finished the job. The knights were gaining. Another witch slipped in the mud, just behind Mela and her parents.

They looked back, only to see a knight cut the woman down, silencing her scream with one brutal blow. Mela simply stared, unable to process what was happening as the towering knight wrenched his sword from the woman's corpse. Edwin turned Mela back around and jolted her forward, placing her tiny hand into Evelina's. Mela looked up to see the two of them speak without words, an imitable sadness in her parents' eyes as Edwin stayed behind. But sadness soon turned into icy resolution as he drew his sword, the long blade scraping against the tough sheath like a warning cry to their pursuers. He gripped it tightly with both hands and faced his oncoming brethren, awaiting the inevitable.

Given a moment of respite by Edwin's desperate stand, Evelina finally pulled Mela across the cemetery's threshold and hugged her daughter tight. Mela could feel the slippery fog already climbing up her skin, while everything went white. In the distance, she heard her father's battle cry and the clanging of swords . . . and a pang of terrible sadness latched on to her heart. The tendrils of mist closing over them, she felt her mother, soft and warm against the fog. It wouldn't be long now; she reluctantly closed her eyes.

Yet, when she opened them, they were still in the same cemetery. Confused, she looked up to her mother and to the tears running down her cheeks. Evelina shook her head, trying to battle back her emotions, but it was an effort made in vain. Realizing this, she wiped her eyes and gently pushed her daughter to the side.

***

Edwin found himself encircled by the knights, their blades darting in and out, searching for an opening, but he gave them none. Pivoting about, his large muscular frame belied the grace and speed at which he brought his blade up and around to deflect their blows. Still, after the chase, his stamina was wearing. The knights sensed it, pressing their attack, until a faint glow stopped them in their tracks. In the graveyard just beyond, a shimmering nimbus of fog spilled outward, hugging the soil, sifting into every crack and every crevice. An electrical current chased this white soup, dancing about in the mist, caressing the homes of the dead.

The knights froze, leaving a wary Edwin to collapse with exhaustion. In between ragged breaths, he turned his head to see what they were staring at, but deep down in his heart, he already knew. The sensation of the special coolness of the fog, of his wife's reach, they echoed in his chest and brought dread into his very being.

Despair flooded his veins as Evelina strode forth to the center of the cemetery, her arms held aloft. He shouted for her to stop, to take Mela and leave, but it was all to no avail. From behind, Edwin heard the other knights suddenly splitting ranks, but he didn't bother turning around, for he already knew the reason why.

The knight-lord had arrived. His king, his sovereign . . . his father. A rich, crimson cloak draped across his plated shoulders, Renton Talmaris strode right past Edwin without sparing him a single glance, lines of bitter disappointment etched in his weathered face. No, the true target of his ire was the witch before him. The other knights gripped their swords tightly, waiting for Renton's imminent command.

From a tactical standpoint, the knight-lord knew that immediately charging Evelina was the best option to be had, before she could muster her unnatural energies, but he wanted them to see. His son, his loyal knights, he needed all of them to bear witness. With their very own eyes, to look on exactly just what evils these Gravewalkers were capable of committing.

***

Evelina eyed her husband's captors, the knight-lord and his retinue, standing just outside the cemetery's gates. She gave a quick glance to Mela, quietly clutching her raggedy doll close to her chest. She could do this. The knight-lord may have known of hatred, but he knew nothing of a woman's love for her husband, for her family.

With that, she closed her eyes, every fiber of her being trembling with the resolve to do what had to be done. Never had she attempted this before; never had she seen it done herself, only heard about it in the wide-eyed tales and dusty tomes of her distant ancestors. But the knight-lord and his ilk would soon know it for themselves as her eyelids slid open, revealing electric-white orbs, a storm inside to match the very heavens above.

In the end, fear overruled reason. Evelina and Edwin's union was judged to be unlawful and immoral, their daughter, a disgrace upon the legacy of the Protectorate. But death, in all its many forms, ran deep within the Gravewalkers' veins, the very essence of their existence. And while legends spoke of their abilities to guide the dead into the afterlife, they could also bring them back.

***

The knights gasped as lightning flashed and danced in her eyes, the very ground trembling all around them. Amid the downpour, the mud began to churn and boil, whipping itself into a sodden, rotten stew. Without warning, the grey rancid flesh of a forearm thrust itself out from the earth, sending clods of wet soil flying. Nearby, a yellowed skull breached the filthy muck, like a man swimming up from the bowels of the earth to gasp for air. Its black eye sockets stared blankly into the night sky as the wind whipped thin straggles of white hair about its fleshless face. Seeing this, Mela moved away from the unnatural legion forming ranks in the cemetery—not out of fear, but in understanding.

***

The graveyard continued to heave forth its long-dead inhabitants, their pained moans striking deep into the knights' mettle. Even the most battle-hardened veterans among them suffered hints of trepidation as the corpses rose up and shook free from the graveyard's clutches.

And despite all this, the ghastly horrors they were all witnessing, Renton looked on with grim approval.

The knight-lord then drew his sword with one great swift motion, his long arms matching the length of his claymore blade. He charged forward, roaring like an enraged grizzly as he led his men into battle. All the apprehension gone now, the knights followed their leader without delay. Lending their own voices to his mighty battle cry, leaving behind a stunned Edwin, sinking to his knees in the wet soil.

The Untoten.

Nothing more than mindless minions, their souls having departed long ago . . . but they felt no pain and they gave no mercy. This is what gave the knight-lord the conviction to see the Trauergast driven to extinction, beginning with the one who had captured his son's heart, the one who had torn his loyalty asunder.

***

As they crashed through the cemetery gates, the Untoten formed a wall against the charging knights, a pale phalanx of rotting flesh, shambling forth to obey Evelina's commands. Instinctively, the knights fanned outward with military precision, as Renton brought his sword crashing down on the first wave of corpses, carving a path through the press of moldering bodies. His men followed, and the initial array of corpses was quickly rent to pieces, their desiccated limbs sliding back into the mud.

Still, the inexperience of the knights against such unnatural foes and their enemy's sheer numbers brought them to a standstill. Renton cursed aloud, searching for an advantage, a strategic target of retribution. It wasn't long before he found what he was looking for, spying Evelina through a gap of bodies, standing behind the bulk of her forces.

With his men now pressed back against the Untoten's resurgence, Renton muscled his way to her, chopping down corpses as he went. Her arms still spread wide, eyes glowing white-hot with concentration, Renton took a chance and slashed downward, but an abrupt fog whisked her away and out of his path.

His sword now buried in the mud, the knight-lord had Evelina's full attention as she rose up behind him in a sudden column of mist. She waved her hands and a heavyset corpse slammed into Renton's side, almost knocking him over. Renton grunted, absorbing the blow, before he finally twisted his sword free of the mud's grip. Just in time, as another corpse recklessly charged in, this one with sharp, skeletal fingers, clawing at his face. Renton dodged the incoming attack, then lopped off the head of the first corpse. Deftly flipping his massive sword in the air, blade to pommel, he caught it—then crunched in the other corpse's skull like an overripe eggshell.

His heart shuddering, Renton took a look around, seeing that his small band of knights was still locked in a bitter stalemate. For every shambling minion they dispatched, three more rose to take its place. Desperate, he turned back toward the Gravewalker, who was now concentrating on raising even more Untoten from the vast cemetery. He charged her once again, but just as quickly, she flitted away in a column of mist, only to reappear teasingly just out of his reach. Her arms swung back and forth, her fingers fluttering about, like a marionette dangling the strings of her puppets.

Renton found himself surrounded as they swiped, clawed, and clubbed at him, instantly pressing him back, their blows raining down upon his armor. To attack one was to open himself to the others, so Renton used his blade to block their incessant strikes, waiting for an opening, until three more corpses entered the fray.

Renton cursed, realizing that Evelina meant to end this fight and she meant to do it now. The Untoten pressing, he took a step back, then another, as it was all he could do to stay alive. Exhausted, he made an impulsive, desperate charge through their ranks, suffering a nasty gash to the side of his head in doing so. Finally crashing free of the bodies, he found himself some momentary breathing room and then something else.

Mela.

Only a few feet away, huddled behind a weathered tombstone. The knight-lord made his choice in an instant, as Evelina panicked, knowing exactly what that intent was to be.

***

Ignored by both the knights and the Untoten, Edwin stumbled into the cemetery, neither a friend nor foe to the two battling sides. He stood there, bewildered by the massive onslaught the two forces had laid against each other, until Evelina's panicked cry roused him from his stupor. He spun around to see his father charging Mela with every ounce of speed left in him, his daughter just standing there, grasping at her doll with cold, wet fingers . . . and there was nothing he could do except watch it happen right before his very eyes.

The knight-lord jabbed his sword toward little Mela, his legs stumbling, but his aim steady and true, just as a great column of fog rose up before him. He felt the long blade slide through soft flesh, his weight pushing the sword to its hilt as he skidded to a knee. From across the cemetery, he heard his son's cry and looked up to see Evelina now skewered upon his sword, the fog dissipating into nothingness all around her. And as her body crumpled, so did the Untoten, sinking back into the earth, back into their soggy graves.

Father and son.

On his knees, Edwin vaguely felt two knights grab him and drag him through the mud toward Renton.

Lord and servant.

Renton pulled the bloodied blade from his son's beloved, eliciting a soft cry of pain from her lips as Mela stood stock-still, her eyes on her mother's prostrate form. Mela was unharmed, but the battle was effectively over. The knight-lord had triumphed.

At the sound of his men's approach, Renton turned around to see Edwin being hauled toward him. He motioned for them to bring him to his feet and then offered Edwin his sword, gesturing toward Evelina. The faint swells of her ragged breath were the only indication that she was still alive.

Beset by a thousand emotions, Edwin considered his father, the sword, and then the unnatural abominations that Evelina had summoned forth from their graves, lying next to the bodies of his former comrades.

But Mela's soft sobs washed all that away, her doll held close to her chest, tears running down her red cheeks. Edwin looked back to the blade and to his father holding it before him. He could very well take it and run his father through. Evelina could still be saved. The surviving Gravewalkers could heal her and they could all still be together.

But in the end . . . he could do nothing.

Thus, the witch . . .

Another bolt of lightning split the sky to reveal a castle towering in the distance as Renton shook his head in disgust. He flipped the blade about and let the hilt come back to his hand.

. . . she lost her life.

And in one blurry motion, the sword rose and fell.

And the knight . . .

Edwin slumped to his knees, utterly defeated, a pool of Evelina's lifeblood spreading out toward him.

. . . he lost his very soul.

Mela's tattered doll fell to the ground as Renton gestured for his men to seize her. Edwin lifted his head toward his daughter, only to see her already looking directly at him. In her eyes, there was only fear, sorrow . . . and anger.

And at that very moment, Edwin knew in his heart that she was lost to him.

Forever.

The knights moved to grab her, but as they reached out, Mela quickly shut her eyes and disappeared in a tiny column of fog, escaping the knight-lord's clutches, denying him of the victory he thought complete.

Edwin sank into numbness, as his gaze fell once more upon his daughter's doll, its threadbare black dress rustling in the cold wind.

But take heart, friends, for this tale . . . well, it's only just begun.

CHAPTER 1

Friends in High Places Aren't Really Friends

Castle Riesenstadt stood as a lone bulwark against the evening sky, the stars bringing black night over the blue of the day. A peaceful interlude, save for the shouts and screams of battling knights, as just beyond the heavy iron gates, an abundant host of rot and decay shambled forth with deadly intent.

Their desiccated skin cracked and split like dried leather, freed from the confines of their moist tombs. Rusted helmets sat atop yellowed skulls, the armor ringing morbidly against their hardened bones. The middle ranks grasped at chipped, dull swords, while the front line brandished great axes to wrench an opening for their deathly comrades in tow.

A small straggle of knights found themselves backed up against the massive gates, the heavy wooden beams at their backs, doubly secured for the sake of the villagers just beyond.

And strewn all around them were the ravaged bodies of their brothers, lying still in the hardened dirt that was now slowly loosening in their blood.

Gripping his sword tightly, one of the knights turned and looked up toward the castle. "Open the gates!" he cried out, his voice deepened by his helmet, echoing over and over in his head. "Sire! Please open the gates!"

***

Considering the knight's frantic pleas from high above, Renton glanced down for a moment, and then looked out to the plains now shrouded in night. Hunting for someone, something.

At his side was a young knight, his armor shining with immaculate perfection, his youthful face smooth and unblemished. Together they stood, towering over the deserted cobblestone streets and grey stone roofs safely ensconced behind them.

After a long moment of deliberation, Alain turned to Renton, his fingers nervously wrapped around the unused helmet at his side.

"Father?" he asked above the ragged shouts of the men below, the clanging of their blades fading away as fatigue began to settle in. Their shouts echoing in his ear, Alain waited for a response as Renton continued to stare ahead into the distance.

"No," Renton answered.

There was a departed stillness to his voice—no compassion, just a simple utterance of a calculating word. Soon the shouts below turned into screams as the Untoten finally gained the upper hand—the whispers of the knights' blades cutting through dead, dry limbs replaced by the wet squelches of the living being chopped to bloody chunks. Renton took in the carnage, unmoved, while his son turned his eyes away, unable to stomach what he was seeing.

"These cowardly forays are beginning to tax my patience," Renton muttered in tired frustration. Alain saw his chance and turned to his father to beseech him once more.

"Why not commit more men to the cause? Surely . . ." But it was a proposition that came out more like a plea.

Renton frowned. "Don't be a fool."

He waited for the rest of his father's admonition, but it never came. Instead, Alain forced himself to turn back toward the slaughter taking place below, where he spied one last knight, standing awash in his comrades' blood.

***

Keldon Berna tore off his gore-caked helmet, the gold markings of his command still shining through. He hastily wiped the sweat and blood from his rough complexion, several scars masking the youth of his face and the early dash to his rank. The outline of his arms showed that, on a normal day, he would have no problems wielding the massive broadsword in his hands, but today was a much different day indeed. As he fought to stay alive, his swings degenerated into desperate, frantic bursts, the remaining Untoten warriors closing in as his strength deserted him. Despairing, he looked up and shouted out with the certainty that someone would hear his pleas.

"Alain! Master Alain! Help me, please!"

Mindless in their murderous pursuit, the Untoten ignored his cries for help and seized the opportunity to swarm him like a pack of wolves leaping upon their prey.

"Alai—"

His body disappeared under their mass, one last scream that ended in a wet crunch.

With Keldon dispatched, the Untoten ceased their movement and stood in complete silence. Then, as one, they turned and shuffled off, away from the castle. Up above, Alain closed his eyes, shaken by Keldon's pleas . . . but the knight-lord's expression stayed the same.

"She's merely baiting us. Testing our resolve."

"She?"

Renton nodded to the far distance, to the shadowy edge of the forest. Alain squinted, trying to spot whatever his father meant for him to see, looking over trees and tall grass—and there it was.

Under a shroud of heavy branches, a glint of steel caught his attention, blossoming into something much worse. Hundreds of still, quiet Untoten soldiers, lying in wait, for some unknown signal.

And in the midst of them, a woman, her face partially hidden by a heavy grey hood. Black diamonds for eyes, sparkling in the dim moonlight like the blades of her Untoten warriors. Alain swore under his breath as he imagined he saw the woman leering at him, but heavy clouds passed overhead, blocking out the moon's silvery illumination. He gasped and walked a few more steps down the rampart, trying to catch another glimpse.

"The misbegotten fruit of your brother's dalliance now comes to haunt us after all these years," Renton said. Alain paled, realizing just what would've happened if they had indeed opened the gates . . . reminded, yet again, of why his father was who he was.

"And with a seemingly endless supply of corpses at her disposal. Corpses bearing weapons and armor, not the moldering puppets we've faced in the past."

"What can we do?" Alain asked, regretting the choice of his artless words as soon as they flew out of his mouth. He could tell by the look in his father's face that his ignorance was showing and that the knight-lord's patience was beginning to wane for the night.

"Until we find the putrid burial ground that supplies her forces . . . nothing." Renton turned to regard his son for a moment. A small glint came into his eyes as he continued, "But that doesn't mean I'm without options."

Wheeling about, Renton marched back down the rampart. "Redouble our efforts to find their camp. Every graveyard, cemetery, burial ground . . . spare nothing," he called back to Alain, who nodded in turn. "And see to it that the bodies below are thrown into the funeral pyre. Quickly," he added with an air of finality that intersected his echoing footsteps.

The torches wavering in the night wind, Alain watched his father fade away in the space of a few long moments before reluctantly turning back to the mangled bodies below.

CHAPTER 2

Memories and Spirits (but Not the Good Kind)

Illuminated by a faint sliver of sunlight from somewhere far above, Edwin sat motionless in the dark gloom of his cell, listening to the muffled talk of his jailers. After all this time, they still feared the knight-lord's reach. Even all the way down in this dark pit, they kept their voices to just above a whisper.

Still, trapped in this cell for what had seemed like an eternity, Edwin's hearing had grown to great extents.

"Just left them out there to die, like dogs," a guard said.

"Aye. I heard he and Alain just stood and watched from above, just—" The guard's story was suddenly interrupted by the scuttle of an emaciated rat frantically attempting to chew a meal out of Edwin's exposed calf. Edwin took in a deep breath and made a tired but precise swing of his fist—eliciting a sharp squeal, followed by a hard crunch as he broke the rat's back. Its dying breaths were still too loud for Edwin to hear what was going on, so he swung down again and ended its misery.

"The witch," the guard said, continuing with the story. "*That* witch." A knowing reference to the prisoner they stood watch over.

Edwin sighed, fingering his filthy, unkempt beard, feeling just how unkind the years had been. His face was covered in soot, layers of filth that sat on his skin, layers that he could actually feel. Rags of cloth hung across his frame, no longer deserving the title of clothes. Yet, while his arms and chest had lost their hard edges, the raw bulk was still there from years of doing rudimentary exercises amid the straw-lined sludge of his prison.

Mela. Was she behind this? If she was, he was sure of why his father was having such a hard time crushing this rebellion, this war of attrition. The guards had been talking about it for months, and while he expected his daughter to have harbored her fair share of resentment, this troubled Edwin. As he did many times before, Edwin mused once again over the events of that fateful night. The other name flitting in and out of his consciousness . . . *Evelina.*

Whatever physical tortures he had suffered over the years, it was nothing compared to the torment of those horrific visions replayed over and over again. Slow as the turn of the mill wheel, they crept about inside his head. Better that he had submitted to the Trial by Swords, but his father had allowed him no such luxury.

He longed for an end, any end, let alone the slow-growing depth of cold steel in his guts. Pain with a purpose, rather than this torture of the soul. *Purpose, where has all that gone to?* And after some time, the cell grew completely dark, leaving Edwin with only the faint flicker of the torches and his memories.

Always the memories.

***

"A toast!" Alain barked to the small assembly of knights, town drunkards, and the other riffraff gathered in the Whistling Pig. "A toast to these brave souls who passed on here tonight!" He lifted his cup even higher, his cheeks flushed bright with too much mead. "And here! For my dear friend Keldon Berna, who fought till the end! No quarter, no mercy!"

Alain paused to fight back some brief vision of horror in his mind's eye before continuing. "Yes, he shall be sorely missed this night and for many nights to come."

Of course, Alain's friend was, in truth, nothing but bloody chunks, and his stomach was beginning to churn with that reminder.

"Now, drink. All of you, you sorry bastards!" he slurred. Everyone in the tavern obediently raised their goblets and cups in recognition of the deceased—the exception being two knights, cloistered in the far back recesses of the room.

"Dear friend, hah!" one of the knights said, his grip on his goblet causing it to bend.

"Indeed," said the other, lifting his cup in Alain's direction. "More like the only one that could stand you."

"The one who hated you the least, you pompous git," the other knight chuckled.

"To the pompous git," his friend agreed, as his grip finally loosened on his drink. "May your head throb with pain tomorrow and may your father beat you extra for it."

They clinked their goblets together and laughed, for at least here, in the shadows of the tavern, they could still conspire to hate their polished commander—as much as the alcohol would allow. The Whistling Pig was the only place where any happiness was seen these days, if you could call it that. Fueled by cheap mead and the need for an escape from the grim reality they were all facing, the tavern had become their oasis.

"Minstrel! A song!" Alain coughed out, but the good minstrel was duly occupied, fending off the advances of yet another drunken suitor. Sitting atop a brandy barrel, considering each lecherous line on its own merits but finding favor with none, she motioned for another drink.

She.

One would have been pressed to notice at first glance, with her sly grin and intermittent mirth, that this was no cavalier bard of legend—but upon a second glance, there was no mistaking that the minstrel that night was, in fact, a woman. She wore men's pants as they should have been worn, loose and comfortable. Her shirt and vest hung in the same manner, wiry flesh, rather than supple curves underneath . . . but the curves were still there. All this topped by a hazel ponytail that spoke of convenience rather than vanity.

She dug into her pockets, searching for a coin or two . . . but came up empty. "Mother of all . . . ," she muttered under her breath.

Her admirer was quick to notice, of course, his greasy jowls quivering with hopeful anticipation of her favor. "No such worries tonight, lass! Drink as much as you like, deep pockets here, deep pockets, I tell you!"

The minstrel coughed out something akin to a barely suppressed grunt, but it didn't deter the man in the least as he continued. "Deep pockets for *large personal* goods, eh, love?"

The minstrel sighed but carried on with the charade, peering into her empty cup. "Yes, yes, I could only imagine, the size, the girth of such goods," she said. "And no doubt, its owner, skilled greatly in the art of—"

"Another stein of ale?" the barmaid asked, cutting into the conversation. The minstrel turned, then gave pause to eye the barmaid's impressive curves and her rouged lips. Her male suitor turned as well, noticing the minstrel's reaction, but in the way that one would notice that their presence was no longer needed nor required. The barmaid caught the minstrel's curious gaze and held it. "Or perhaps you'd prefer something else?"

"I said, minstrel!" Alain interrupted with impatience. "If that's what you're truly calling yourself, that is . . ."

The target of the young man's indignation finally turned her head away, her annoyance hidden with the aplomb of a seasoned actor.

"Yes, sire?" she asked, as she slapped away the suitor's hand, his interest renewed even more.

"I said . . . a song, minstrel!" Alain barked out. But then, a bit softer, "A song for my fallen friend," his anger clashing with his drink and his sadness.

The minstrel weighed the intent behind Alain's impertinent glare before eventually turning back to her inebriated admirer. "Of course," she said, as she patted the man's head and whispered, "Later, m'dear, later," before turning back to Alain. "Of course, sire."

The minstrel then snatched her lute, a thing of ale-soaked wood and frayed strings, and nimbly leapt atop the bannister of the bar, stepping over grubby hands and spilled cups. "A song for the fallen Keldon Berna and his men!" she yelled out to the crowd, as she crossed over to stand atop another barrel. "As no brave knight should ever be forgotten!" she continued, lifting her arms to the raucous cheers of the tavern's patrons. "And always to be remembered in his passing," she solemnly tacked on.

Swinging her lute from around her back, she flexed an array of long, nimble fingers and plucked just once at a single string. Its long resonance washed over the crowd, silencing them, as her rich, lilting voice filled the sudden vacuum.

"What would ye say, fair people, fair folk,
considering a brave man, his life taken in one stroke.
Fighting for true love, fighting with no hope,
for the Knight Proper—"

"Curse you, bard! I said I wanted a tribute to Keldon Berna, not some flowery poetry!" Alain yelled out. The human flesh was still swirling around in his mind, floating about in a pool of blood and gore.

The minstrel took a slight bow, the less intoxicated men raising their head for a peek of opportunity, as she smiled ever so graciously. "Of course, sire, of course . . ." Her mind darted about for perhaps better words, better phrases, but there was none to be had. The moment escaped her, and it didn't appear to be the first time. "If you would just let me finish, you see . . ."

Alain sneered, then slammed down his cup atop the bar and took out his sword. "Let me finish it for you, dog!" he shouted, wavering on his feet. More than a few patrons cheered Alain's challenge, desperate for someone else's misery besides their own. The minstrel's rejected suitor sprung up to her defense, but his chivalrous charge ended before it began, as he stumbled, smacking his head against the wooden bannister of the bar.

The minstrel rolled her eyes, then quickly looked to rest of the crowd for support, but their lust for spilled blood seemed to now override their patronage for the arts or even the sight of her cleavage, however hidden away it was.

"Ha-ha! Gut the bitch, lord knight!" A cry rang out from the crowd, followed by "Aye! Gut the wench for her insolence!" The minstrel took in their reddened faces and the indifferent knights, then quickly swung her lute back around.

"Of course! Silence the very person who would bring a fraction of inspiration into your miserable, insipid lives!" the minstrel yelled back. More boos shot through the air and more hands began snatching at the minstrel's feet.

Emboldened by the crowd, Alain stumbled forward, his blade leveled directly at the minstrel's chest. "You hear that, wench?" Alain slurred. "Now the real performance begins!" Woman or man, it mattered not. He could see his enemy, and this time, it wasn't hundreds of feet below him. Now she was right in front of him and he would skewer her as she deserved.

The minstrel hopped over a few more tables, sensing the inevitable finale to this so-called performance. She thought of appealing to the other knights' sense of chivalry, but she knew her boyish appearance wouldn't allow her such luxuries. She thought of pulling her blade out but, indeed, thought the better of it.

Then there was a crash at her side, as her former suitor lurched to his feet and pressed through the bodies, knocking over stools and tables in the process.

Amid the chaos, his flushed face emerged from the sea of angry glares, the minstrel in his sights. "You'll have safety in my bed tonight, dearest minstrel!" he said with a drunken grin. "No slashes or lost limbs . . ." He tilted his head closer. "But perhaps a few bite marks and scratches."

The minstrel blew him a kiss—a smirk more than a smile. "Mm, thank you, but no thank you, milord," and suddenly launched a meaty gob of spit, which splattered directly upon his sweaty face. With that, she turned and hopped over a few more heads, taking advantage of his distraction to skip toward the door.

Wiping the spit off, he shook his hammy fist in her direction. "Why you, you brazen slut! I'll show you! And don't think I didn't see you looking at that barmaid, you lusty little trollop!" he slurred, his face growing even redder, if such a thing was possible.

Nearly at the exit, the minstrel turned and gave one last bow to the jilted patrons. "Cassandra Lethellon, my loves! Cassandra Lethellon! Remember the name, for I'll soon—"

There was a loud crash, as a mead cup broke into a thousand splinters against the wall next to her. The minstrel took the hint, shaking her head as she ran the length of the bar and out the door.

CHAPTER 3

Freedom, an Overrated Thing, Really

A tiny sliver of sunlight crept across Edwin's face as he lay huddled in the corner. The ball he had clenched himself into had provided just enough warmth to grasp some sleep. That was until a deluge of cold water crashed upon his head and jerked him wide awake. Edwin coughed and shook his head, droplets of water flying from his straggly hair and beard. Hearing a low chuckle, Edwin wiped his eyes with grimy hands to see Alain standing just beyond the metal bars holding an empty water bucket.

"Good morning, Brother," Alain said, the toll of last night's drinking easy to see in his flushed cheeks and dreary eyes. He massaged his brow, then leaned in a bit closer. "Be thankful it wasn't another round of horse piss this time, eh?"

The knights at his side chuckled in agreement as the small rivers of water turned Edwin's cell into a pool of stale sewage.

Edwin could only shrug at the squalid sight of it all. "Truly merciful. It's been a good while since I've had a proper bath."

"Oh? That so?"

Edwin nodded. "We all don't get to soak in lavender and lilacs like you do, whelp."

The knights at Alain's side began to chuckle again, but this time at the other brother's expense.

Alain couldn't just ignore their mirth. He searched for some retort to put Edwin back in his place . . . but there was no need. Cocking his ears toward the end of the passageway, he heard the echo of heavy footsteps approaching and leaned closer toward Edwin. "Look lively," he whispered. "Father wishes to speak with you."

Alain took delight in seeing the other knights bolt to attention, along with the darkening of Edwin's demeanor. Like storm clouds settling over sunny hills, his father threatened to dampen the day far worse than any bucket of piss. The knight to his left snapped his steel-plated boots with enough force to rattle his ears as he barked out, "Make way for the knight-lord!"

The corridor reverberated with the clanging of many suits of armor, as every knight down the hall hastily followed suit. One by one, Renton passed them by, not a wasted step in his stride.

Edwin didn't need to see the knights' stiff postures and stern expressions, already well aware of the respect that his father commanded. When Renton finally arrived at Edwin's cloistered cell, Alain stepped to the side and lifted his head just a notch taller, while the others bowed their eyes at the knight-lord's presence. Lined on both sides of the musty corridor by a phalanx of armor-plated knights, Renton took a moment to consider Edwin's sorry state, much like he had on that fateful day in the cemetery.

And in his eyes, nothing had changed.

Another moment of absolute silence before a drop of water from Edwin's shaggy mane splashed down into the muddy pool below.

Renton's nostrils flared, like someone smelling spoiled fish in the hot sun.

"I thought you would like to know that your vile seed, that wretched creature . . . ," he began, as Edwin slowly raised his eyes to meet his father's.

"Mela," he said slowly. "Mela."

"Yes . . . Mela," Renton said with a curl to his lip. "Mela, who butchered a score of our men, just last night. *Our* men!"

The anger rising in his voice, Renton continued.

"Mela, who's subjected an entire kingdom to her murderous rampages. Our people, hobbled in their homes by fear, by despair." He reached out to the cell bars, his mailed fist gripping them tightly. "Mela, who's plunged the countryside into chaos! Innocent folk plagued by their loved ones crawling forth from their graves to obey her murderous commands!"

"We've already had this conversation, Father," Edwin muttered.

"You!" Alain yelled, lunging forward. "Watch how you address the knight-lord, you traitor!"

In response, somehow defying the physical logic of fifteen years in a cramped cell, Edwin suddenly rose up and snapped to his feet. He locked eyes with his brother through his wild, mangy hair, instantly taking a bit of wind out of Alain. He called out to him softly, "Here then, Brother. Come here and teach me how to properly address your knight-lord, won't you?"

Despite the show of bravado, Edwin was much more weathered than he let on, the burn in his muscles almost forcing him to cry out. Still, he didn't budge.

A few moments of tense silence passed before Renton finally interrupted the standoff, fixing Alain with a pointed glance. "Perhaps if you spent as much time training as you did drinking, your threats might mean something." Mortified, Alain shrank back into place, as Renton turned back toward Edwin.

"And what . . . you think your daughter would greet *you* instead with open, loving arms? Serve you cake and cider over a warm hearth? Surely she holds you to blame, just as much as she does me."

Edwin tensed for a moment longer, then stood down. Remembering his daughter's last expression of scorn and sorrow, he knew that his father was right. *He's always right.*

In response, Renton shifted his demeanor as well, releasing the iron bar to instead hold his hands out before his son.

As if the knight-lord of Riesenstadt was about to plead for his favor.

Alain was the only one to notice it, the other knights' eyes still cast to the ground . . . but notice it he did.

"Join us, Edwin. Come back to the Protectorate, to your Brotherhood. The people of Riesenstadt, they desperately need the strength of your sword arm."

Unable to stomach what he was hearing from his father, this sudden outpouring of acceptance for Edwin, Alain shifted his weight back and forth as Renton continued.

"My son . . . redemption can still be yours."

Edwin stared down at the floor and looked nowhere else, while the knights in turn lifted their eyes, scarcely able to believe what was about to happen after all these years . . .

But the moment passed.

Edwin took a step back, then another. Silently retreating to the shadows of his cell.

Renton nodded, the iron lines of duty and service returning once more to his weathered brow. "Never again," he muttered, before turning to look Alain directly in the eye. "Never again."

As one, the contingent of knights wheeled around and followed Renton out of the corridor, leaving Alain alone with Edwin.

Relieved, yet shaken by the mere suggestion that Edwin could be forgiven, Alain edged a step closer to Edwin's cell, lowering his voice. "You hear that? That was the sound of your freedom, Brother. Escaping you for good."

He waited for a response, but there was none to be had.

Sensing that nothing else he could say would rouse Edwin from the depths of his cell for the time being, Alain turned and followed his father down the corridor.

And once again, Edwin was alone.

CHAPTER 4

Have Horse, Will Travel, but Only When He Wants To

Sunlight had given way to a tiny peek of waning moonlight . . . and Edwin had not moved once. He kept his customary vigil in the corner, watching the shadows grow, to later vanish along with the dawn. Just him, the guards, and the penance of his thoughts—

Until he was thrown to the floor in a startled heap. The very ground, the walls, were rocked by an enormous explosion. Above the immediate din, he heard the guards running and screaming. Edwin heard a sound he'd never thought he'd hear in his lifetime, like the entire castle was collapsing atop its own ponderous weight, tons and tons of mortar and stone rumbling about. His prison cell continued to shake all around him, his body sent hurling into the wall. His head bounced off of the stone and dazed him, as he coughed and choked amid the sudden torrent of dust swimming in the air.

Then the guards fell back into a semblance of order, yelling confused orders back and forth as they ran in every direction, their shadows bouncing in the corridor's faint torchlight. While not quite in the same state of military preparation, Edwin found himself latching back on to the discipline of his former life. The shock was now wearing off, his battlefield experience starting to rise from within. Shaking his head clear, his cramped muscles forgot their previous fatigue and he sprang to his feet.

"Grab a bucket, get to the water troughs! Go!" one of the guards yelled. He could hear more voices through the grate above.

"Secure the gates!" a knight ordered his men.

And then another muffled explosion shook the cell.

Coughing amid the flurry of dust, Edwin closed his eyes and resigned himself to his fate. His daughter had finally come for her vengeance, and despite his acceptance in knowing that, he still found himself saddened that he wouldn't at least get a chance to say—

"There you are," came a voice from behind. He turned on the spot, swiveling on his heels, but saw nothing through the cell bars. Incredulous, Edwin took a step forward, trying to make out the speaker through all the dusty dim light. And there, just outside his prison, stood a woman. Wearing a loose ponytail, her hands on her hips while the shadows flitted across her face.

A lute was strapped to her back, a needle-thin rapier tucked into her belt. And in her hands . . . the dungeon key ring. Edwin fixed his eyes on that key ring, having seen it previously attached to a guard's belt. The woman fiddled with it, riffling through the various metal odds and ends. Finding one that seemed to meet her specifications, she then slid it into the bulky keyhole of Edwin's cell. She turned it . . . but no luck.

"Hmm," the woman muttered, as all the while, Edwin stood silently by. The shouts and cries of the knights continued to reverberate from outside, still scrambling to engage whatever had accosted them.

The woman looked up, taking a pause from her efforts. "You know, for a moment, I thought I was in the stables by the stench of you. Bathe much?"

Edwin hesitated to reply, incredulous, before his curiosity got the better of him. "Who . . . are you?" he asked. The woman glanced in his direction, then gave the quick but theatrical bow of a stage performer.

"Cassandra Lethellon, milord. Or just Cass, if you like. Master bard and crusader against sobriety, I am," she answered, before nonchalantly returning to her business at hand.

"A . . . bard? What are you doing here?" Edwin asked, even more confused.

Sudden shouts from down the corridor quickly ended Cass's indifference as she quickened her pace, riffling through the endless menagerie of keys. "Why, I'm here to perform for you, milord! Isn't it obvious?" she muttered, now keeping her attention solely on the keys. Then, after a few more curses, a wide smile reached her ears. She fingered one and jammed it into the lock, forcing it to twist open with a loud click. The door swung open with a creak of protest.

Unsure of what was going on, Edwin took a few steps back, retreating toward his cell wall. "Bloody hells. Really?" Cass asked with impatience.

Edwin took another moment. Setting his jaw, he finally stepped forward and out of his cell. "Good man. I was beginning to wonder," Cass said, slapping him on the back. Edwin fixed her an annoyed glance, then peered down the corridor, as if he fully expected to be thrown back in his cage at any moment.

"My father will have you killed for this," Edwin said.

In return, Cass snorted with amusement. "You say it just as he or your brother would, sir knight."

Edwin considered her words, then—

"Fah! Enough of this idle chatter!" Cass said, cutting him off. "Time for us to make our grand escape, eh?" Gauging Edwin's reaction, she leaned in. "You do want to escape, yes?"

But Edwin's answer was indifferent silence.

Cass muttered under her breath, then reached into a pouch. With a flourish, she pulled out a dented silver flask, then turned back to Edwin. "But first!" she said, uncapping the flask. "First, we steel ourselves, we gird our loins!" She took a long swig and wiped her lips with no small measure of appreciation. "This . . . this is what glory is made of, eh, sir knight?"

As if he still didn't believe that escape was an actual reality, Edwin just stood there, his shoulders slumped in resignation. "Why are you doing this?" he asked.

Cass put the flask away. "I've several different reasons, if you will, but none of them as important as the notion that there's a story to be told, milord . . . your story. But *you* have to finish it." Cass took a quick look around, then turned back to Edwin. "Now then, could we please get moving? Preferably before the guards return and stake my pretty head on a pike." She flashed a gleaming set of white teeth and then ran off down the corridor, the sounds of the guards drawing even closer.

Edwin stood still, until Cass's voice rang out from the end of the hall. "Really, any day now, sir knight!"

Edwin looked back to his squalid cell, gritted his teeth in frustration . . . then staggered down the corridor after Cass. It was at first, a sequence of spastic lunges, his newly freed legs recalling the mechanics of how to run . . .

But run, eventually, he did.

***

Edwin pushed through a small portgate to see chaos . . . pure, unbridled chaos. Townsfolk, guards, and knights alike were running pell-mell through the cobbled streets, bringing sloshing buckets of water to the castle's enormous oil cauldrons, both bellowing flame and heavy smoke. Smaller fires and gobs of bubbling oil littered the perimeter around the cauldrons. No bodies, though, and no Gravewalkers or Untoten shambling about . . . and for that, Edwin was as grateful as much as he was impressed by his rescuer.

"That was you?" Edwin asked, as he took in the view.

"Spectacular, I know," Cass said, as she put her hands on her hips in pride. She looked ahead to the massive ironbound gates of the castle wall, gaping wide open. But even as she did so, the space began to fill with foot soldiers, scrambling to close them.

In the distance, a mangy old horse tied to a wooden post bucked wildly against its tether. Cass turned at the noise of the struggling beast. "A faithful steed as any, I assure you." Without warning, she sprinted toward the so-called steed, leaving Edwin to himself.

"Oh, hells . . . ," Edwin mumbled under his breath, then chased after her once again.

***

"Yah now, settle down I say!" Cass barked out as she struggled to gain control over the horse. Edwin nearly keeled over as he reached the pair, his muscles now really starting to feel the strain of countless years without proper exercise.

Bent over, trying to catch his breath, he saw movement from the corner of his eye . . . the gates were closing.

Leaving the questionable safety of his cell was one thing, but the thought of being thrown back in struck some primal chord within, as he yelled out to Cass in between ragged breaths, "Damn you, bard, do something quick!"

Cass looked and saw the gates drawing shut as well. Quickly, she grabbed the reins with one hand and drew her rapier with the other. The point glistening in the night's fires as she held the blade directly to the horse's eye.

"Curse you, you miserable, villainous beast . . . are we at an understanding?" The horse snorted once in defiance, but then calmed down. Cass shoved her rapier back into her belt and climbed up onto the saddle in one graceful leap.

Edwin took Cass's outreached hand and struggled to climb aboard. "Ha! Fat and lazy after all these years, eh, milord?"

Edwin gave Cass a fierce gaze but finally heaved himself up onto the horse. The animal bucked, protesting against the extra weight, but Cass gave it a solid kick, which sent them off into a full-tilt gallop. "Hold on, sir knight!" she cried.

All around them, the fire continued to lash out at the knights attempting to drown it, hot whips of flame reaching out from the walls of the inferno. The chaos was growing, surrounding Edwin and Cass as they charged the gates. A single footman stood guard, debating whether or not to stay at his post or fight the fire as he saw the two escapees and their frothing horse bearing down on him.

"Halt!" he yelled. "Halt!" His spear shook as he prepared for the attack when the horse lowered its head to his. There was a moment of perfect clarity as everything came to an absolute standstill—

Then the guard felt the crack of his skull, but not the ground he fell toward.

Cass spurred her horse on, as Edwin looked back toward the fallen soldier. He could hardly think of a worse way to abandon your post as he watched the gates finally close behind them. Still, no one was chasing them, and no one had even noticed the poor bastard, in all likeliness, stone asleep in the mud beside the steel gates. He fervently hoped that the man's helmet had protected him, for the only thing worse than being knocked out by a horse would be the indignity of being killed by one.

Especially this horse, he mused.

"Well, milord, I—" Cass began, before Edwin corrected her.

"It's Edwin," he said, still lingering on the visage of Castle Riesenstadt slowly receding into the distance. The haze of fire and smoke were now beginning to die down, the mandate of the knight-lord's military discipline once again asserting itself over the initial panic and chaos. Having seen enough, Edwin turned back around. "And thank you."

Cass nodded in silent acceptance.

She snapped the reins to keep the horse at a gallop, and they pushed forward through the night.

CHAPTER 5

Getting the Dead of It

Rocks and roots jutted out from earthen walls; a lightless tunnel stretched on into the depths below. Two figures draped in grey cloth marched its length, their hurried footsteps echoing off the walls around them. Eventually, light bled through the darkness, faint specks of fire blossoming in the distance.

Her face hidden under heavy robes, one of the Gravewalkers noticed that the echoes of her footsteps had changed, becoming flat and dull, as the stench of rotting flesh pushed in through her nostrils. Just ahead, unseen guards stood watch against the walls, neither breathing nor moving in the black gloom. Acacia's heartbeat quickened, for she enjoyed this morbid surprise in the dark. She detected the smell of rust from the guard's blades, a shiver of delight running down her spine.

To Acacia's left, Elaine slowed her own heartbeat and took shallow breaths. As long as she had worked with putting the dead to rest, she could not, and would not, ever get used to the rancid smell of these risen soldiers. As Acacia and Elaine approached them, the Untoten became illuminated, faint spots of their armor and weapons gleaming in the torches' fires. Still, the two Gravewalkers kept up their pace, passing door after door, each with its own set of skeletal guardians.

Elaine had to admit, this underground fortress, it served its purposes well. While most sisters preferred the exercise, they could've just as easily teleported themselves anywhere within its confines, given their immediate access to the emotional residues permeating everything around them. Here, they were nearly unstoppable and couldn't fathom the size of the army that would be needed to storm their sanctum.

Yet as they continued, Elaine couldn't help herself from thinking how much she missed living above, under the stars, under blue skies and billowy clouds. Walking in the fresh air rather than scurrying about like a rat in these never-ending tunnels. She sensed that Acacia shared her sympathies, but she knew it was not for the love of nature or fresh air, but instead her ever-present paranoia. Elaine had spent a great deal of time working on becoming calmer around her, but just like her younger counterpart, she knew that neither would ever trust the other.

A light thump suddenly interrupted her thoughts, followed by approaching footsteps. Acacia's and Elaine's ears both perked up at the noise that heralded the arrival of another Gravewalker, this one with the nimble features of a cunning stray. Pausing for a brief moment, the girl glanced at both of them in the dim torchlight. The two sisters caught the glint in her eyes, then watched as she quickly pushed her way past.

Elaine shared a knowing glance with Acacia. The young scout had beaten them to their destination and delivered the news for which they had been hurrying so much to tell.

That Mela's father had escaped.

Normally news traveled fast throughout their dominion, but Elaine and Acacia had sought to reach Mela first, in what they had hoped would've been a more tactful fashion. In these lower tunnels, teleporting about was considered bad form, but they both regretted their decision in not doing so. The scout already quickening her steps behind them, Acacia and Elaine continued down the tunnel but slowed their pace, given that there was no point in hurrying now.

Elaine was not entirely sure how Mela would take the news. She was convinced it would threaten to fog the girl's mind, but just how far the disruption would go, Elaine couldn't say. But now that her father was free, her mind would be cluttered with even more distractions. *Men,* she thought. For every adversity her sisters had endured, men always seemed to be at the heart of it . . . but what were they to do?

While it was impossible for a sister to give birth to an infant boy, in addition to the Gravewalkers' traditions forbidding males from living among them, there was still the fleeting dance of courtship and mating. The process of selecting a mate was still one of the few things left to chance, left entirely to the whim of each sister, and the men who sired their daughters were each wholly unique and special in their own right, for enticing a young Gravewalker in the prime of her pale beauty was no small feat.

As thus, while her sisters made do without men in almost every other capacity, they were still taught to honor the memory of their fathers and their lovers. Occasionally, some would find it hard to do so, to part ways with the men who had captured their hearts, but it was never a cause of concern for her brethren. Eventually, the lure of the burial ground, the gratifying sensation of harnessing the emotional residues within, it was too strong to resist for their kind.

Like fish to the sea, the birds to the air, she mused.

What none of them could anticipate, however, was a sister bedding the heir to the very knight-lord himself. Whatever uneasy truce they had enjoyed before, that unexpected union had nearly resulted in their extinction.

Men.

And now, despite his captivity for many years, now Mela's father was free. Given that Mela still harbored understandable resentment from seeing her mother butchered before her very eyes, Elaine couldn't guess how their leader would react. The young should be allowed to live and make mistakes, not be tasked to lead others in a war. Mistakes were unavoidable at any age, but the young were prone to making them, and in her opinion, the sister next to her was especially so. The familiar uneasiness crept inside Elaine even now, as she thought of Acacia and her wild, reckless behavior.

***

The time has come, Acacia thought. Certainly the freedom of Mela's father would now spur their leader into an attack of some sort, she was sure of it. There could be no other answer for the man who had abandoned her, who'd idly stood by while her mother was slaughtered. Even as a little girl, Acacia remembered the stories of how they had found Evelina's corpse lying facedown in the mud. Thus, even if a few peasants suffered along the way, it was Mela's rightful vengeance to be had.

Of course, the clucking hen beside her didn't share the same views, but she was nothing more than a temporary annoyance. Her constant lectures of patience, holding back one's power, and other fits of old age was enough to drive Acacia crazy. Elaine had never approved of Acacia's appointment to Mela's side, and it had driven the two of them to a stalemate before.

The heavy wooden door was approaching quickly; the guards were becoming more imposing in stature and better armed. Soon, she would see where they stood. *Soon,* she thought, *there will be real war.*

***

Mela sat at a wooden table, staring into the empty eye sockets of a yellowed skull. Candles spread small doses of light about the room, wavering shadows intersecting all across the moldering stone. Her arms were crossed; she rested them upon the table and continued to peer into its depths.

"So he has finally escaped," she said. "After all of these years, my father has finally found a way out of his prison." She closed her eyes and let the gears of thought grind in her head.

"So he has finally escaped," a hollow, somber voice repeated. Mela opened her eyes and watched the skull's jaws shudder to life. "After all of these years . . ." It dragged out the word *years,* as if it understood just how long Edwin had spent in captivity. ". . . my father has finally found a way out of his prison." It finished with a click of its jaw, as the bones closed up on themselves. Mela stared back at the motionless skull and contemplated its words.

"What does this mean?" she asked herself.

"What . . . ," the skull began to speak.

"No, not that!" Mela yelled, and the skull closed its mouth. Her tone let it know this was not a sentence to be repeated.

Peering closer, Mela could see eyes slowly emerging from the darkness of the skull's empty sockets, flickering sparks of light blue, staring out at her in curiosity. As if they wondered why she had banished them to the abyss, to be trapped inside this dead, hollow thing. Mela lingered on these thoughts for a moment, then pushed them to the back of her mind and watched the eyes sink back into the darkness and fade away.

She didn't have time for such memories. Those kinds of thoughts were not going to help, but she knew the more she dwelled on the conundrum of her father escaping, the more the past would return to haunt her. She didn't even know for sure what her father's escape meant. Would he seek her out? Would he run away to a far-off land to escape her grandfather's wrath? *The knight-lord,* she thought, a small crinkle of dark humor dawning in her eyes.

A candle hissed as its flame began to drown in wet wax. Mela reached over and snuffed its light out, then grabbed for one of its unlit brothers. She tipped the wick into the flame of yet another candle and set it down in the other's place. *One problem replaced by another,* she considered. There were always new ones to replace the old ones, and she would soon have to find new answers for each of them.

"What will be next? It matters not," she said aloud. "Things are moving in the direction that they should for the moment as we continue to test their defenses. All according to plan." The skull began to repeat back to her when the door creaked open.

Elaine entered but didn't bother with any honorifics. "Mela, what have I said about you conversing with that thing?"

Conversely, Acacia sauntered into her chamber, strategically offering Mela a slight bow as she did so. "My lady," she purred.

Mela regarded both of them with a curt nod as Elaine waited for an actual response. Regardless of their differences, Elaine and Acacia were her two closest advisors and both had offered a remarkable degree of insight over the past few years, even though they had two entirely different outlooks. And today, she could tell, it was Elaine's outlook that would be expressed in its entirety.

Her disapproval was easy to see. Her face redefined her age as she looked on in dismay, each wrinkle creasing in on itself. Still, Mela found herself suddenly short of her usual patience, given the events that had transpired as of late. "And what did I say about not caring?" Mela responded, with more brashness than she had intended. She paused for a moment, then turned around in her chair. "We've discussed this before. It's not worth your while to argue otherwise."

Elaine started to speak, but Mela quickly cut her off. "Elaine . . ."

Not yet fully resigned to Mela's decision, Elaine pulled her hood back, revealing the heavy streaks of silver in her hair. It was thin and starting to fall out. *Less and less every day,* Mela thought. Most of the sisters hadn't seen the change, but observing things where others did not was Mela's gift, and it gave her a clear advantage. As wise as Elaine was, she continued to lose control of her younger sisters to the more youthful and seemingly progressive Acacia.

"Of course. This is what you call progress," Elaine said.

"It's my experiment and I'm keeping it," Mela added as a way to end the point.

Grinning at the exchange, Acacia pulled her hood back, revealing her long golden hair. Both Mela and Elaine couldn't help themselves from staring, as Acacia's fair tresses were always a jarring contrast to the dark locks representative of their kind.

"I rather like the trinket skull," Acacia casually added to the conversation. In truth, she liked the tension she could feel in the room more. Elaine took in an audible breath of dismay while Acacia slipped out of her robe and let it fall to the floor, showing off her limber, supple frame. The cloth dress Acacia wore was simple, but it said what it needed to, with its ability to hug each of her curves.

But the candlelight dancing upon her face also revealed a flaw in her soft skin. A fleshy ridge that ran sharply from above her eye, all the way to the crest of her nose. It had remained thin throughout its entire existence, but in the candle's long sifting shadows, it ebbed and flowed like a tidal crest.

In turn, Acacia's attention was solely focused on Mela. *Her hair always rides along her body in just the right way,* Acacia thought. *Her grey robes fool no one; her figure can't be hidden.*

"Yes, well, like it or not, it's not an experiment—it's a mistake, something that never would've been created had you better control of your emotions," Elaine countered back.

Acacia raised her eyebrows in delight.

Elaine noticed Mela's withering glare, but she couldn't help herself as she continued on. "The legends of our people are very clear on this and they hold truth to them, none so perverse as the Toten-Geist!" Elaine scared herself each time she used the phrase—not because she feared the legend, which of course she did, but because she was disturbed by how it had grown easier and easier to say out loud. "Creating mindless Untoten out of duty, out of self-preservation, is one thing, yes, a horrible thing . . . but this?" She gestured angrily at the skull. "This is what happens when we lose control of our emotions." She looked over to Acacia. "When we fall prey to our basest desires."

"I think we're far removed from whatever danger you're thinking of, Elaine," Mela said, though she knew she was closer than she portrayed. In truth, she had not pursued the idea any further than the skull. It had not moved past basic repetition, but Mela felt that there was a real possibility in the legend of an Untoten creature gaining complete sentience, given that its creator possessed the right balance of talent, discipline, and self-awareness. Elaine was indeed correct that the emotional outburst that had created the skull was uncharacteristic of

Mela's normally even temperament . . . but it was still a flawed creation. What thrilled her and terrified her was the possibility of getting it right.

"Far removed or not, it shouldn't have been pursued in the first place," Elaine said, in a tone growing more stern by the minute. She could feel the heat blossoming under her heavy robe and began to take it off. "The possibility of a dead mind is extremely dangerous. There would be no control over it." Elaine turned and hung her robe on the door hook.

I cannot stand how Acacia stares at Mela, Elaine thought. *Like a hunger, it hangs in the air and Mela just ignores it.*

Acacia decided to sit down and take in the show. It was an old one, but it still entertained her. She watched as her two sisters squared off, Mela sitting calmly, Elaine straightening her back and squaring her shoulders. Acacia swung one leg over the other and flicked her foot to the beat of the argument.

"It's bad enough what you've done already, defiling soldiers' bodies to work, to fight in our stead." Elaine said with disgust. "But to run the risk of creating real life from a corpse is unforgivable and dangerous to us all!"

"Those dead soldiers have created this, our home, and they have struck fear into the hearts of our enemies," Mela said coolly. "They've held the great and mighty knight-lord at bay." She straightened up and pressed her hands into her thighs. "Those walking corpses have given us our freedom."

"Those slaves, you mean," Elaine said. "Those damned bodies of labor. How do you earn freedom through the forced cooperation of others?" she argued. *We cannot win on the labors of others. Doesn't she understand that?* Elaine asked herself.

"They are things—not souls, not men, just things. There is no enslavement here, you can't enslave an object," Mela barked right back.

Well struck, Mela! Acacia thought, still focused on the young Gravewalker. *That old bat hasn't got a clue how powerful a tool you are, how strong those fearless corpses are.*

But Elaine still wasn't about to back down.

"You think a soul cannot feel its former body being controlled, being used against its will? Mela, those men were laid to rest after years of wandering the ether, after we came along and blessed them . . . but for what? To only curse them later?"

"You don't know what a soul feels, Elaine—none of us do. Don't be so dramatic," Mela said, growing tired of the same old argument. *Will she ever come up with something new? The same old phrases, the same old worries . . .*

"Yes, I do, all too well." Elaine said. The melancholy did not last, though, as she could feel the fire burning inside her again. "This is not our way!" she yelled at the top of her lungs, finally exploding.

"It is now," Mela said plainly.

"All according to plan," the skull cut in.

"What did that thing say?" Elaine asked, spooked by the skull's unexpected retort. *What is that thing doing? What is that girl doing?* Elaine thought, her mind racing. Distraught, she turned to see what Acacia was doing in response to all this, but found her idly playing with her golden hair.

"It's just finishing repeating what I said before," Mela said. "The interruption may've seemed strange, but it does that from time to time." *And it catches me off guard every time,* she thought.

"It's more than strange," Elaine said, coming back to the argument. "A voice like that, reaching out from the grave, it makes my blood freeze over." *Stay calm, Elaine, don't show too much emotion lest it starts to run away with you,* she thought. Her body stayed perfectly still, like a deer in the sight of a hunter. "It holds nothing to the sensibility of its former life," she added with certainty.

"He was a dog," Mela said firmly.

"Well, I miss the poor boy," Acacia chimed in. *Though his body wasn't poor,* Acacia chuckled to herself. She had grown weary of where the argument had been going, but the talking skull had opened a doorway for some fun.

"Leave it alone," Elaine said, sensing Acacia's direction of mischief.

"No, really," Acacia started. "He was a remarkable source of entertainment," she finished with a glint in her eye. *Fun, fun, fun!* she thought, with so many things in mind at once.

"I certainly hope so," Mela said, without turning from the skull. "He cost you a piece of your beauty."

Unable to help herself, Acacia reached up and felt her own face, her hand sliding down from above her eye, until she felt the ridge in the skin.

Mela smiled at her small victory. *Take your fun and keep it,* she thought.

"True, sister, he had his price," Acacia said, as she rose from her chair. "He was . . . an expensive endeavor." *She possesses more cruelty than I thought,* Acacia mused. *Not a bad thing, I suppose, but even I didn't deserve that.*

Still, even as she had been struck, Acacia felt a hint of excitement about the whole thing. She waited a moment for Mela to press forward, but when she didn't, Acacia headed for the door. *This game has played itself out for today.*

Mela heard her sister's footsteps departing out the chamber and smiled, allowing herself the tiniest sliver of satisfaction.

"Well, I hope all of that was worth it," Elaine said, sounding more like Mela's mother than her tutor.

"All of it is," Mela said, now tired of conversation. "I suppose you originally came to see me because of my father?"

"I did."

"It's not of any concern to me."

Elaine frowned, knowing Mela was just being condescending to her. *Acacia's influence, no doubt.* Not wanting to let it die just yet, Elaine looked back to the door. "I don't know why you give her so much power, Mela. She's dangerous."

"You think everything is dangerous, Elaine."

"And you think everything is under your control. You've had too much success with that for your own good. But this *thing* . . ." She turned to the skull to make her point. "That should remind you that you won't always be so fortunate."

She waited in vain, as Acacia had, for a response. When she didn't receive any, she made for the door as well. Slowly pulling her robe from the hook and onto her body, she added, "One day, something—or, yes, someone—they'll once again get to you, my dear girl. There's an emptiness in your heart and you're desperate to fill it. Your father, the respect of your sisters, another lover . . . who knows. But it will happen." She took a short breath with calculated effect. "And I'm afraid by then, it will be too late for any of us to do anything about it." And with that, she left, leaving Mela alone to herself.

"Too late," the skull echoed, as blue orbs rose up once again from the blackness of its sockets.

Eyes of misfortune . . . and truth.

CHAPTER 6

Not Whither, but Whether

Cass's horse was moving at a brisk trot, its gums pulled back with exhaustion. It bucked slightly to signal its annoyance, but Cass already had her hands on the reins, bringing them to a sudden stop.

She looked back to Edwin, wrinkling her nose. Edwin took the hint and swung down to the ground, stiff on his feet. The bard breathed a sigh of relief at the removal of Edwin's stench as she nimbly hopped off her horse in turn.

At the edge of a forest lay an abandoned fortress, its true size obscured by the rampant growth all around it. Moss and lichen had worked themselves into the cracks in the mortar, and trees hugged all around the edges as if they were trying to hold the building close, like a mother would a child.

Edwin lingered on the fortress, taking in its decrepit state. "What's this?" he asked.

Cass let out a slow breath as she tracked Edwin's vantage point. "Home," she answered. "For the last few miserable winters anyhow."

Cass's gaze suddenly dropped, wandering over the grounds as she took a few tentative steps forward. She caught the look of confusion on Edwin's face and pointed toward the woods. "They roam at night."

"They?" Edwin repeated, raising an eyebrow.

"Stray corpses, left behind by the Gravewalkers. Let's just say they're not exactly in the practice of, eh, laying the dead to rest anymore." She chuckled to herself as she continued. "Unrest is really more like it."

"I fail to see the humor."

"Then I suppose I'm just too clever for anyone's good," Cass replied with another laugh—until Edwin abruptly reached out and grabbed her by the shoulders.

"They were human once, no different than you or I," he growled, an inch away from throttling her. He brought his face in close and dropped his voice to a strained whisper. "Not fodder for your blasted amusement."

"Hm. Perhaps too clever for my own good then," Cass offered with the tiniest smile, but received no such expression in return. Seeing this, she tried a different approach. "Perhaps a little more respect was in order?"

"More than a little, I think," Edwin said, his voice dropping even further. He was too tired to stay angry for long, and he released his grip on the bard.

Cass caught herself and straightened up. With an uneasy cough, she reached for the reins of her horse to tether it to a nearby stump. In doing so, she spied Edwin scoping the grounds in earnest, a veteran soldier still, despite the years that had passed.

"Over here, milord."

After a few tense moments, Edwin reluctantly turned and followed the bard to a heavy thicket of underbrush. Cass prodded it a bit with her foot before kicking the loose vegetation aside, revealing a wooden trapdoor underneath. As she pulled it open, Edwin could see a stone staircase descending into the ground toward a warm glow. He looked back to Cass's horse, lazily chewing the tall grass in the clearing.

"Your horse?" Edwin asked.

"Let them try," Cass snickered. The irritable steed echoed Cass with a loud snort and a toss of its mangy head.

As Cass dropped beneath the earth and down the staircase, Edwin gave one last look to the expanse behind him. The crescent moon was barely illuminating the earth, lending the senses more to sound than sight. Edwin could discern the weeds rolling back and forth in the breeze. A rodent was scampering beneath them, cresting the brown warmth of the dying plants in the dark of night. It all appeared very clear for Edwin, everything the way it should've been for the moment.

One more glance, then he made his way after her.

***

The steps were steep and the space not very accommodating; Edwin's shoulders brushed against the stone walls all the way down to the growing light beneath. A cobweb caught his cheek and worked its way into his mouth. Barely able to reach for it in the tight quarters, he gave it an irritable puff as he continued downwards.

At the bottom was a corridor much wider than the staircase, but one just as littered with cobwebs. Edwin followed Cass's torch to the end and reached the source of the light, a great, wide chamber that shot up and out to the sides.

His attention was immediately drawn to the dome ceiling above, painted with figures he'd never seen before, a tapestry of dark shades of crimson and evergreen. Their details were nearly impossible to make out, but they charged his imagination. Like in the days of his childhood, his mind was wandering toward great and far-off adventures. Creatures of the dark robbing kingdoms of their princesses and having only Edwin to stop them.

Evelina, he thought, *my princess lost, and Mela, my lost princess.* His imagination once again faded into the past, into the shadows. As his gaze dropped downward, he saw that the floor, the furniture, the walls, that they were littered with artifacts. An underground museum of antiquity illuminated by the dull shine from hundreds of flickering candles. Dust hung about most of the relics. They were propped on wooden stands, crammed into shelves of cabinets, piled into corners. Others showed care, hours of love spent in cleaning them to former glory. Old rusty swords rested against shields that bore crests of families long extinct, while some were emblazoned with images from a different time, all unfamiliar to Edwin. All from a time before the Brotherhood had done away with all of that, a time when blood had ruled all. A time before a family of men allowed the unification of high and low, all under one banner.

It all seems trapped in a circle now, he mused.

There was also a sea of literature that rolled about the room. Scrolls of yellowed parchment and books with cracked leather-bound covers spilled out before him, scattered among a menagerie of cracked skulls and melted candles.

"Could fancy me a collector of historical odds and ends, I suppose," Cass said, as she plopped down on a makeshift couch. It was worn out in a loving manner and probably the cleanest thing in the room because of it. Cass grabbed a bottle from the floor and pressed it to her lips; a hard swallow followed. "But not of decent wine," Cass sighed. "The depravity of being piss-poor."

"Try something else besides pilfering burial grounds," Edwin said as he continued to gaze around the room.

"Not just burial grounds, you know," Cass retorted.

"Of course. Where else then?"

"As of late, the Fields of Sorrow," Cass answered as she swung from her couch to a low-standing wooden table. "As I'd like to call them anyway."

She cleared away books and goblets and slapped down a map. Her finger pointed toward a hastily drawn skull nestled between two mountains. "There's something about it that I haven't quite figured out yet, but for your intents, we'll just call it the site of just another vain, insufferable war, duly forgotten along with so many others." She took a deep touch from her wine bottle to the same grimace as before. "Forgotten to all those with exception of the, ah, intellectual sort."

Edwin's frown made Cass pause. "Ahem, well . . ." She pressed on after catching Edwin's stony expression. "Speaking of grand tales . . . we have yet to discuss yours."

"There's nothing to discuss," Edwin grunted back.

Cass smiled, something that Edwin had already decided annoyed him, as if he was being manipulated. He wasn't some lovesick fool and he was tired of being charmed as if he were. Stranger still was the thought that a woman could make him feel that way, almost like a piece of meat to be coaxed and tenderized . . . but the lute was already in Cass's hands. She laid back into the couch and began to strum, her fingers plucking and pulling with deft, quick strokes.

"No?" Cass seemed to sing out the question. "There's no merit to the travails of the Knights Proper?"

Her words cut sharply into Edwin. "No," he insisted. "And stop saying 'the Knights Proper.' It's the—"

"Konig Protectorate," she finished for him. "Of course, milord." Cass didn't let him off the hook, though, as she waited patiently for the rest of his response.

"The matter's settled, there's nothing left to do."

Cass's smile grew even wider, the grin of a conniving jester more than anything else.

"Whether the weather is whetted for heroic endeavors . . . ," she began to sing, plucking her lute a bit harder now.

"Or wet for to wither your miserable bones
run hither or thither but never ye shiver
it matters not whither, but whether you go."

As she finished, Cass simply got up and walked down another corridor. "Come, Sir Misery and Suffering."

Edwin's jaw tightened, but he nevertheless followed Cass into a small stone chamber that looked fit for a servant's sleeping quarters. A meager cot sat at the back with a water basin tucked beside it. A few candles were spread about, but there, on the wall, was the one thing that captured Edwin's true attention.

A magnificent suit of armor, along with a burnished sword . . . now free from the cemetery muck where Edwin had last made use of them. They glowed with reflected brilliance, the artifacts capturing what little light remained in the chamber.

"Recognize these?" Cass asked, knowing the answer and smiling wider than ever.

"Where did you . . . ," Edwin started.

"A collector, remember?"

Edwin finally pulled his gaze away from the suit of armor to look Cass directly in the eyes. "Speak plainly, bard. This. All of this. What's it for?"

"I told you," Cass said, her expression a touch more serious now. "You have a grand story in the making, and I want to tell it."

"And I already told you . . ." Edwin's impatience was mounting. "There's nothing I can do."

"Well, what if I said there was a way . . . a way to see your daughter again?" Cass asked, her own patience being tested as well.

Edwin froze. "How?"

"Bah." Cass's smile began to rise again in her face. "Details aren't important. It's whether you're willing." She walked over to a wooden chest that Edwin missed when he first walked in.

"Whether or not you have the conviction to finally tell her how you truly feel," she said.

Edwin's eyes narrowed at her last comment, but he remained silent.

And when Cass stood up, her expression seemed to have been devoured by her own newfound conviction. No laughter now, no smiles. Serious and taut, she spoke without joke or song. "Because surely, if saving the good people of Riesenstadt wasn't reason enough for you . . ." She grabbed Edwin's hand and forced something into it. "Then perhaps the chance to finally set things right would suffice instead."

She paused before continuing, letting the moment wash over Edwin. "For the Knight Proper knows the meaning of love, just as much as he knows the meaning of duty."

Edwin looked down into his hands. Soft and tiny, there it lay . . . Mela's doll from years past. Rescued from the cemetery, cleaned with the same care as the armor.

He heard Cass's footsteps trailing out the door as he continued to stare at the doll.

"Consider my words, Edwin Talmaris," Cass's voice echoed through the stone walls. "And by the Gods . . ." Edwin turned quickly to see the bard's face peeking around the doorway. "Will you please make use of a proper bath? I thought the dead were outside, not in here."

Her head disappeared from the doorway again and her voice returned to echoes from the hallway. "Words of gold, sir knight! Words to consider!"

CHAPTER 7

A Bedtime Story

Mela rolled and moaned beneath the sheets of her bed, an ornate thing of old wood and corroded nails. The posts swayed with every movement of her body, constantly threatening to give way and collapse altogether. Then the moaning stopped, replaced by her heavy breaths.

Cocooned by the pitch-black of the chamber, she felt her hair lightly touching her face, like a ghost seeking warmth. The dream was fading away, pieces at a time, as she tried to hold on to the horror. She didn't know why she had been so scared and she never would if she couldn't train her mind to embrace these nightmarish visions.

Bloodied, severed limbs strewn about. A gate of some sort.

And then . . . nothing.

She pulled away her covers and swung her legs over the edge of the bed. The stone floor was cool on her feet, not freezing as she always suspected it would be—just enough to help calm her nerves. She blinked, still seeing nothing in the dark as it pressed on her eyes. There were little streaks and clouds of color, but she knew it was only her mind inventing things to replace the void before her. Letting her feet feel her way across the room and to her desk, she reached her hand out toward the stool and grabbed a hold of the warm wood. As she sat down, she felt for the matches on the desk and soon had one lit. The scratch and hiss finally brought light to her eyes, then to the wick of her candle.

"Why do I know you?" a flat voice asked. Mela felt her nerves stand on end but stayed stuck to her stool. "I know you from somewhere," the voice continued. "But what somewhere?"

Mela's eyes slowly turned toward the mounted skull, not quite sure where it had gotten that. *I never asked such a thing.* A small hint of panic crept into her thoughts.

"Please," the skull started again, "please tell me." The voice rustled in her ears like dry air on a hot summer's day.

"It's a long story," Mela finally answered, unable to think of anything else to say.

"Long," the skull stated as if it were deciphering the meaning. "Tell me the long story." It droned as flatly as Mela had ever heard. She could see the blue eyes creeping out from the dark sockets once again, and then she heard a voice for the first time in a long time. His voice.

"Remind me how I know you, Mela," the skull commanded. At its words, at *his* words, she could once again feel the chains on her skin. The memory of the cold iron and the sound they made as they clinked against their surroundings. His chains would always remain in her mind just as they stayed in her room, hidden beneath her bed. His voice grated on her, just as the memory of the chains did.

She paused for a moment, but her initial anxiety was now a thing of the past as she fully embraced the melancholy she was feeling. "I found you wandering," she said. "Found you on the outskirts of our camp, lost and hungry."

Mela stared straight into the bone and traced its shape as she gathered her thoughts. *This is real, I can feel it,* she thought, while her subconscious organized her story.

The candle burned straight and narrow. There was no wind in the room anymore, no draft from above to tease the flame. Just as the air had gone out of her, so had the room emptied of everything but her and the skull.

"We hadn't been there long, but we knew that we had to stay and make it our new home," she said. She rolled her toes on the stone floor but felt the barren soil of days past crumble beneath her feet. "A vast battlefield, its fallen warriors a gift to our cause. The knight-lord was still searching for us, to end us once and for all . . . but we were tired of running."

Mela looked up to the earthen ceiling above, its contours molded and sculpted in a way that suggested a guiding hand. "There was much debate—Elaine, of course, always clinging to the old ways, but our survival won out. We raised the dead, these combatants of ages past, traded in their broken swords and shattered shields for shovels and pikes . . . and we began to build this. Our fortress."

She turned back to the skull, a trace of wistfulness in her voice. "The rains had gone on for days and you had lost your bearings while riding out the storm. I could see the genuine confusion in your eyes." *I always saw everything in your eyes—except for her.* "You had been herding sheep but had been unable to keep them together in the great storm. All you had were the clothes on your back and a walking stick, no idea of where you were." Everything was starting to flood her memory now, and Mela was trying hard not to let it overwhelm her.

"Close as you were to discovering us, my sisters were ready to dispatch you, but I stopped them. You collapsed before me, but I caught you and brought you gently to the ground." *You had been so weak in that moment.* Mela could remember how shallow his breath had been as she held him. *I let that cloud my judgment and always thought of you as weak and gentle.* "We carried you down below and into my room." *Even then it wasn't much different,* Mela couldn't help thinking.

While there was plenty of work to be done, their personal chambers were among the first tasks to be completed. Mela had taken the largest room at the end of the tunnel, and Acacia the room to her right. At first, Elaine had refused to live in such a tomb and Acacia rarely spent time underground anyway, so for all intents and purposes, Mela was left to herself.

To him.

"I had only brought in a cot at the time and we placed you on it." She could still remember the creak and groan of the makeshift bed under his weight. "We placed you near the wall and I chained you to it to satisfy my sisters' concerns. As I'd said, we hadn't been here long and were in no mood to be uprooted again by loose tongues alerting others to our location." *It was so different to have thoughts of comfort in those days, to find a place and want to call it home.* "After enduring the knight-lord's crusade, my sisters had traveled for many years and I felt for them. Their concerns were mine and I rarely found any happiness, except in theirs." *Happiness?*

The illuminated skull sat motionless before her, simply taking it all in. Mela wasn't sure if it was listening anymore or if it had gone dormant, but she'd started this story and she was going to finish it. "Many discussions were had as to whether or not you were one of Renton's spies. I was convinced of your story, despite my own untrusting nature, but convincing the other sisters of your innocence was no easy task. It didn't help that Acacia had sided with me, seeing how many of the sisters didn't lend her much credence. While I awaited their final decision, I spent my nights feeding you, bringing you back to health." *Long nights of stories, wonderful stories.* "You told me of your family and the stories you shared with each other. I couldn't see how you would be a serious threat, but I could appreciate my sisters' hesitations to let you simply go back home." *If I had, I could have been rid of you.* "Eventually a compromise was reached that if you were to stay alive, you would need to remain here, imprisoned. With me. I volunteered that you would stay where you were, as I had grown fond of you and was comfortable enough sharing the space."

I wanted you with me.

After the prisoner's fate had been decided, efforts to create an underground stronghold had begun in earnest. The Gravewalkers and their endless supply of skeletal minions built and built like they hadn't before. Elaine and a few of the other sisters had been set on continuing to live above in tents but finally submitted to moving below for fear of alerting others to their presence, especially with their frequent trips to the river for fresh water. Knowing that Renton and his men would search the surrounding areas, they instead had a trench dug that brought the water directly to them.

"Life had turned nearly normal after several months. You remained chained to my wall, but now you shared my bed." *It was always warmer for it and has never been warm since.* "You had become my confidant and lover. In a fashion, you had become my teacher as well. I would spend days down here, only answering the door for food and water. Both Acacia and Elaine tried hard to get me to leave more often. I didn't know it yet, but I was losing the respect of my sisters, who rarely saw their leader."

Meetings were held every night. A roundtable of discussion, a chance to tell the old stories and voice concerns, even if most of the early nights were spent with only that, concerns.

What was Renton going to do next, could he find them here, and what was their leader going to do about it?

Given her propensity for bloodshed, Acacia had thrived on all of it. Old stories that reawakened the spirits of the sisters and rekindled their desires. Stories of the Toten-Geist, a chance to bring a real threat against Renton and his forces. Yes, they currently harbored a legion of soldiers, but eventually they would have to find a new source of corpses, while the Toten-Geist could perhaps bring them complete victory. Acacia told these stories again and again, as they watched the embers burning in her eyes, as they stared at her unnatural blonde locks. The will to fight was rising as the sisters grew restless with each passing night, with every retelling of violent retaliation.

And over time, Mela eventually dwindled from the sisters' minds and stories that flew furiously around the fires.

"I had grown too comfortable where I was. With you and with the peace that we had seemed to find in this place." *Warmth.* "One day, I was wandering the tunnels, when I nearly collided with a sister by accident. She looked up at me without knowing who I was, 'Sorry, sister' being all she said. There was no respect in her voice, no contemplation of who she had just walked into."

I wasn't myself anymore. I didn't know it yet, but I wasn't who I needed to be.

"'They've forgotten you, Mela,' Acacia told me afterwards. She had seen them each forget, one sliver at a time as I had spent so much time away, down here, with my lover. I remember how she'd said that very word—*lover*—with such disgust, for a sister never takes on a partner, only a coupling or two to give us a child." *To have a child now.* "I wasn't ready for that, my own childhood being reason enough." *I was strong for the wrong reasons then.*

"It was time to be with my sisters again. I had to show them that their leader hadn't left them, but I wasn't going to leave you either. I put my hatred aside and joined with them before their fires. I brought them stories, stories of our lore, of our traditions, of healing and ceremony, passed down to me by Elaine. Of our roles as caretakers of the dead and caretakers of the living, to those who had lost their loved ones."

They were not hiding—they were surviving, and Mela had to show them that. Survival meant keeping their stories alive and their practices strong. But each night, the younger sisters would ask for the stories of the rising dead, of power, and of bloodshed. Acacia's imagination had struck deep into their cores and Mela was having a hard time persuading them otherwise. When Acacia could be found, the sisters sought her out and asked for her stories. They respected Mela just as they respected Elaine, but they hadn't found their leader yet. She had been lost and forgotten, and they needed to find her again.

"One night, after struggling to keep my sisters' attention on our tradition, but losing them to boredom, I headed back to my room earlier than usual. I stayed lost in my thoughts and the flicker of the torch lights hanging from the walls of the tunnel." *I guess that's why I didn't hear her.* "When I opened my door, I found that I had lost more than my sisters. There she was, flaxen hair swinging about in treachery and deceit, as you lay there with her on top of you. That's where she had been while I was trying to bring my family back together. That's what she had been doing while I blindly droned on about peace and survival. You and she had been desecrating my bed every night before I lay in it. Before I came back to you!"

How utterly foolish I'd been.

"I grabbed her by that hair of hers and pulled her from you to the ground. I stared at you, your chest heaving in ecstasy, your eyes wide and reflecting me at myself." *Never again.* "I reached to my desk as you pulled at your chains. The knife was just there waiting for me. I plunged it into you again and again. You moaned and I plunged harder and faster. Your moans growing louder in my ears, just as they had every night we had spent together, only now it fueled only my rage." *I'll never feel passion again.* "When you stopped and all I could hear was the knife churning your insides, I collapsed.

"'Well, at least now that's over,' I heard Acacia say. I turned to her naked body on the floor with all the anger that still pounded inside of me. She could see my fury. I knew it because of what she said. 'You wouldn't kill a sister, Mela. You can't kill a sister.'

"I could feel my muscles relax as I approached her. I told her I knew I couldn't as I gently swept her beautiful hair from her face. I told her I wouldn't, even as I raised my knife to her face. And I felt myself smile as I cut her." *What that unleashed still reverberates to this day.* "I let her bleed on my floor and turned to your mangled body. And then I had my true moment of weakness. Tears that built up inside me but never escaped, a scream that never released as my knees slammed into the stone floor. I reached back into my memory, back to when Acacia and I were younger. A day when, in our arrogance, we sought to create a Toten-Geist but found ourselves sorely lacking."

Mela leaned in closer. "You know what the legends say about our abilities, don't you? How they work?" The skull remained silent. "Emotions, nothing more. All the spent tears, all the sorrow, it's the kindle to our fire. But what they don't know is this . . . that our own emotions have an effect as well, that they can rule our powers beyond control. Not just fear or anger. It's what makes you angry. What makes you laugh. What makes you fall in love. What makes you feel pain. I felt true pain, the pain of your heart's betrayal. I felt all this and more . . . and I breathed a half-life back into your body."

Mela reminisced to herself, of how a bloody and naked Acacia ran out into the dark that night and screamed out to all the sisters. "She's done it!" she shrieked. "Mela has brought us our revenge!" The sisters rushed to the entrance of the tunnel to see what Acacia was wailing about and were met with a horrible and wonderful sight.

Mela stood there, blood on her hands, a pair of blue eyes glowing from behind her in the darkness. He walked out into the firelight and confounded them all. His hollowed-out gut dripped onto the soil as he stumbled toward them, his head cocking this way and that as he took them all in.

"The Toten-Geist shall bring us our revenge!" Acacia screamed to the heavens, nearly choking on her own blood-matted hair.

"But she was wrong. You were not the Toten-Geist she prayed for; you were incomplete. Just as I was, after you took a piece of my soul with you." *That piece that all first loves get.* "I couldn't stand the sight of you, so I had your flesh boiled away and watched your eyes explode in the heat. We disposed of all your bones but your skull, I placed it here as a trophy, something Acacia suggested." *I'm thankful she did, I suppose.* "One night, while I pored over maps, mumbling to myself, you spoke to me, but with my words. Every night since, I've spilled my thoughts to you and had you keep them, to speak back to me whenever I asked for them." *A tool of the most macabre.* "But tonight . . . you spoke your own words and, somehow, with your own voice." *Something much worse.* "And now I'm not sure what I am anymore, if I can't figure out who, or what, you truly are."

Mela rose then from her stool and blew out the candle. As she walked back to bed, a voice reached out to her, that familiar, haunting voice.

"I find you wanting," it said.

"What did you say?" Mela demanded as she spun on the spot.

"Found you on the outskirts of our camp, lost and hungry." The skull continued in its regular, flat voice. "We hadn't been there long, but we knew that we had to stay and make it our new home." Mela calmed down and realized the skull was now reciting back to her as it always did.

It's late and I haven't been sleeping enough. It's all playing with my head, she thought, but she was not able to convince herself completely. She crawled back into bed and listened to the skull recite her tale to the darkness, to her. *Perhaps this is what it's coming to,* she mused. *Perhaps we're all mad.*

CHAPTER 8

Slow to Rise for Quite the Surprise

The Gods were battling in the air while hapless mortals could only watch from below.

At least that's how Cass envisioned it. As majestic swords struck each other, ripples of golden lightning sprayed out into the air. She slumped back on her couch, while her eyelids fought to stay aloft as a heavy pulse thrummed in her head, keeping the beat of the fight above.

Of course, the small part of her brain somehow unaffected by alcohol recognized that it was just the morning light, soft and gentle, streaming into the vaulted chamber through the circular windows above. Cass appreciated the slow movement of the sun's rays, not quite ready for the harsh light of day just yet. Her mind wandered to thoughts of why one's focus was so minimal in the morning, especially after too much drink. The stories of a time passed by played out above, then blended into curious thoughts and disappeared altogether as she could no longer focus on either.

To her fingertips, the sloping glass of the wine bottle was cool and soothing. *More than I could ever say about the contents,* she thought. She barely felt the rest of her body, but she knew she would have to do something soon to make sure it stayed that way.

Then, faintly, there was the aroma of steel in the air. Cass couldn't directly place it, but it was definitely nearby, invading her nostrils. Indeed, it felt as if it were just above her head. There was the smell of soap as well. She tilted her head back, feeling her pulse shift from one side of her head to the other as she spied a human column of polished metal.

"You're slow to rise this morning, bard," Edwin said, staring down at Cass.

Cass drew a sharp breath, for the haggard, bearded beggar that she had seen the night before was now resplendent in a burnished suit of armor, clean-shaven in a way that brought home the regal bearing that Edwin had inherited from his father.

"I'd imagine in your old age, sir knight, that you'd share the same predicament," Cass said, weakly laughing it off as she sought to cope with Edwin's transformation. Soon enough, though, the pain rattling in her head put an end to her gawking, as did Edwin's raised eyebrows.

"Slow. To rise? In the morning? Or really just anytime in particular," she winked, finding it was much less painful than laughing.

"Yes," Edwin said, unamused. "You're quite the poet, aren't you?"

"Feh! Poetry is for lovesick little girls. And, ah, lend me a hand, won't you?" Cass implored with yet another wink. Edwin didn't answer, but instead reached down and rolled her off of her couch. "Gods!" she moaned as her face pressed against the cold stone floor. "Humor, have you heard of such a thing, sir knight?"

"Yes," said Edwin.

"Yes," Cass mimicked. Edwin then reached down and hauled her up into the air, face-to-face. "A much better look for you," Cass said as she considered Edwin's appearance with genuine interest. "Yes, quite good," was all she could add, her mind growing fuzzy with all the sudden movement.

Edwin said nothing as he continued to hold Cass aloft.

"Ah, are you hungover as well, friend?" she asked. "Your vocabulary is about as ranged as mine at the moment." Edwin finally threw her back onto the couch, where she landed like a sack of potatoes and didn't budge.

"I've been thinking, bard. On what you said."

Cass blinked in acknowledgment. Her entire dedication was focused on trying to hear Edwin over the pounding in her head, and answering with words would require too many functions at this state in the morning.

"You were right," he said.

As Cass looked on, the light grew brighter by the moment, causing Edwin's armor to shine like a blazing torch. *A knight truly stands before me this morning,* Cass mused. "Excellent! Because you look quite ready to cleave some heads, I'd say," Cass finally let out over the pain.

"Yes," Edwin replied.

"Yes . . . ," Cass mumbled to herself as she felt around for her own sword. "Ever the master of words."

"Suit up, bard. We're going to find my daughter," Edwin rumbled, his old rank resurfacing.

Cass moaned as she pushed herself up from the couch. Her muscles were starting to hurt, yet it was time to take action. She shuffled across the room to a bookshelf and reached out for a hefty volume. "Well, I too must gird myself this morning, sir knight," Cass said as she pulled the book from the shelf. The leathery cover groaned open and Cass flipped just a few pages over to reveal an amber bottle hidden inside.

"More spirits?" Edwin said, as he saw the bottle emerge from the pages.

"A draught of healing," Cass corrected him. "Aged fifty years," she added with a great grin. She shuffled back toward the couch and grabbed a glass from the table at its side.

"Do we really have time for—"

"Shh . . ." Cass stopped him. "A moment, please."

And Edwin watched as the bottle was uncorked, poured into the glass, and then consumed, as if it was all one motion. Cass closed her eyes and savored the moment. She could feel the liquid working through her body quickly, warming, loosening, and charging her with new life.

"Like after a warm afternoon's nap, sir knight," Cass said, finally opening her eyes. "Now then. Ready to start the day?"

She corked the bottle and laid it gently back into the pages. Edwin watched her stride across the room to place the book back upon the shelf and then back toward him, grabbing her rapier before continuing to the grand chamber.

Edwin shook his head and called out after her, "I hope you know how to fight with that pig sticker of yours."

Cass came to a complete stop, then turned around.

"Pig . . . pig sticker!" she exclaimed.

"Yes," Edwin said. "Pig sticker."

For once, Edwin thought, he had finally captured the bard's attention with something else besides threats of physical harm. The slightest of smiles upon his face, Edwin gripped his scabbard tight and marched by a dismayed Cass, toward the stairs above.

***

Soon they were on the road, with Cass atop her horse and Edwin marching ahead. Traveling under blustery clouds that hung over miles and miles of wet, grassy knolls, they climbed and descended, the wind rising and falling just the same. Marching in full plate, Edwin did his best not to show fatigue, but he was still only two days removed from a jail cell; his breaths turned more ragged with each climb. Further darkening his mood was the absolute absence of life; the landscape was as empty and forlorn as the skies above. Cottages were boarded up and abandoned; farms were choked with weeds. Grumbling through the discomfort and the chafing, he gritted his teeth and marched on.

After what seemed to be yet another stretch of endless hills, Cass finally broke the silence. "You don't have to walk, you know." She waited for a response, but Edwin continued to plod on in silence, pausing only to wipe heavy beads of sweat from his forehead.

She shrugged in resignation. "You really *do* enjoy suffering, don't you?"

"Good exercise," Edwin stated flatly, speaking for the first time since they had left the fort.

Cass chuckled. *If he wants to make it harder on himself, then so be it,* she thought. Even Cass's steed seemed to realize that it was much better off than the knight as it raised a bloodshot eye to Edwin's reddened face and snorted.

On a whim, Cass reached into her saddle bag and withdrew a matted black book, stuffed with unruly slivers of yellowed parchment. Reaching back in one more time, she also found a feathered quill, slate-grey with bluish black, as sharp as the falcon it came from.

"Now then," Cass intoned. "Let us speak clearly and without equivocation. Your father . . . an arse biter of heroic proportions, wouldn't you say?"

Edwin gave no response, continuing to dutifully march ahead.

Cass pursed her lips and readied the quill for another attempt.

"You're his son, his very own flesh and blood . . . yet he still threw you ass over end into a piss pot of a jail cell. I mean, when one says, 'knight-lord,' it does carry a certain weight, a certain expectation of benevolence, yes? At least to one's own kin?"

Cass chose her pauses carefully in the hope of grabbing Edwin's attention, but still the knight continued to trudge on in silence. Seeing that she'd have better luck interrogating her horse, Cass gave up, placing the quill and her book back into her saddlebag.

"Did you know your father, bard?" Edwin suddenly asked.

"Oh, I knew my father, all right. The problem was he didn't know me," Cass replied.

Whatever retort Edwin had planned next, it dissipated as he looked at Cass, intrigued by her admission.

A gleam of hope shined in Cass's eyes as she reached back into her saddlebag for the quill and the book. "An exchange it is, then! Unless you expect me to compose a heroic tale derived entirely of grunts and nods . . ."

Not wanting to give Edwin the chance to say no, Cass dived right back in before he could respond. "Noble blood, you see. It runs in my veins just as well. And as such, my father expected me to paint my face, wrap myself in ridiculous dresses, and happily marry some flatulent pig, all for the grand finale of an ignominious death, after a lifetime of squeezing out his ungrateful little brats."

"And what does that make you?"

"Some might say that you and I are one and the same, sir knight."

Edwin scowled, but found there was nothing he could say in response.

Cass snorted with amusement. "Oh, relax. At least your father still wants you back, or so I've heard. No, I'm a bastard, through and through, milord, even if it's for entirely the wrong reasons."

"Then tell me," Edwin said. "What right has a bastard of asking another person about such things?"

"Eh, I see . . . ," Cass said, a little stung but also getting a better answer than what Edwin had provided. "But if we really want to discuss bastards, what of your brother?" She readied her quill once more.

"Half brother," Edwin corrected.

Cass shook her head. "I'm guessing your family gatherings must've been such joyous occasions, declarations of love and affection from everyone's lips. Is this how you were with your daughter as well?"

Edwin stopped in his tracks, pausing to wipe his brow. "Cease your endless prattling and remind me again where we're going," he said.

Much to Edwin's dismay, Cass smiled back. "I never said."

"Perhaps you should."

"Perhaps you should remember that it was you that made a solemn vow to set things right."

"Perhaps I should just strangle you now and be done with it."

Cass gave a nervous laugh in return, a finger drifting to her rapier.

"And I never took any blasted vow, curse you and your pretty little words," Edwin growled, inching closer.

Cass's horse snorted with delight, apparently not at all concerned for its owner's well-being. "You want pretty little words?" Cass said. "How about—" she started before she was interrupted by the telltale sound of someone cutting wood, the first sign of life that they'd seen all day. Cass and Edwin both turned their heads, looking forward to the small farm just ahead.

There, a rail-thin farmer put his axe aside and gathered up the logs lying at his feet. Struggling to hold them aloft, he trudged his way over to a wooden pyre. Lying atop was a woman of middle-age and a young boy of no more than five or six years. Cass and Edwin both watched as the farmer finally reached the pyre and added the last of the logs before reaching for a lit torch nearby.

"By the spirits, what's he doing?" Edwin asked, horrified at what he was seeing.

"No one buries their dead anymore," Cass explained, glad for the change in conversation. Edwin stared on in confusion, but Cass led him on further. "The fire prevents . . . ah, unexpected visits from loved ones, I suppose you could say."

Edwin shook his head in denial. "She wouldn't raise these people," he said, more to himself than to the bard. "Raising soldiers with weapons and armor . . . yes, I see that, but women and children?"

"Every *body* is fair game," Cass said as she scribbled in her book, apparently far too jaded for an event such as this to strike her. "You can take some consolation in that it's not just your daughter raising the dead, though. All of the Gravewalkers are finding it to their fancy these days."

"Consolation?" Edwin spat. "What use is a mother, a little boy?"

In the distance, the pyre came to life with a whoosh of flame and smoke as the farmer threw his torch on top and took a step back. His frail shoulders slumped in utter resignation, as the flames grew about the woman and child before engulfing them completely.

Edwin watched in dismay, until the stench of burning flesh reached his nostrils and turned his stomach. He had endured the smell of burning flesh before, but they had been men, warriors, or brigands. The acrid perfume of this family was unbearable. *They didn't deserve this fate,* he thought.

Cass raised her hands and tried to explain. "It is simply the way things are done now, sir knight. It's been so long now that it feels sometimes that this has always been the way." She shrugged, then reached down into her saddlebag to retrieve her flask. She lifted it to her lips only to find it empty. "Curse upon curses . . . ," she started.

"I know," Edwin said, with sorrow in his voice. Cass refrained from the rest of her comment and let the knight be.

Edwin hung his head for another moment, then turned back to Cass, his eyes blazing with renewed determination. "How much farther, to wherever in the hells you're taking us," he demanded.

"Not much, milord, not much," Cass said, thinking it better to just give the man an honest answer, as she looked into the distance. Her gaze followed the adjacent river, dwindling into the heavy vegetation and crooked trees of a swamp.

Edwin nodded and marched on, just as the pyre began to collapse upon itself. As they reached the edge of the farm, the man who was watching his family burn stood silently by, motes of ash drifting into the grey skies behind him. Edwin solemnly nodded his head toward the farmer in respect. The farmer responded by launching a thick gob of spit, which landed at Edwin's feet. The man then stood his ground and watched as the two travelers passed him by.

"He no doubt blames your father and the Knights Prop—" Cass said, before correcting herself. "The Konig Protectorate. There's no way he could know who you are, milord."

Cass offered a brief smile, trying to lessen Edwin's distress, but the knight wasn't buying it. As they continued down the road, Edwin turned back to the farm and the charred remnants atop the funeral pyre . . . and lingered for a long time.

"I'll change that," he said. "Whatever it takes, I will change all of that."

CHAPTER 9

Stage Tricks

Not long after, Cass and Edwin reached the edge of the swampland. The moss-green miasma of the bog lay before them, an expanse of fetid gloom broken up by arching trees and curtains of sickly yellow vegetation. Within its depths, tiny points of pale light flitted about in erratic patterns.

Atop her horse, Cass couldn't help but wonder how anything could thrive here, as even the insects that called this place home seemed to be stricken ill, feebly lurching about from place to place. She covered her face in a vain attempt to siphon off the cloying rot that assaulted her nostrils, but it was simply no use. As for Edwin, despite his renewed sense of determination from earlier, he was bent over, gulping ragged breaths.

"Stay a moment, sir knight," Cass said, at which Edwin nearly collapsed to the muck underneath him. The bard dismounted and grabbed her horse by the reins, but it refused to budge. She pulled harder the second time but only received a determined snort of disapproval. "Suit yourself," Cass said, as the nag flared its nostrils in return. "Damnable beast," she muttered before turning to survey their location.

While their immediate surroundings consisted of nothing but miles and miles of dense wetland, one last reminder of civilization lay before them. A modest roadhouse, its windows boarded up just like the other dwellings they had previously encountered. There was also a dock, jutting out over the river, which had now dwindled to a miserable specimen of its former strength. Like everything else here, the swamp's influence had seemingly brought it to heel.

Cass pointed ahead to a small boat adjacent to the dock. "There, we'll take that inland. Not far now." She drew her flask out, only to remember that it was empty. She cursed her luck, but as her gaze drifted to the roadhouse, her dismay turned into a wide-open grin.

"A boat?" Edwin asked, his hands still on his knees. He looked down to notice his boots slowly sinking into the wet soil, along with a trail of blood spread across the dirt, crimson droplets spotting the fallen leaves. Edwin looked closer, then called back to Cass. "Wait . . ."

But Cass was already at the roadhouse, peering through boarded windows.

"Right, right. Just get the craft ready, will you?" Cass gave the knob to the door a slight twist but found it to be locked. "Heh. Nothing a little finesse won't fix." Taking out a set of small steel picks from a pouch on her belt, she began to size them up against the door's lock. "No, no, no," she muttered as she matched each one up. Then her eyes opened wide, the possibility of refilling her flask suddenly becoming a very real possibility. "Yes, there you are, my dear." She held up a slender pick between her forefinger and thumb.

She was angling it toward the keyhole when she was distracted by a sharp whinny. Looking up, she saw her horse bolting back the way they came, clods of wet muck flying from its hooves. Cass wrinkled her brow, but turned back to the lock. "Bah. The wretch will be back soon enough," she muttered. Shifting the pick gracefully between her fingers, she plied the keyhole once more, eventually being rewarded with a click as the lock gave way.

Edwin watched Cass's horse gallop off into the distance and took a wary look around, his fatigue suddenly forgotten. "We need to keep moving," he said, still eyeing the blood on the ground.

"Just going to take a little look inside," Cass answered as she stood up and put her lock picks away. She gave the rusted knob a twist and peeked her head in through the door.

In the distance, Edwin shouted, "Damn you, that means now, bard!" but Cass's quest would not be denied.

What she saw, however, was far from any stockades of mind-numbing drink. Instead, a mass of huddled strangers filled the tavern floor, just barely visible in the darkness of the room. They stood still and silent among a clutter of broken tables and chairs.

Cass reeled back and covered her nose, gagging against a reek that surpassed even the stench of the swamp. And as one, the shadowy figures slowly turned toward her.

Her eyes widening in surprise, Cass fought down her nausea and slowly retreated. "Eh, pardon me, will you?"

***

Edwin threw his hands up in disgust and turned toward the heavy rope that held the boat fast. As he plied his thick fingers helplessly against the intricate knot, he lamented that there was simply no talking sense to his companion. *I swear that she'll come running out any moment now, screaming for help like some bleating sheep . . .*

And Cass didn't disappoint; Edwin suddenly heard the bard's shrill shout. Turning to see what the ruckus was about, he saw that Cass was indeed running, running toward the boat and Edwin like her very life depended on it. And as Edwin looked just beyond the sprinting bard, he swore violently under his breath when he saw what the bard was fleeing from.

Erupting forth from the roadhouse door was a steady stream of rotting flesh, caked with the dirt of their once-occupied graves. Men, women, and even children, with their ragged, shriveled arms reaching toward Cass. Edwin thought back to the funeral pyre from earlier and realized the folly of his ways. That same anger snapped him out of his stupor as he gritted his teeth and pulled his sword free of its scabbard.

"Damn this, damn this all . . . ," he cursed under his breath.

This was just as Cass sprinted by with nothing more to say than a squeak of terror. The bard reached the boat and began to furiously work the knot—until a low moan caught her attention. A husk of a former farmer closed in on her, its jaw hanging by a fleshy thread, swinging back and forth. Cass yelped, the knot still in her hands as the creature grasped at her with blackened nails and ivory stubs of bone. That was until a sword cleaved the corpse in half as Edwin rose up in front of her.

"Move aside!" Edwin ordered. Cass obliged and lunged away, as Edwin brought his heavy sword down for a second time to split the docking rope. Cass spun back in time to see another misshapen corpse lurching toward her . . . and then she suddenly collapsed.

"Bard?" Edwin called out in confusion.

The corpse, seeing the lifeless body of Cass, turned its attention toward Edwin as two more Untoten minions entered the fray. Caught by surprise and now starting to feel the fatigue of the day's march return, Edwin barely managed to avoid their skeletal claws, slashing and parrying as even more Untoten staggered in his direction.

While Edwin was battling for his life, Cass slowly opened one of her eyes to register the situation. Sensing an opening, she stood up and made a mad dash to the boat, only to collide with yet another corpse—a woman, her burial dress hanging in ragged tatters, as was the flesh from her face.

"Gah!" Cass cried out in horror. She backed up as fast as she could and drew her rapier. With the fine point of her weapon, she stabbed at the creature, but she only succeeded in peppering its misshapen torso with tiny holes. Desperate, Cass reached for a nearby rock and threw it; her aim was true but the rock merely rebounded off the creature's head. Her Untoten adversary soon seemed to realize just how futile Cass's attempts were, reaching out for her throat. Cass froze, but once again, Edwin saved her before it was too late. With a slash of his blade, he took the creature's hands off by the wrist and pulled Cass back.

"Get in the boat!" he wheezed, almost out of breath. This time Cass did as she was told and scrambled into the boat while Edwin continued to hack away at the onslaught of Untoten. Not bothering to wait for the knight, Cass grabbed a pole and pushed it hard into the murky water.

Edwin saw this, and desperation gave him the strength to finally free himself of the corpses and run toward the vessel.

"Hurry!" Cass exclaimed, as she pushed down on the pole again, the boat drifting away from the dock.

"Damn you!" Edwin yelled in frustration. "You wait for me!" As he reached the end of the dock, Edwin leapt into the boat, nearly causing it to capsize with his bulk.

"You lunatic!" Cass cried out, as she placed her hands on either side to steady their vessel. Eventually it settled and Cass let out a sigh of relief. They both turned to see if their monstrous adversaries were following them into the water, but the corpses just stood motionless on the shore, watching the boat float away with their sunken, shallow eyes.

Cass lingered for a moment before she caught Edwin's venomous stare. The knight gulped down a few more breaths, then gathered the strength to speak. "Next time you decide to play dead, I'll make sure it's no ruse."

Her eyes returned to the silent ranks of the Untoten continuing to watch them drift down the river. "That 'ruse,' I'll have you know, has deceived many a discerning audience member—"

"This is no theater production, you fool."

"Made it, though, didn't we?" Cass said with a sheepish grin.

Edwin made a start, as if he was about to throttle her right then and there, but he was simply too tired, and he brought his hands back down to his seat.

Cass knew better than to press her luck. With that, she finally took her eyes off their ghastly farewell party and pushed deeper into the swamp.

CHAPTER 10

When Drink Is Not Enough (If Such a Thing Was Possible)

It occurred to Renton that every day there were new casualties of the war, both the men and the families that they left behind. As such, a large share of his time had been taken up walking the cobbled streets of Riesenstadt, visiting those families to honor their loss. They were brothers, sons, fathers, and men of distinction . . . and none felt their absence more keenly than the knight-lord himself, each death a gaping wound in the ranks of the Brotherhood.

A small number of knights traveled with him in an effort to bolster the spirits of the citizens while he saw to the matter of attending the families. Ever the master of efficiency, Renton also saw it as a chance to learn more about the newer recruits in his service.

On this particular day, he was to visit the home of Lady Berna, the mother of young Keldon Berna. Among the others, this visit would merit extra consideration, something that stayed on Renton's mind as they made their way through the maze that was Riesenstadt's working-class residences. Not just for some special privilege that Lady Berna enjoyed, but for the selflessness she had shown in her many years of service to Castle Riesenstadt, even as far back as Edwin's birth. She still served there now but lived here in the city in the home of her late husband.

After a few more twists and turns, they came to a stop, standing just outside a simple cottage. As dense as this particular street was, with all of the homes tightly packed together, it wasn't long before a crowd of onlookers gathered around the knights. There was more than a fair share of chatter and noise, but they kept a respectable distance. They'd seen enough of these processions to know exactly why the knight-lord was standing outside Lady Berna's home and what he was about to do.

"Not a stop I ever wanted to make," Renton said to the trio of knights behind him.

"Not a stop any of us wanted you to have to make, milord."

Renton turned around to face the speaker, Jonas, one of the guards assigned to the procession. One of the youngest knights in their ranks, Jonas, along with his older brother Luther, came from a lineage of men who had admirably served Riesenstadt for many years. He was incredibly gifted with his twin blades, a fighting style that was unique among the Brotherhood but well respected nonetheless. Indeed, taking a closer look, Renton found himself thinking of how much Jonas reminded him of his son Edwin at that age. Young but impossibly skilled beyond his years.

"Milord?" Jonas asked, snapping Renton out of his reverie.

Renton shook his head and offered curtly, "Of course," before facing the door. He knew what was behind the young knight's sentiment, as this was a home most of the knights knew well. Lady Berna always took in the newly initiated and comforted them, as the Brotherhood didn't allow for any such showings of sympathy. Still, she was insistent. "Even tough men need comfort," she would always say. As such, young Keldon gained many friends through the kindness of his mother, and many followers, including those in Renton's current retinue.

***

Just as Jonas felt the dread of this moment, so did Aras. Only a few years older than the other knights, Aras mourned Keldon's loss just as much, but unlike Jonas, he wasn't up for talking about it. In fact, he'd manufactured every possible ruse to excuse himself from being a part of this day, but his close kinship with Keldon had ensured his accompaniment.

Distracted, he ran his finger over a cold crest atop his shoulder plate. The night he had earned the crest had been a hard one. A march through the Schwarzes Moor was an act of passage and most of the knights had endured it with success, but that night Aras was the only one to return, losing his companion of many years in the process. Their footing had been compromised and Brighton had begun to sink into the black muck. The gurgling goo pulled Brighton downward with the speed of a serpent devouring its prey. Aras had held on to him as long and as hard as he could but eventually watched his friend sink below the surface.

After hours of crawling through the Schwarzes, Aras had reached his brothers. They'd tried to comfort him with compliments of his bravery as the blacksmith engraved his accomplishment on his shoulder. He had let it all wash over him, but he'd felt a sickness fester inside. Keldon had seen the sickness, the loss in Aras's eyes, and had dragged him to his mother, Lady Berna. A motherly hug was the beginning of his healing, but it would still be many nights before he returned to proper health.

But here he was now, and where was Keldon?

***

Renton continued to stare at the front door, trying hard to not show hesitation in front of his men. The knight-lord's armor shined brightly in the sun, the steel barely peeking out among the many gold badges. He stood there, just as if he were on the edge of a deep canyon. The breeze picked up the scent of the pink blossoms that grew just outside the home. *A rare comfort in these times,* he thought, just as the blossoms were overpowered by the stench of the cremation pyre off in the distance. What beauty still survived in this world had been pushed to the point where the color had been driven out, only to be replaced by the sullenness of a grey survival. The knight-lord let his armored hand fall heavily upon the door just once before he pushed his way through.

***

The feeling inside was not much better than what they left outside. A fire was burning away in the hearth but shared little of its light with the rest of the room. Renton strained to see, until the door shut behind him and the fire offered a bit more of its light.

Lady Berna was sitting alone in her chair. Her eyes were like glass and her breath was heavy. She clutched a large mug that sweated thick, heavy drops all over her palms. Renton knew she must have been up all night with the comfort that only mead could bring.

"Lady Berna," Renton said, feeling the words fall like stones in the thick air of the room, sinking down to the floor instead of reaching her ears. He tried again, but in a whisper. "Anna?"

The name traveled light as a feather across the dense air and rested in her ear. She blinked hard and took in the sight of her guest.

"Knight-lord," she said, coming slowly out of her stupor.

"You know my name, Anna," Renton said, trying to keep her comfortable.

"I'm sorry, milord. Renton, of course," she stumbled out. The familiarity of their first names was not something they had shared for many years. They felt strange to say out loud and stank of dishonesty. It wasn't the place of these two people to share themselves that way, the lack of their formal titles, but the moment had been thrust upon them whether they wanted it or not.

"May I sit?" Renton asked as he gestured toward the only other seat in the room.

Anna's eyes wandered toward the floor and the rugs that so many young men had sat on before, men in heavy armor and with heavier hearts. She doubted that Renton had been a boy for very long and was even less likely to have sat patiently on a floor to listen to anyone. *How lonely his mother must have been with him as a child,* she thought.

"Yes, of course," Anna said, mirroring Renton's gesture toward the chair. Renton pushed his cloak out of the way and took a seat, resting his hands atop his knees.

"Here it is then," he said, in an attempt to start a conversation. Where exactly this was going, he wasn't sure, but he knew that it would have a certain direction. Given Anna's drinking, he knew he would have to keep his patience.

"Where?" she asked.

"You and I, on a day we both hoped would never come," he answered, a way of clarifying his position. "Young Keldon gone." He couldn't bring himself to string too many words together. There would be time to get to where he was going, but it wasn't now.

"Gone to the wind," Anna said. "Ashes in the breeze." Her head felt full with too many things as she too struggled to put the words together. She sipped from her mug, hoping Renton would say something to fill the empty space between them.

"I can tell you that his loss is being felt by all the men. I know that doesn't help things much, but it's true, and that's something."

"Things," Anna said without any feeling.

She drank deeper from her mug, knowing that this conversation was going to be longer than she wanted it to be. It already was. The firelight spit and sparked on a wet log. Renton tilted his head at the hiss it made. Slowly, he twisted his neck until it popped, his head twitching like a tick.

The jerking move sat oddly with Anna. It wasn't a characteristic she had seen from him before. *He must be nervous about something more than my son's death, more than trying to comfort me like he knows he can't,* she thought. He may have gotten all of the other families convinced that their children had died for a cause, but he wouldn't get her that way. Let Keldon's brothers mourn his death, let their leader feel that weight. *Damn him for not opening the gate,* she thought.

"We must all stand for something," Renton started.

"Fall for something," Anna interrupted. Renton could appreciate the double meaning behind what she said. Her son had fallen to the enemy, but not for a cause.

"He was never duped, Anna," Renton said more defensively than intended. "He was a smart man. He knew what we're fighting for."

"Don't start with me, Renton. A mother will never explain away the death of her child. No mother worth a damn!" she spat in return.

"Believe what you want about him and his death as you please, but do not lie to yourself about the grief his brothers feel for him," Renton struck back, his voice growing louder yet more controlled with each word. "*Your* boys are grieving."

Anna lifted her chin and stared Renton straight in the face.

"Yes, I know what you do for them, Anna," he said.

"It's important to find some kind of comfort in this world. Even if it's nothing more than a kind word."

"It *is* important," Renton said, lowering his tone. "They need their den mother and I need you to realize the importance of that."

"So you can keep them fighting, you mean."

"Yes, of course!" Renton yelled, starting to lose his temper. "This war isn't over yet and I need them to have their heads on straight!" He rose from his chair and slammed his hands down on the table, nearly capsizing the pitcher of mead. "I don't want to lose any more of them than you do, but if they're stuck in their grief, they're useless to me. I need them to blubber or whatever it is you let them do so they can get over it."

"You look down on them, don't you?" Anna said, knowing she had crossed the line as soon as she had said it.

"How dare you!" Renton growled as he advanced on her. Anna rose as fast as the alcohol would let her, but Renton was on top of her in a heartbeat. His hands shot straight to her head stopping just a breath away from her skin. Anna could feel the energy from them as they shook with anger, the rattle of his armor chiming all around her.

"Figure yourself out, woman. If you don't, their blood will be on your hands." He took a deep breath. "Do your job."

Anna began to cry, silently at first, then uncontrollably sobbing. Renton's hands dropped to her shoulders and held her fast. He guided her back down to her chair. There was no point in staying any longer and Renton made his way for the door.

"I'll do it," she choked out.

"And, as always, you'll have our appreciation," Renton answered. The light blinded him as he stepped out, despite the growing clouds in the sky.

At Renton's reemergence, the trio of young knights awaited some response, some command, but there was nothing.

Jonas watched the others just stare silently ahead and it drove him mad, these moments of helplessness.

"How'd it fare, milord?" he asked.

"I'll walk myself the rest of the way," Renton answered, skipping Jonas's question altogether. "Go see to her."

Aras and the other knight made for the door, but Jonas hesitated. He had waited here for what had felt an eternity. He could feel for men like Aras, and he had heard the stories from his brother Luther, but he wasn't here for her.

Renton made his way down the cobblestone street, while Jonas watched the other knights enter Lady Berna's home.

"Wait, milord!" Jonas yelled out.

Renton stopped and turned toward the young man, directly addressing him for the first time.

"It isn't necessary, Jonas."

With every bit of willpower that he could muster, Jonas fought down the delight of the knight-lord's mention of his name. *So I have made an impression.* Jonas caught himself and quickly straightened.

"I insist, milord," Jonas answered. "This, what you're doing, is very necessary."

"Very well, young knight. Come with me," Renton said, unwilling to let the day's events rob him of what still mattered. "Let us comfort the willing and drink with the grieving, side by side."

This time, Jonas couldn't help himself, the slightest hint of a smile breaking over his face . . . and then it was gone, for duty called.

CHAPTER 11

Inspiration Doesn't Come Easy in a Swamp

The stench was growing stronger with each passing minute that Edwin and Cass traveled farther into the swamp, the current of the river having now completely run its course. Following their narrow escape at the dock, Cass remained unusually quiet while she pushed the boat along, each dip into the water sounding more like soupy mud than anything else. The sun was beginning its descent and the hazy gloom that lingered at the edges of the bog was creeping ever closer.

Cass spared a nervous glance toward Edwin, slumped against the prow, his posture seeming to admit defeat in that he wasn't a young strapping knight anymore. Perhaps it was the weight of memories more than the years, but the years couldn't be ignored. Noticing Cass's attention, Edwin instinctively straightened up, pretending as if the bard hadn't seen him relaxing.

"That pig sticker of yours, it has enough of an edge to cut those corpses to pieces. If you knew how to use it, that is," Edwin said, hoping his taunt would preserve a sliver of his dignity. "Your feints and thrusts might work against costumed fops upon a stage, but against the foes we face . . ."

Cass muttered some nonsensical sounds, more to herself than to Edwin.

"Or perhaps you'd prefer to just throw rocks at our enemies, because that certainly brought them to heel." Still mildly irritated that Cass had caught him off guard, Edwin wanted to press his point further, but figured the time could be spent at least teaching the bard how to properly handle a blade instead. "Here." He lifted up his heavy sword with one hand and slashed downward, angling off into a precise horizontal line. "*Slash, slice* . . . those are the words you should add to your book. An arm here, a head there, that's what will take our opponents down to size."

"Right, right. Of course . . . ," Cass mumbled, adding to the other sounds her mouth was making. Her eyes continued to stare down into the swamp water, a thick sludge of dark green.

"Would it be that I didn't have to bore you with such details," Edwin grumbled. The knight's eyes scanned the swamp as he sheathed his blade. He could tell from the pole's reach that he might be able to stand in the river if they were overturned, but he didn't like his chances. With his armor, he would be little match for the dead, unable to move about in the muck below. Tired, annoyed, unsure of what he was doing, where he was going, and who exactly he was going with, Edwin closed his eyes and lay back against the prow once more, the bard be damned.

"If only she were still here . . . ," he said quietly to himself.

At his words, Cass raised her head, somewhat surprised that the knight was now plainly admitting to his fatigue and frustration.

". . . to make sense of all this madness," Edwin finished, each word softer than the last.

Whatever thoughts had previously held the bard's attention, they were now a thing of the past. If Cass knew one thing, it was never to turn down the chance to hear a good tale.

"Care to indulge an audience?" Cass queried, her eyebrows raised.

"No," Edwin said, curt enough to make his point.

"Master Edwin," Cass started, having received Edwin's missive but duly ignoring it. "As you may or may not have noticed, I've been without drink for some time now and, well, I'm nearly to the point where I'd be willing to consider sampling the delights of swamp piss myself." Her upper lip curled as she considered the thought in earnest. "So, please. Just . . . regale me, won't you?"

Edwin raised his head to glance at Cass, realizing that it had indeed been some time since he had seen the bard raise a flask to her lips. Still, that wasn't enough reason for him to spill his guts to a woman he barely knew. Cass remained undaunted, however, pressing onward. "Just let the words come out, milord. Just let the words come out. That's all there is to it."

Edwin waited another moment, then finally relented, turning away to stare into the dull reflection of the muddy water below. "She always knew how to handle such things. She was . . . confident. Assured. And what she saw in me, I'll never know."

"Surely there had to be *some* virtue that stood out," Cass remarked, unable to help herself.

Edwin turned from the water to regard Cass. "Perhaps. Or it may have been that she simply pitied me."

"How could one of noble blood be pitied?" Cass asked with a tone that spared neither curiosity nor sarcasm. The man before her may have had some light to shed on the woes of noble life, but Cass doubted it, given her own personal experiences. Better that she'd been born to dirt-poor parents, accepted for whom she aspired to be, rather than what others wanted her to be . . . but no one cared and no one bothered for the problems of overstuffed nobles. Still, this was the present, the now, and the dramatist in her always kept her curiosity right at the surface.

If there was something new to be gleamed in the knight's musings, she wouldn't ignore the opportunity.

Edwin let out a long sigh and turned his gaze back to the slick water, imagining his father's stern face in the sheen of the river. "Because, unlike most nobles, I cared."

Thinking back to her own plight, Cass huffed but let Edwin continue.

"My mother . . . was a commoner." Rising next to Renton's image in the water, Edwin saw his mother, a plain woman of simple beauty. Her wedding veil swept over her pale face, taking in quick breaths of anticipation. Edwin smiled, for he knew her face like it was his own. He remembered every moment of happiness in his mother's life, accented by those same shallow breaths. "And when she died, my father gave no thought to arranging a proper burial for her."

His mother's face sank back into the swamp, replaced by his, arguing with his father. Edwin's cheeks turning red with frustration as he yelled and yelled to no avail.

"She was merely one wife of many, he said. That one day, I would come to understand . . . just as he did." Stout castle walls rose around the figures, and Edwin watched his younger self storm off down the cold stone hallways. "So I took matters into my own hands."

The revelation entranced Cass, the terrors of the dark swamp all but forgotten, as Edwin sank deeper into his story. She hadn't given up on the pole just yet, but their pace had slowed considerably as she continued to listen.

"Of course, it was said that only superstitious peasants buried their dead with the Trauergast. That they were charlatans, swindlers," he continued.

The fortified walls of the castle gave way to Riesenstadt Cemetery, looking as bleak as it'd ever been, but this time, there was a crowd drawn about its entrance.

"But I believed in their promises."

Edwin remembered the villagers standing in line next to wagons bearing coffins and bodies wrapped in linen. At the front of the line, a hobbled old man hands over a small leather pouch to a Gravewalker. His eyes are lined in red as tears stream down his face. Next to him, a woman lies still atop a cart; her wrinkled face is only partially covered by a soiled cloth. The Gravewalker first considers his tears then the cart's wheels caked with the mud of many a rutted road.

Handing the pouch to one of her sisters, she nods to him with warmth and compassion, tears welling in her own eyes; she holds them back for the old man's comfort.

"The promises of a decent burial . . . ," Edwin continued.

Placing her hand upon the old man's shoulder, she signals her sisters for assistance. They lead the cart into the depths of the graveyard.

"Or perhaps it was because I simply had no other choice."

In the water's reflection, Edwin now saw himself at the front of the line, his high noble collar standing from his shoulders to his chin. He sticks out from the rest, his attire a sharp contrast to the peasants' and farmers,' but his grief is all the same. He has no cart or servants to help; he carries his mother's body in his arms. A funeral shroud hangs hauntingly like her wedding veil over her face, her eyes closed to the world. A hooded Gravewalker approaches him with soft steps and a gentle stride, pulling her hood back to reveal the face of his beloved Evelina.

"Gods, she was the most beautiful thing I'd ever seen."

Evelina takes in the sight of Edwin's mother, her limp form curled up in his powerful arms. She looks back up at Edwin, and this time, there is more than sympathy in her eyes.

"And she saved my life."

Cass fumbled her grip on the pole and drew Edwin's gaze as she nearly lost it to the depths of the swamp. "Er, please continue, Master Edwin." She coughed.

Back to the water's reflection, Edwin imagined the cemetery again, but this time layered with a thin coating of pure white snow. The moon hangs in the darkness as it shines down upon each headstone and its own unique story. Edwin is walking among the carved stones, waiting, biding his time. A soft movement in the corner of his eyes catches his attention and there she is. Standing beneath a tree, its bare branches casting thin shadows over her body. A smile spreads across her face, breaking through the shadows and giving Edwin's heart pause.

He could see himself smiling back, that same smile on his face just now. "Because for the first time in my life, I knew true happiness . . ."

The graveyard disappears and a warm chamber dancing in candlelight comes forth. Evelina is once again smiling with sweat beading upon her brow and Edwin holding her hand. Exhaustion shows upon both of their faces, but their pride and happiness keeps them from succumbing to it. A Gravewalker carries their child to them, deep wrinkles carved into her face, but her elderly hands stay still and true. The baby wriggles in her dark wrappings as if she knows she's about to meet her parents.

"... for she showed me love, kindness ... all the things that my father was unable to give."

Both Evelina and Edwin hold their baby girl in the warmth and bask in the miracle that is given to them.

By now, their boat had settled into a slight drift, some unknown current once again leading them forth. Cass pulled the pole in, glad for the chance to give Edwin her full attention.

"For a time—a short time, anyways—they were my life, my everything."

Grey clouds encircle the warm chamber, shrouding it back into the past, while a sunny cemetery rises in its place. Edwin sits with Evelina upon a rough wool blanket spread across the tall grass. Behind Edwin, there is a sudden puff of fog with a tiny electric sizzle as a little girl with mischief in her eyes appears. She wears a black dress similar to her mother's and clutches her favorite doll.

Mela sneaks up on her father and clasps her tiny hands over his eyes. Edwin's grin reveals his happy surprise at this familiar game. He turns to grab her, but she disappears with another flash of fog and a sizzle as his arms close around empty air. He turns around again, but whoosh! She's gone, only to reappear just to the right of him. Another puff and spark, then she's at his left. He quickly turns again, and just as a column of fog begins to rise in front of him, he grabs Mela from thin air, guessing just the spot where she'll be. She giggles in his arms and Evelina joins in the laughter while shaking her head.

But then Edwin notices something just beyond the iron gates of the cemetery.

"My father. Naturally, he thought it to be an abomination. An assault upon his morals, his ideals ... his legacy."

It's Renton, suited in full armor atop his horse.

"His reason for waging war."

The knight-lord's raised visor reveals his sour look of disappointment.

"If I had just shown courage, to leave my old life behind for a new one . . ."

His father turns and rides off at a full gallop in a cloud of dust, pulling the bit deep into his steed's mouth.

". . . perhaps she'd still be here today."

In the reflection below, Edwin saw Evelina looking to him in worry. But in the quickening current, her face was breaking up, drowning in the filth beneath him. As it always was, he was unable to reach her, unable to change the past.

With that, he faced Cass, who now had her book out, scribbling words into the parchment as fast as she possibly could.

"Oh, quite good," Cass said, still writing. "Quite good, if I might say so myself, sir knight."

Edwin grimaced, unsure whether or not he'd just committed a huge mistake in sharing his story, until Cass interrupted his contemplation.

"Will things be any different for you and your daughter?"

Caught by surprise, Edwin said nothing as Cass's question lapsed into awkward silence. Not wanting to press the issue, she turned back to writing in her book. "Ah, disregard, milord. Just a thought I had."

Edwin made no mention of it. Secretly glad for the reprieve, he watched Cass continue to scribble away. "Tell me, bard. This tale of yours. What will you call it?" he asked.

"I don't quite know . . . but I'm sure inspiration will strike me somehow," Cass answered as she slowly rose back to her feet, minding her balance in the rickety boat.

"Well, I find it hard to believe that you would risk such dangers for a simple ballad."

"Not just any simple ballad, sir knight."

"One no different than any others you've written."

At that, Cass gave a slight cough and looked off into the swamp.

"You *have* written others, yes?" Edwin asked incredulously.

"Why the sudden concern, sir knight?" Cass jibed back. "Afraid I won't do your 'simple ballad' any justice?"

Edwin snorted, once again reminded that the bard was just as deadly with words as he was with a blade.

"Well, what of your future? If you were to wed the man of your choosing, would you have children of your own?"

Edwin asked to change the focus on her, but he also wanted a better measure of Cass's character. The complications of a drunken bard should not have been so difficult in his opinion, but the woman was maddeningly difficult to figure out.

Cass snorted as if Edwin had gone insane. "I'll pass, for obvious reasons, as I'm sure you can appreciate."

The last comment stung Edwin just a bit, but he also sensed he was drawing nearer to something. "But who will remember you after you're gone?" he asked.

"I'll be remembered for my words, my songs!" Cass exclaimed with an assured look about her.

"But not for your actions?" Edwin wondered aloud in curiosity. "Or your good deeds?"

Cass's assuredness waned for a moment as she took up the pole again, holding it like a staff in front of her. She seemed ready for a fight in that moment, but that was just before her mischievous smile returned.

"The only 'acts' I know of are the ones that lay in the pages of plays, sir knight. 'Acts' are just pieces to a bigger story, and that is where I live," Cass answered with a sense of finality in her tone.

"But life isn't a story," Edwin said, still unable to understand just where Cass was coming from. This woman was in a world of her own, it seemed, unable to truly live in the now. She was not a person Edwin could grasp, but perhaps that did not mean he couldn't trust her.

The boat suddenly lurched to a halt as its bow ran aground and became stuck in the mud of the swamp's banks.

"Here we are," said Cass, but Edwin wasn't sure if she meant that they had reached their destination or if the bard meant the impasse they'd just arrived at.

A strange woman, Edwin continued to think, *a strange woman indeed.*

CHAPTER 12

Same Roundabout, Surprise Ending

The air had grown stale in Mela's room. In truth, she knew that it was always stale, given their whereabouts, but today Mela found it especially so. She also knew she had been locked away too long, but she still wasn't in the mood to be around her sisters. A map of Riesenstadt and its surroundings lay before her, droplets of wine staining it here and there.

The skull looked on in long moments of silence until it was called upon, parroting back her words. The ideas bounced about in Mela's head, and as each one was vocalized back to her, she grew more discouraged. The sound of the skull had begun to grind on her mood, deepening her despair and frustration. That night in the pitch-black still sat heavy and fresh with her, the memories that were dragged to the surface, bloody and raw. Her sisters had slipped notes beneath her door here and there, but the routine updates of the state of their home felt redundant and as musty as the air she was breathing.

The time for action, for a breakthrough against their enemy . . . this had been upon them for a great while. Mela knew that she didn't need to stall any longer. She knew the enemy's strength. She knew that she wanted the knight-lord gone. What she wasn't sure about, however, was the issue of her father and what exactly to do with him.

The man had failed to save her mother so many years ago and had seemed to be content to rot in a cell for the rest of his life. So why the escape? Why now? More frustrating was that she still didn't understand why it bothered her so much. Looking up from the map, she took in the skull's empty sockets. Her eyes were growing bleary from the ordeal, so she tried to center her sight on the darkness within. There were no blue orbs emerging now like they had done before. She wasn't so sure she had wanted them to, except that in the back of her head, a voice quietly willed it. Despite that tiny voice, there was no haunting to be had. Perhaps she was just too tired to care any longer. Or perhaps the tiredness had nothing to do with it.

Her hand slid across the map and grasped her cup. It was burdensome, despite its lack of being full. Slowly, she pulled it up to her mouth. The wine felt heavy on her tongue, and dryness set about her mouth as she swallowed. There was a knock at her door, light and sharp. She turned to await another note of boring missives, but nothing came. Then there was another knock, harder this time.

"Come in," she called out. She could hear every creak of the wood as the door slowly opened. It had been so long since it had swung on its hinges that it seemed to groan in defiance at its being finally forced to open. Cool air rushed inward and Mela felt herself sucking it in. Light on her skin and fresh air in her lungs saw the wine's effect being washed away. She could feel life coming back to her, an invigoration of will creeping back into her bones.

And that was entirely helpful, for once again she would have to contend with her two advisors.

Mela saw Acacia's golden hair before anything else. She mused on how everyone could spot her in an instant. And if the hair didn't do it, no one forgot her once they had laid eyes on that scar. Even after all of these years, Mela still caught herself staring at it.

Behind her was Elaine. *Of course,* she mused. A forgettable woman when it came to her appearance, but Mela knew her influence among the other sisters was anything but. Grateful as she was for the change of pace, it was still an onerous matter to see these two together in her room.

Their hatred for each other keeps them attached at the hip. And they never stray very far from my headaches.

Everything was a grinding headache in Mela's world these days, not the least being the constant bickering of her two sisters. The same tired arguments, over and over again.

"I really don't have time for this," Mela said, desperately trying to cut them off at the pass. Her hand drifted behind her in search of her wine bottle. Her stomach growled at the proposition, hunger fighting outward in contention with the dry heaviness of her drink.

"You can't just ignore it, Mela. It needs to be addressed—and now," Elaine replied, doing her best to sound like her mother.

She has never been able to let go of that particular sentimentality, Mela thought.

Acacia didn't even try to hide her disgust at the tone Elaine was already setting. Her eyes rolled in her head while she clenched each hand into a fist, letting each knuckle crack individually.

Like two old cats.

Mela finally found her bottle and began to scratch at it in thought. Her stomach growled again in a plea for something more sustaining. Her eyes were beginning to feel as dry as the map on her table just then. She could only really focus on the fact that she did not want to be caught in the middle of this debate again.

"Mela, you know we need to strike," Acacia argued. "Something big, something seriously bloody, and it needs to be soon." Acacia's heartbeat fluttered when she saw Mela raise an eyebrow, sensing that she was perhaps leaning her way. *She wants it and she knows it. I just need her to focus on it and get rid of that old bat.* Acacia let her knuckles crack again, but this time, she counted off a rhythm to bait Elaine.

The old woman wasn't going to have it. She wasn't giving in to the hateful girl who stood next to her, and she wasn't going to let go of the straying girl in front of her. *They're women now. I need to remember that.*

The fear of the Toten-Geist grew inside Elaine each and every day. When she slept, she dreamt of it; it was a dark figure in the background quietly stalking her sisters. When she awoke, her mind desperately tried to put a face to it, as if it were a distant certainty and she needed only to know who the poor soul was to be and how she could prevent it. Throughout the day, it danced inside her head, grinding on her mind like a mill wheel, slowly tearing away at her sanity.

"And at what cost?" Elaine said, turning to face Acacia. She knew deep down Mela had the logical mind to recognize the disaster of such destruction, but Acacia, even if she did see it, chose to ignore it. The fight was old and—as they had so many times before—they would follow the same strings of reasoning. The trick now was to come up with something new. *I need a different angle. Nothing has changed thus far.* "The destruction of the knights solves nothing, Mela. Not if the people still hate us. What do you think the death of their precious Knights Proper will do to them? Are you actually proposing that we take their places as the keepers of peace and prosperity?"

Elaine saw Acacia flinch, knowing she had struck a blow. This is what she had to make clear, arguing for the future rather than some single attack as a whole. "The fear, the hatred, it'll live in those people for generations and this will never be over. Your revenge will turn into the never-ending hunt of our kind."

"Here's my solution, then . . . we kill all of them," Acacia said plainly. Immediately she saw that she'd erred, as she noticed Mela's interest wane. She knew she needed a way to convince her that the people were as much her enemy as the knights. *I don't care how many we kill. I'll do it myself if I have to.* Her bloodlust was rising inside her; she could feel her face grow flush with the excitement.

Elaine could feel the heat coming off of Acacia. *There is a lust there that will never be sated.* In response, she could feel herself growing colder. The heat scared Elaine just as much as the Toten-Geist did. Someone like Acacia, free to carry out her murderous whims, could be far worse than such an unnatural creation when it came right down to it. No master but destruction and the power to do it. She knew Acacia was stronger than she'd ever let on—perhaps even more powerful than Mela, but she still feared their leader and that kept her at bay.

Mela watched the two sisters in dull assessment. They hadn't really presented anything new to her. New to them perhaps, but what did they think she did alone in here for all these hours? Every situation had to be looked at from as many angles as possible.

This war has already gone on too long. An angry populace will not do. There must be a way of eliminating the knights and keeping the people as a whole safe.

But she couldn't dismiss the notion that Acacia's need for an all-out attack was well reasoned, as defeating the knights in combat would most likely send a clear message. Mela had even considered a way to accomplish such a task, but it would require a number of factors to succeed—deceit and treachery being chief among them. Mela was no fool to think that even with a massive host of Untoten soldiers she could best the knight-lord's forces in an open field. They were too well armed and too well trained.

Plus, in order for them to succeed, her sisters would have to be close by to issue strategic commands to the Untoten. Generally, one could raise an Untoten and send it off with a general command to attack whomever it encountered, but such single-mindedness would not fare well against the discipline of the knight-lord's forces.

In addition, there was the notion that devious acts never won people over in the long run. It only bred further furtiveness from both parties, and her ultimate aim was simply for others to leave her kind in peace, not to foster a war without end.

She shook her head in dismay. In truth, a lot of it had stopped mattering to Mela. Too much time spent alone with only her thoughts, thoughts stuck in the same circle. Even when she did have visitors, it was only these two sisters with their own circles to repeat. She watched as they continued to move closer to her as they argued, their volume growing in an ever-escalating war of words.

Mela began to scratch the wine bottle again, looking for something to do with her hands. She had already made up her mind that she wasn't going to have another drink, her stomach insisting on sustenance instead, her mind throbbing with the tremors of all this muddled deliberation.

"Well, what are we to do?" Acacia asked, bringing Mela back into the conversation. Mela let her head lull a bit.

"I'm still thinking it over," Mela said, hoping that would lead the sisters to the door but knowing it wouldn't. They didn't care that she was tired and stressed. They were tired and stressed, and they had her as their outlet. Mela's mind began to wander toward her bed. Not for rest, but for a good boff. A good roll between the sheets was what she needed—a false love with a lot of sweat, how she missed it.

Seeing that she was lost to some daydream, Acacia kneeled down before Mela and whispered softly to her. "We need a decision, sister," she said. "One way or another, it has to be reached and you're the only one who can reach it."

"She's right, Mela," Elaine said, surprised at her own words. The truth was that a choice had to be made, and even though Acacia had said it first, there was no disagreement to be had on that point.

"And you two don't think I know that?" Mela said, starting to feel some anger grow in her. She was partially thankful for the annoying statement, happy to have some sort of tangible, concrete emotion breaking through the fog.

"No, of course you do," Elaine replied, secretly pleased to see that they had finally reached her.

And reached her they had, as Mela's eyes narrowed with her rising anger. "You come to me for decisions, only to remind me that I'm the one who has to make them. How thick do you think I am?" The rage felt good and so she went with it. *They need to be reminded of their place.* "What is it exactly that you think I do in this chamber, day in and day out?"

"We've come to wonder," Acacia said firmly, rising from her knees. "You don't communicate with us anymore."

"What is there to communicate?" Mela barked back. "How the Toten-Geist will doom us all?" She looked at Elaine, derision in her eyes. "Or that we should set off to bathing ourselves in our enemy's blood?" she said, snapping at Acacia. "Anything new at all? From either of you?"

"Well—" was all Elaine managed to say in the shock of Mela's outburst.

"Well what?" Mela said.

"What," said a hollow voice. All three women turned to look at the source of the melancholy sound. "What are you doing here, Acacia?" the skull upon Mela's desk said.

"Not again," Mela said more to herself than to anyone else. She clenched the wine bottle in her hand.

"Still beautiful in every way," the skull continued. Acacia smiled at the compliment as the skull droned on. "I hope that wound was worth our time together." It seemed to take in the sight of her scar. Even without eyes, the entity managed to make everyone feel as if they were being watched.

"Always so sweet," Acacia cooed, a different kind of heat rising up inside her now.

Mela looked back and forth between her sister and the treacherous skull. She realized now that this was new. This was different.

As she watched, the tiny blue embers came to life within its hollow eye sockets, sending a chill down her neck. The neck of the bottle was snug in her grip. The rage was building again, and there wasn't an end to it. Everything leading up to this last decisive moment had been easy. Now everything was solid and sure. *I hate the lot of them.* The whining, the reliance, the treachery, all of it had reached its zenith, and Mela was through with it.

Elaine gasped in recognition of what was happening, that the skull was showing the most tangible proof of sentience yet.

"I don't mind it, you know?" it said, almost in a love-struck manner. "The scar, I mean. It only furthers our connection."

"That's it!" Mela screamed. With the bottle raised over her head, she charged at her desk. With surprising speed, Mela brought it crashing down upon the skull.

"Why?" was all the skull could let out, before it shattered into a thousand pieces. Mela breathed hard and fast as she gazed down upon the destruction she had caused.

"What did you go and do that for?" Acacia asked. "He wasn't hurting anybody." Her smile had nearly reached her ears. Mela's head snapped away from the desk and toward Acacia.

"You want blood, sister?" she asked, her eyes creasing to slits. "I will give you blood!" Her patience was gone now, shattered along with the skull; nothing mattered anymore except for the emotions running through her body that instant. She stepped forward, ready to do more than give Acacia a few more scars, but something stopped her.

Her feet froze, as if shackled to the floor, and something pulled at her navel with invisible strings. Acacia stood ready to receive her sister, while Elaine seemed to freeze right at the same moment. The older sister watched Mela's body go rigid, held by an imperceptible power, and she feared it more than anything, for she was at a complete loss as to what it could be. Mela felt a new heat rising up from her feet. An electrical sting ran up her legs, her heart racing at the mysterious sensation. It jumped up to her pelvis and she felt a warmth that seemed divine in nature, a sensation that sent her eyes rolling.

Elaine and Acacia stood transfixed, watching Mela's expressions to the invisible sensations exert themselves like compulsions. It was as if she were having a pleasurable fit of some sort.

The warmth then left her pelvis and drove its way into her chest; her heart stopped as the current lingered there for a moment. The air in her lungs escaped, and then there was a buzzing in her head. As the buzzing ceased, Mela finally understood without thinking what was happening to her. A rapid fog rose up from the floor as the electricity left her head and raced downward to meet the rising column of mist.

"No!" was all Mela was able to let escape before she disappeared in a storm of blue current. Elaine and Acacia were left standing in the middle of the room, worried and afraid, but for altogether different reasons.

CHAPTER 13

The Art of Lining Your Pockets

Revitalized by their arrival, Cass nimbly bounced up from her seat and onto the shore while Edwin slowly pushed himself up. The thin boat jerked this way and that with each of his movements, his armor clanking about as the boat creaked and sloshed.

"Come, come, sir knight, grab your pole, won't you?" Cass said as she extended the wooden stick. As Edwin reached out for the pole, Cass gave him a wink and a smile. "Gently now, milord, it is our first time. Best to be careful with any sudden jerking motions . . ."

Edwin was not amused with Cass's humor and grasped tightly to the wooden shaft, securing the boat in the mud. He stepped onto the bow with one foot and swung his other to the shore. His weight pressed into the soft soil and he was quick to step away onto more solid ground.

He pushed the pole back to Cass and took stock of the silvery foliage of ferns and mosses surrounding them in the darkness. "Always with the quick answers, bard. I'm not sure I appreciate the humor in this place as much as I should."

Cass chuckled as she fastened her sack. "Whatever I can do to bring some cheer to that saddened face, sir knight." She looked up at Edwin for a clue as to whether or not her remark had helped or hindered, but it seemed to have done nothing at all. Not willing to admit defeat, Cass redoubled her efforts. "We are on an adventure, milord! Take it with some enthusiasm."

She gave Edwin another wink, but the knight wasn't having it. His gaze instead turned to a trail marked in gravel, a footpath above the mud and rot. A sharp scrape of flint against metal and the snap of a spark of light brought his attention back to Cass.

"Here," the bard said, offering Edwin a lit torch, its infant flames pushing back the darkness around them. The swamp had just enough light of its own to see, but the torches certainly helped. A warm light instead of the eerie, unnatural yellow glow that had been their constant companion thus far.

In the distance, Edwin could now discern that the trail led to a heavy stone door shrouded by a coat of moss and leafy vines. Two monoliths of hooded figures stood to the left and right of the door, the weathered statues appearing to emerge from the stone and through the moss. Poised to charge ahead rather than stand still at attention and wait for a fight, Edwin was transfixed. A loud bang shook him from his stillness as Cass had thrown the pole back into the boat.

Cass stepped past Edwin and onto the graveled path with a grin, knowing she had startled him from his reverie.

Edwin called out after her, "I want answers, bard."

She turned with the grace of a dancer, her toes pivoting on the spot. "Answers?" she asked, with a hint of childish innocence.

"Yes," Edwin said sternly. "Like, what does any of this have to do with finding my daughter?" Cass gave an easy smile, but Edwin cut her off. "And this time, I mean it."

The bard sighed and threw her hands up in defeat. "Very well. An artifact of sorts. That's what we're after."

Edwin narrowed his eyes, but Cass continued on.

"Your wife's ancestors established safe havens, like these . . . ," she said, pointing to the stone door with a flourish. "Sanctuaries said to house an apparatus that allows them to summon their kin in times of need."

"But I'm not a Gravewalker," Edwin growled in response.

"Not a Gravewalker?" Cass said in exasperation. "To think, all this time, after all the trouble I've been through . . . ," Cass finished with a smile that slowly crept across her face.

"You know perfectly well what I meant," Edwin said, trying to gain control of the situation and end his mockery.

"Yes, sir knight, I am very well aware that you're not a Gravewalker, but you do share their bloodline. Well, at least your daughter's anyhow. Of course, we could just stand around and bloody well scream her name from the top of our lungs until we collapse, if you'd prefer that instead . . ."

Edwin's hand gripped his sword, twisting the hilt in frustration. He held up his torch a bit higher and started to make his way down the path. As he trudged toward the door, Edwin noticed that the ground may have been more solid than the banks, but it still held the sick moisture of the swamp despite the tiny stones at their feet.

Now all alone, Cass watched as the shadows closed back in. She coughed up a nervous laugh as she ran to catch up to Edwin. "Ah, wait, milord! Just one more thing you should know!"

Edwin halted and turned around, the torch's warm light revealing a long look of uncertainty on Cass's face. "Speak,"

Edwin commanded, his patience growing thinner with each passing moment.

"Heh, well, I was thinking . . . they wouldn't . . ." Cass's voice stumbled as if struck by some revelation over and over again in quick succession. "Eh, they wouldn't leave such a place unguarded, would they?"

Instinctively, Edwin turned back to the stone guards by the door. For a moment, he thought he saw the statue breathe. "Pray, when were you going to tell me?" Edwin asked as he drew his sword, the blade scraping the length of its large sheath.

Cass quickly walked to his side, trying to divert Edwin's attention. "Ah, I don't think we'll be fighting statues, milord."

Edwin kept his eyes on the monolithic figures, but indeed, they stayed still as the very stone they were carved from.

"I mean . . . Gravewalkers, right?" Cass said with a quickly fading smile.

Then, in the next instant, as if Cass's utterance had commanded it, bubbles began to rise from the water to each side of the gravel trail. "Er . . . ," Cass said to the frothing swamp water.

Edwin clenched his jaw tight and brandished his torch like a shield, a fiery counterpart to his heavy blade. A misshapen hand rose from the depths, its three pickled fingers grasping a rusty, corroded blade.

"What was that you were saying about adventure?" Edwin rumbled, his mood strangely lifted by the chance to finally fight something. He raised his sword high and charged down the trail.

"Wait for me!" yelled Cass as she whipped out her rapier, the thin blade whistling from its scabbard.

Ahead, the first wave of corpses had already made their way onto the trail well in front of the stone door. Their skeletons were caked in slimy mud that dripped from their bones in globs, holding what little flesh was left on them in bits and chunks. Sodden moss hung at length about them like battle dresses. Clenched in their fists were chipped weapons, glinting with a wet shine, a far cry from the unarmed corpses they had fought at the dock.

Edwin dropped his shoulder as he came upon them, bellowing as he attempted to barrel his way through. He crashed through two of them, then came to a stop, his feet carving great ruts in the gravel before he brought his blade down on a third. He swung upward toward another, slicing him from the groin to his shoulders. The Untoten warrior slumped into pieces, but its brethren were still rising from the water, each one more gruesome than the last. Ascending from the true depths of the putrid swamp's underbelly, they carried with them a smell worse than death.

"Ha!" Cass yelled as she plunged her sword into a corpse. "Victory, you black-hearted fiend!" To her surprise, however, the corpse simply pressed forward as the steel sliced deeper into its body, its pierced organs oozing black rot. Cass froze, momentarily stunned by the reek of the shambling corpse. The Untoten warrior lunged toward her and bit down on Cass's exposed arm.

"Agh!" she screamed in pain, her blood highlighting the corpse's skull in crimson.

"Limbs!" Edwin shouted to Cass, as he ran to the bard's side and smashed the creature's skull with his hilt. The bone shattered, leaving its teeth in Cass's flesh. "Limbs, woman!" Edwin ordered.

Still wincing from the bite, Cass gritted her teeth and held her thin blade out with her good arm, just as another Untoten warrior charged in. Cass dropped to one knee and, with a flick of her wrist, severed the corpse's leg from its body. It fell to the ground, where Cass, with another flick of her wrist, cleanly beheaded it.

"Right, yes, of course!" she said as the revelation hit her.

"Yes, bard!" Edwin shouted in approval, while fighting off another corpse hefting a chipped battle-axe. "That's the way to do it!"

Cass tested her wounded arm once more, then grinned back. She continued to delicately sever limbs in blinding fashion while Edwin shattered whole bodies with his powerful swings. Having cleared some space, Edwin pummeled his way to the stone door. Cass followed as quickly as she could until a skeletal hand reached up from the mud and grabbed her ankle.

"Ah!" Cass yelled out. She slashed at the hand to no avail, as the thin blade kept rebounding off the calcified bone. Losing her focus on the bigger problem at hand, Cass was now being surrounded by shambling corpses.

"Bard!" shouted Edwin. "Look up, damn you!"

Cass raised her head and immediately understood the knight's concern. Desperation flooding her veins, she deftly whirled in a pirouette. Her blade flashed in the air, severing all of her foes' heads, while her other foot came down on top of the skeletal hand, crushing it with a mighty crack that sounded throughout the swamp. As the bodies fell about her, Cass ran toward Edwin, shaking fingers loose from her boot.

His torch lying on the ground, Edwin already had his boot braced against the side of the heavy stone door, his face flushed red with the exertion of trying to pull it open.

Cass shook her head and sheathed her rapier. "Push, not pull!" she said, as the Untoten swarmed even closer. Edwin scowled before shifting his weight to push the door inward.

"Perhaps you could've mentioned this while we were still in the accursed boat?"

Feeling the door sliding slowly in the dirt, they shoved as hard as they could, both being able to hear their Untoten foes dragging themselves closer in the murky gloom. Finally, Edwin was able to start squeezing through the gap they had created. Cass could hear Edwin's armor grinding against the stone as he shuffled and twisted his way inside. She grabbed the torch from the soil and kept her back to the door to cover Edwin's escape.

"I'm through!" he yelled.

"Well, my dearly departed foes . . . ," Cass said as she stepped back through the door. "I do bid you a fare—"

Edwin reached out and unceremoniously yanked her inside.

"Cease your prattling and help me close it shut!" Edwin barked. Cass complied and soon the door began to close, sliding slowly through the dirt and sealing them inside with a faint shudder.

"The . . . ," Cass sputtered. "The worst is behind us now, eh?"

Edwin didn't answer as he was too busy catching his breath as well, trying to see beyond the small radius of flickering torchlight.

Cass took a moment to remove her blade from its scabbard and wipe it clean of rot and grime against her pant leg before sheathing it again. But when she turned around, her blade sprung right back out again as she took in their surroundings.

Embedded in the earthen walls around them were hundreds of skeletons lying still in decrepit alcoves. Some were barely protruding from the dirt while others looked as if they had nearly worked their way free of the soil's grasp.

"Hells below . . . ," Cass whispered.

"I suppose we should have expected something like this," Edwin said as he abruptly wrested the torch out of Cass's hand. He imagined that he could hear the dirt falling away from their yellowed bones even now, but shook it off. "But if they were to attack, they would've done so by now."

"Or they're to wait until we're so far into the belly of the beast that we've been digested and don't even know it," Cass said, more matter-of-factly than in concern. There was no going back now. The door was far too heavy to pull open if they needed to escape, and even if they did get it open, they still had the shambling carcasses waiting for them on the other side. "Nothing to do but press on, sir knight."

Edwin nodded his agreement and sheathed his sword. They strode forward, his heavy footsteps clamoring down the narrow corridor, echoing off the bones like some morbid symphony.

"Exemplary swordsmanship back there," Edwin said, while they continued down the long passage.

Cass nodded, eyeing their skeletal hosts within the walls. Without breaking stride, she would occasionally, and very gently, tap a skull or two with her rapier as they passed by.

"For a woman, you might say?" she asked nonchalantly.

"For a bard," Edwin replied, not taking the bait.

"Mm . . . ," Cass answered, not quite paying attention. "Well, yes, thank you, milord."

Annoyed by Cass's distraction, Edwin glanced over to see the bard still tapping the occasional set of bones with a studied look on her face, her tongue between her teeth in concentration. "What are you doing?" Edwin asked.

"Oh, most likely inviting disaster down upon myself," Cass answered, without any tone of sarcasm or humor. Edwin shook his head, now doubly sure that he would never understand her. He was a man of straight answers and Cass was anything but.

Cass's tapping ceased for a moment as she spied a particularly large skull, the glint of a shiny bauble reflecting in the dim torch light. She tapped it upon the forehead once more, and a dull ruby gem plopped down into view.

"Ah, why thank you, good sirrah," she purred contentedly, reaching out toward the riches only to have her hand brought painfully down by Edwin's heavily armored gauntlet.

"The dead are entitled to their dignity, not to line your greedy pockets," Edwin scolded.

Cass frowned in return, as if she'd been insulted in the worst possible way. "I didn't see you bestow any such dignity outside."

"We put them to rest. It was the proper thing to do," Edwin answered back, nudging Cass forward.

"Such certainty," Cass retorted.

"Simply the tenets of the woman I loved."

"Tenets that apparently weren't passed on to your daughter, eh?"

"Mind your words, bard," Edwin answered curtly, before coming to a sudden halt. "There. You see that?" Edwin pointed down the corridor, where a crystalline pinprick of light shimmered in the distance.

Her irritation quickly forgotten, Cass gasped in surprise. "That's what we've come for, sir knight. That's it!"

They both quickened their steps as the light grew stronger. Cass whispered to Edwin, "It knows you're here, milord, I'm sure of it."

Edwin didn't respond, but he couldn't deny that with each step they took, the light's radiance seemed to be greater than before.

After a few more paces, they stepped into a rounded chamber, lined with just as many cobwebbed skeletons as the corridor behind them. The walls, and the dead, rose up into the chamber's vaulted ceiling, with legions of hollowed eye sockets silently staring down at them. Occasional beams of moonlight struck down through tiny holes in the ceiling, but they were nothing compared to the radiance of what lay in the center of the chamber.

As their deathly hosts looked on, Cass and Edwin approached the small dais where the light shined the strongest. There, rested a skeletal hand of crystal bone. Despite its own layer of dust, the hand sparkled and shimmered as Edwin drew closer. It seemed to hum with its own peculiar kind of energy, as if it were alive.

"There," said Cass, pointing to the hand. "The Knochenbau. That's what enables the Gravewalkers to summon their kin, no matter the distance." She looked around as small gusts of wind danced about the chamber and whistled through the moonlit punctures above. "And completely safe. Heh, I mean, what fool would dare to arouse the wrath of a Gravewalker"—Cass ran her eyes over the endless rows of corpses stacked around them—"in a place like this?"

Edwin ignored Cass's nervous chuckles and leaned in closer to the skeletal hand. "How do we know it still works?"

Cass shrugged and gingerly extended a hand toward the dais, her finger slowly uncurling in its direction. Without warning, the artifact sizzled and snapped with a spark of blue energy. The dust disappeared in a flash and the crystal ran blue with electric current, as Cass quickly jerked her finger back with a loud yell.

"Mother of all!" Cass cursed as she emphatically wagged her finger in the air, the skin now a shiny red. "I'm overjoyed to report that yes, it will still kill hapless mortals as intended, milord," Cass announced to Edwin as she cradled her hand.

Edwin paused a moment, then straightened to his full height. "I have to try."

Determination etched in his face, he approached the crystal hand. As he removed his gauntlets, the hand hummed louder and louder with each step that he took. What appeared to be blue veins of current inside the crystal grew brighter with each pulse of energy.

Once there, Edwin took one last look back at Cass, still cradling her singed finger. Resolved to see it through, he turned around and reached out toward the eerily beautiful skeletal digits. The humming vibrated in his ears as the hand's crystallized fingers began to reach out to his, as if yearning for the contact. Edwin's fingertips gently touched the crystal, which felt warm and smooth, like the softest human skin. The skeletal fingers lunged forward and grasped Edwin's hand tightly, the electric veins bleeding blue beneath the hand's surface.

Edwin waited for some inevitable sorcery to occur, but nothing happened.

A few more moments, but still, Mela was nowhere to be heard from or seen.

He frowned as he released the hand, its humming trailing off to a soft buzz.

"Perhaps we haven't had enough to drink yet?" Cass offered as an explanation. "Maybe if we just looked around for a bit, we could—"

But Cass was suddenly cut off, as all of the air seemed to rush out of the chamber. The faint whistles of the chamber now turned to screams as the wind built up and swirled toward the ceiling. Both of them struggled for breath as a pillar of white fog rose before them. A blue storm silently raged within the fog as blue bolts darted this way and that. As each of them thought they might pass out, the air returned and the fog pillar dissipated to reveal a dark-haired beauty.

"Mela," Edwin gasped.

***

Enraged at her abduction, Mela quickly took in her surroundings. Her eyes darted around the room and then . . . she saw the knight.

"If your mother could only see you now . . . ," she heard him say in a reverent whisper. His words told her exactly whom she was looking at, but how did he do this? Her eyes drifted to the skeletal hand and then back to Edwin . . . and she had her answer.

***

Cass nodded in rushed agreement along with Edwin. "She's quite the vixen, sir knight!" she said, moving away from the wall for a moment. But only for a moment, as Cass stopped gawking at the Gravewalker and returned to the safety of the wall's distance. There, she watched Mela's eyes grow wide with anger after she glanced at the skeletal hand, then Edwin. The Gravewalker let out a low hiss, and the skeletons surrounding all of them began to suddenly creak and twist in their dirt entrapments.

Cass looked about, her eyes growing wide with fear. The dead were wrestling with the earth to her left and right, but she remained frozen to the wall. "Ah, milord . . . ," she called out to Edwin, but the knight was preoccupied with his enraged daughter.

"You!" Mela screamed at her father. "How dare you!"

"Mela . . . ," Edwin said, trailing off into silence. Taken aback by her fury, Edwin struggled to find the right words, but he was still her father and she needed to remember that. He straightened himself and looked at her directly in the eyes. "Mela, you have to stop these attacks, this foolishness! It's not what your mother—"

"Do not!" Mela yelled at the top of her lungs, dirt falling all around her from the ceiling as the skeletons continued to dislodge themselves. "Do not speak of my mother. Ever! You have no right, you and your honorable knights—"

Edwin stood still, stung by the words that kept coming out of her mouth. "All you could do was watch them gut her like some animal! You let it happen right in front of you—I was there! I saw it all!"

"Mela, that's not true," Edwin said.

"Heh, really, it's not, milady!" Cass chirped from the back, finally finding her courage.

Mela's head whipped toward the sound of Cass's voice, glaring at her with white-hot orbs of electricity. In response, the corpses at her side burst their way free of the earthen wall in a sudden rage.

"Er . . . ," Cass said, pressing herself back even farther into the dirt.

"Mela. I know that I . . . ," Edwin stammered to pull her attention away from Cass, but it wasn't working. Realizing that perhaps he'd taken the wrong approach, he lowered his voice and raised his arms to plead his case. "I could have done more. It haunts me every day, it does."

He took a step away from the now lifeless crystal hand toward his daughter. "But I'm still your father. And I'm here now. And I'm telling you, asking you, please . . . stop this madness."

Mela glared back at him, but for the tiniest of moments, she softened as she took in the sight of her once-proud father, begging for her forgiveness. The skeletons surrounding Cass paused as well, as they too reflected the change in her demeanor. The whole room began to feel slack.

"Is that it, then? Is that all you have to say?" she asked.

Cass's eyes nearly bulged out of her sockets as she tried to mouth the right words to say for Edwin, but the knight just simply nodded his head in confirmation at Mela's question.

"As I thought," she said. And then, just as quickly as it had begun, the reprieve was over. Mela closed her eyes for a moment, and when she opened them, they were glimmering like white suns. "Good-bye, Father."

Cass shouted a warning to Edwin, but she was drowned out by the shrieks of skeletal jaws grinding against each other as they all pushed free from their resting places. Then she discovered that she had other things to worry about as the Untoten began to lumber in her direction.

Spit began to fly from Mela's mouth, her face growing more deranged by the minute. Edwin began to lose sight of his daughter, as this creature of hate boiled up to the surface from inside her.

"Mela!" Edwin yelled. "No! This isn't the answer!"

Cass breathed a sigh of relief and snuck away as her attackers suddenly turned their attention toward Edwin. Still, she knew it would only be a temporary respite as more and more Untoten swarmed the chamber from the corridors beyond.

"Not good," Cass muttered. "No, not good at all."

"You were a fool for coming here, Father . . . a fool." Her mouth twisted into a cruel smile as she advanced on Edwin and Cass.

Just then, Edwin heard something zip past his head and a small black bolt struck Mela just below her collarbone, sickly yellow ichors dripping from the wound.

Mela didn't even cry out; instead, she hazily glanced at the bolt protruding from her shoulder. "C . . . coward," she said, as she looked up at Edwin. Her strength faded fast.

"Mela!" Edwin cried out as she slumped to the floor. Her skeletal minions followed suit, collapsing where they stood.

From above, scores of corpses that had only partially worked their way free came crashing down, disintegrating into dust upon impact, or swung loosely by their legs and feet—dead chandeliers embroidering a dark mausoleum.

Edwin coughed amid the cloud of debris, and when he looked back up, he saw Renton, Alain, and a group of knights standing by the chamber's entrance. Nearby, a small mist began to rise around Mela . . . only to then fizzle away.

"If she gets her strength back, all this will have been for naught," Renton said, his voice echoing deeply in the chamber. "Bind her quickly and remove her from this place." He gestured his knights toward Mela's limp form.

The knights rushed past Renton and quickly set to fastening Mela's limbs with iron cuffs. "I'm sorry that you had to see for yourself, Son." Renton addressed Edwin. "But now you know." Renton paused, a genuine look of concern on his face. "She meant for your death, for all our deaths, and there's nothing you could've done to change her mind."

Edwin glanced about, still utterly confused by their arrival. He spied his old comrade Luther and thought that at least he'd get some answers from him.

Sensing Edwin's disquiet, Renton quickly gestured to Alain, then to Cass.

Alain's confusion momentarily joined Edwin's, however, when he realized exactly who the bard was. "You," Alain hissed, thinking back to that night at the Pig, where he'd been humiliated by Cass's sudden departure.

"Now," Renton commanded. Gritting his teeth, Alain loosened a leather pouch from his belt and tossed it to the bard, who nimbly snatched it out of the air. Edwin heard the clinking of coins, even as the pouch landed in Cass's hands.

Cass looked back to Alain, the slightest hint of satisfaction in her eyes. "Not exactly a member of the war council, are you, Master Alain?"

"My keys, woman," Renton said. "The performance is over." Taken down a few notches, Cass grudgingly pulled the set of jail keys from her pocket and tossed them back to Alain.

The logic of what had just happened finally permeated Edwin's confusion as he turned around to face Cass.

"This whole time?" growled Edwin.

"And why not? She's an actor, a mere pretender," Renton answered for Cass. "It was the only way you would come to see the truth, Son." Renton raised an eyebrow at Cass, who by now had backed away several paces from Edwin. "As if she'd been able to stage such a preposterous escape herself."

Cass's sheepish look turned to embarrassment as she began to stare down at the floor.

"You self-serving bitch!" Edwin yelled as he charged Cass.

Anticipating his son's temper, Renton quickly blocked his path.

"It's over, Edwin."

Edwin lunged again, but his father embraced him in his arms and held him still. "You made a valiant effort, but it simply wasn't meant to be." His arms wrapped even tighter around his son. "It's over."

Already upset over his father's revelation regarding the details of Mela's capture, Alain took notice of Renton's affection for Edwin . . . then followed the other knights out as they carried Mela's limp form from the chamber.

***

After some time, Renton felt Edwin relax in his arms and let him go. The crystal hand suddenly hissed in the damp air, sensing the same blood that flowed in Renton as well. Renton frowned, then drew his sword.

Striding over to the dais, he brought the blade's hilt down upon the hand, shattering the crystal in an explosion that littered the ground beneath them with countless fragments.

"It is done," Renton said as he turned away from the broken relic and faced Edwin, who stood with his shoulders slumped in defeat. "Come. The people of Riesenstadt await your return."

With that, Renton marched out of the chamber and toward the corridor.

Edwin closed his eyes, then opened them to see where Mela's blood had pooled in the dirt, mixed in with oily traces of poison. Filled with regret, he turned slowly to Cass.

"Did you find your inspiration, bard?"

Cass remained silent, staring at Edwin, but not saying a word.

"Edwin . . ." His father's voice echoed from the corridor.

Edwin waited a moment more, then walked out of the chamber to follow the hallway back to the surface.

Left to herself, Cass shuffled over to the dais. Reaching out with her wounded hand, still red and blistering, she held it over the shattered bits of crystal. The clear pieces began to twitch and vibrate, sensing the bard's approach. A small bolt suddenly leapt out and struck Cass's hand, then another, and another until there was a cluster of electric sparks rebounding off her flesh. Cass grimaced, but continued to hold her hand in place as she watched her hand blister with empty eyes.

A few moments more, then she made her way toward the exit.

CHAPTER 14

Rotten Cores and Open Sores

The sun had risen hours ago, but just now was it peeking over the high walls of the alleyway in which Gertrude slept. The hem of her dress was soiled with dirt and worse, but given her situation, it was the least of her worries. The rays of sunlight were starting to attack her eyes, warming her eyelids and stirring her awake. It had broken through the plague of clouds that normally cursed the sky this time of year. She could hear the sounds of the city now, people going about their day. Carts rolling in the streets, a blacksmith in the distance hammering steel, a mother chasing a misbehaving child.

Gertrude's stomach ached from the drink the night before. It had been too sweet, but it had done the trick. The man who had given it to her had wanted something for himself in exchange and she had let him take it. Here in this alleyway, she had let him inside her while the drink had kept her lightheaded and warm. Her hand slid down her dress and she could feel the stiffness of his stain. She rolled back, closer to the wall, but the sun had already taken over the entire alleyway. The depression was sinking in again, just as it did every morning. It seemed to grow out of nothingness, just as she knew it would fade back into nothingness once the drink had worked through her system. She would have it again tomorrow because she would devour its calling again tonight.

Gertrude's luck had remained the same for months now. She was aware her life was meaningless; it had probably always been, but up until a few months ago, it hadn't felt like it.

She'd had her parents, loving and warm, and her brother, strong and kind to his sister. But he hadn't been strong enough for the Gravewalkers. The filthy witches who had set those bloodthirsty corpses upon him. He had been on guard duty, trying to be noticed by the Knights Proper. He had wanted to do more than simply stand on guard at the city walls. Maybe that's why he hadn't backed down when the Untoten appeared. Instead of pulling back and fighting with the knights, he'd pushed forward, swinging, fighting, until he was swallowed up in the horde of corpses. She knew those witches had been watching, watching while her brother had been torn apart, and she hated them even more for it.

Her head still felt light. She was thankful that it didn't ache as bad as her stomach. She wished she could crawl into bed with her mother like she had when she'd been younger. A mother who now cursed worse than the men at the Whistling Pig. Fighting with her husband every day.

After their son died, they'd fallen apart right before Gertrude's eyes. She hadn't known what to do when they fought. She had tried hard to be a good daughter and to do whatever she could to keep them from each other's throats. She cooked and cleaned as often as possible, but they found new things to fight about. There was always something, a tone of voice, a roll of the eyes, or a sigh of tiredness. The arguing drove Gertrude mad to the point where she would hide outside, no matter how cold it was, to cry so hard it made her sick.

Her mind suddenly pulled a knee-jerk instinct, and she felt her waistline. There it was, her safety, tucked tightly between her dress and her skin. You wouldn't call it a blade, certainly no blacksmith would, but there it sat, a piece of a half-made, broken sword from a workshop floor. She had scrounged it from a blacksmith's rubbish and had kept it close ever since. And for good reason, as she had already struck a few men in the calf when they had gotten too rough.

Her thoughts wandered back to all the nightmares her mind wouldn't let her have while she was asleep. Tension built up inside her as she remembered her parents, the screaming voices cracking under the stress and anger. Her stomach ceased aching at that point and gave her back last night's drink. She caught the whole of it in her mouth but swallowed it out of habit. She didn't gag; she never did. She just let it slide back down. She thought of the rotten piece of fruit that she had stashed in her pocket, but she desperately wished for something that hadn't come from a trash heap.

Gertrude wept for a moment, the depression worse than ever, the reality of it all sinking in too deep. This life was something she hated, the mornings most especially, but when the night came and the drink flowed heavily enough, she was placated. If the man of that night had more talent than the usual, then she might actually enjoy those hours in the dark. She would still wake up in the morning and regret everything, but then decide—as she always did—that she didn't know what else to do. The times were harsh; those accursed witches had brought it all down on her people's heads. There wasn't going back from any of it, and she wasn't sure if there was a forward or a future anymore. Just the torture of her daily cycle. Truth or lie, she lived it now and it was all for naught.

***

Later, she awoke to the sound of hurried footsteps out in the cobblestone streets as a steady crowd made their way to the city gates. She rolled away from the wall and onto her stomach. Her eyes rose toward the street and saw firsthand the owners of the footsteps. She began to push herself up from the ground, first to her knees, then steadying herself with her hand sliding up the wall. As she straightened, her head began to clear a little; perhaps the air was better up here. Her feet shuffled along to the end of the alleyway and out into the bright street. She shielded her eyes against the sun, taking in all the people in such a hurry.

"What's going on over there?" she asked to anybody that would answer.

"They caught her!" a man yelled out as he ran past.

"Caught her? Caught who?" Gertrude yelled back.

"The witches' leader!" the man shouted before he turned away and sped off.

Had they really gotten her? How? Gertrude turned toward the city gates and ran for all she was worth. The one responsible for all of their suffering was finally going to get her due, and perhaps Gertrude would get her life back.

The air rushed past her face, a semblance of living free once again. She felt the blood pumping hard through her body and her lungs taking in great gulps of air. She felt her waist again, one hand pressed there to hold the blade fast. She reached the crowd and started to push forward. Most were working hard to get to the front without losing their own spot, the others sinking farther into the back.

Gertrude weaved her way forward, choosing a few select moments to throw an elbow or two to make her way. When she reached the edge, she held her spot with the same elbows that had gotten her there.

Then she saw the knights entering, the knight-lord himself leading them through the gates. His sons rode at his side, both looking sullen, but Gertrude felt pride. Edwin must've finally come to his senses, choosing his people over his malicious daughter.

Several knights passed her before she caught sight of the wooden cart that held their captive, the Gravewalker herself. She found herself filled with an intense longing to get close to the witch, uncaring of the consequences, unworried about being stopped or just how she would get up into the cart itself. Spirits curse them all, she would have her revenge and she wouldn't be stopped.

She stepped out into the street when a hand suddenly pulled her back.

"Not yet, Gerty," a deep voice whispered into her ear. She recognized its owner right away, despite how long she'd been away from him. Her father turned her on the spot. For a moment, Gertrude forgot about her revenge and took in the sunken sight of her father. The long hours with the knights' auxiliary had taken their toll on him, but he smiled at her nonetheless.

Gertrude found herself smiling as well, but the sound of the prisoner's cart rang loudly in her ears. The wheels seemed to clatter along the cobblestones, calling out to her. She turned away from her father and made toward the cart again. Her father pulled her back and held her close.

"Now isn't the time."

"But—" she started.

"But she will get hers tomorrow, my dear. And we'll be there to do our part." His head turned into the crowd and Gertrude followed her father's gaze.

There stood her mother.

"Tomorrow, we will stand as a family," he said. "And together we'll give that bitch what's coming to her." Gertrude's mother never even looked at her, but kept her stare on the Gravewalker. Even from here, Gertrude could see the tears sliding their way down her mother's face, her stare growing harder with every passing every moment.

Gertrude felt her father's hands on her, squeezing with empathy, and for the first time in a long time, she felt a sense of hope. She nodded in assent, but there was still at least one thing she could do.

Reaching down into her pocket, she grasped the piece of moldy fruit and pulled it out. Before her father could stop her, she whirled around, and with every conceivable ounce of hate and fury that she could muster, she let it fly toward the cart.

***

Mela stood in the rickety cart, the team of knights and their horses ahead. Teetering this way and that, held up by a guard's arm while the poison kept her mind clouded, she was unable to distinguish much that was in front of her. She could hear the jeers and jaunts from the crowd as the first rotten bit of fruit exploded against her face.

Even if she'd been able to think clearly, she knew there was nothing left to her but the knights' mercy, and that was hardly a consolation worth considering. For the first time in her life, she found herself utterly powerless and completely vulnerable. Bereft of a proper graveyard or cemetery to draw from, she was as helpless as any other unarmed woman in Riesenstadt.

Despite suffering the same barrage of rotten fruit and worse, the knight's grip tightened with excitement around her wrist. His steel gloves dug into her skin and pulled blood. Her wooziness grew as the garbage continued to fly at her face.

Renton led his men through the village, Alain and Edwin riding just behind him. The knight-lord signaled both of his sons to move up to his side. Alain straightened up and smiled as he pushed his steed forward. Edwin watched his younger brother and sighed. This wasn't his glory, but it was going to be the closest he would ever come. When Edwin reached his father's side, Renton leaned over and clasped an armored hand on his shoulder. The crowd cheered as Edwin gave a regretful smile.

Alain turned in his saddle to see their embrace. Not quite sharing the same enthusiasm, he yelled, "Victory!" to draw the crowd's attention. They screamed again in approval, and Renton took the opportunity to raise Edwin's arm high into the air. More screams followed, but Alain only felt defeat. He bit his lip harshly and pulled back behind his father and brother.

Mela watched as her cart gained on the knight-lord's youngest son. Alain was hanging back, letting the other knights ahead of him to raise their own arms up in triumph and receive their cheers. The cart drew level with his horse, Mela's body, level with his own. The rotten fruit continued to fly at Mela despite the presence of the knight-lord's son.

"You know that you're only making them angrier?" Alain asked Mela, who could only respond by gritting her teeth. A large tomato caught her square in the face and the villagers let out a great raucous laughter. Mela answered by spitting out into the crowd, catching a villager on the forehead.

"That's the spirit!" Alain guffawed as he watched the thick glob of spit run down the man's face.

Mela stared straight ahead, ignoring Alain and his comments.

"We'll see if you stay this strong through the night, witch." His tone grew stern. "You'll have a much smaller and tougher crowd then." He slammed his heels into his horse and galloped back up to the front.

***

A dark cell laid open in wait for the Gravewalker, receiving her thrown body with the open embrace of a cold stone floor. She couldn't lift herself up while the poison was still flowing through her. She settled instead for wiping the blood from her mouth, an impassioned gift from her captors.

"No rotting corpses to save you now, witch," Alain leered, unable to keep his emotions in check. "This . . . ," he said as he knelt next to Mela's body. "This was your father's cell." Mela didn't move a muscle. "I hope you enjoy it as much as he did."

Mela turned her head to see that Renton had joined them, standing over her and his son.

Finally together for the first time, the two of them seeing eye to eye in that moment, Alain couldn't miss the utter hatred in Mela's gaze as she looked at Renton.

"Grandfather," Mela said plainly.

Renton showed no emotion, ignoring the barb altogether. "I am anything but unmerciful," Renton started. "Tell us where your forces lie and I promise swift justice."

"The same justice you gave my mother?"

"It is your choice to make. See to it that it is the right one."

Mela tensed at his arrogance. How she wished him dead—more than that, how she wished it to be at her own hands.

"Be as angry as you like, child," Renton said, answering her body language. "But even you can see it is all over now. You have only the opportunity to choose the nature of your end, here in my domain."

He turned and walked out along with Alain, leaving Mela to curl up into a ball. This was just another of the many firsts she'd experienced today, this utter despair that began to creep its way into her heart.

CHAPTER 15

Sit and Stew on Just What to Do

The heavy wooden sword slammed into the battle dummy with a tremendous crash. Despite the speed of each blow, there was a stupendous weight behind each stroke. The dummy itself, despite its countless sessions of use, was only now showing signs of wear thanks to Edwin's relentless strikes. He landed each hit with the precision of many years of practice and with the fury of incessant worrying after an equal amount of years in prison. He didn't have to fight for his life like he had to do in the swamp. Here, he needed only to cause hurt on his mental anguishes. They were all there with him: his father, Alain, the bard. His mind's eye let them stand to each take a turn at the chopping block.

Despite his anger, his mind also made room for Mela and her mother. There, the two of them witnessed his hatred and frustration rise in the physical torment of the wooden dummy. Watching, staring at him in judgment.

Large beads of sweat were starting to run down his forehead as he picked up the pace. The strikes were growing wilder and less precise. The sweat snuck in under his eyelids and stung him. The fade made him worse for wear; his sight grew fuzzy. The battle dummy momentarily doubled, then tripled in number. Unable to focus on any of the dummies, Edwin made a great arcing swing until he found the true target. The wooden sword made contact and snapped in the same instant.

Edwin grinned in pleasure at the sound. He let the hilt drop to the floor, letting his muscles relax, allowing his breath to slow. Beneath his training leathers, he could feel the heat and moisture rising, like he was wading through yet another foul swamp. He closed his eyes to feel each bead slide over his skin. Like a sick rain, he let it all wash down his body.

When he opened his eyes, the ghostly images had left him alone in the empty training room. He walked over to the dummy and picked up the splintered blade from its feet.

It's been a good long while since I've done that. Fighting to relieve stress, rather than fighting to stay alive . . . but perhaps it is one and the same.

The broken blade was warm in his hand as he palmed it. He strode back for the hilt, his body tingling from the exertion of the workout. With the pieces reunited, he took them to join their brother practice blades, a testament to their service. Making his exit, he passed the dummy and shoved it to the ground in one last fit of disquiet.

Perhaps it was true that the battle was still being fought, but a small smile grabbed his face and he felt strange for it. Feeling like he had when he was younger, it brought an entire mix of emotions to the fray, crowding up against the sentiments of betrayal and anger. All of this duplicity, the outlandish times that had bred it all, his losses weighing down on him, it sparked a rebellious sense of youth. It made him think of

Evelina and how she had sparked that same rebelliousness so many years ago.

It was only then that he noticed that his exit had been blocked by someone else walking into the room. He looked up from the floor to see Lady Berna standing in the entrance. Her dress bore the crimson colors of the knight-lord, as did everyone else who served in the castle, but tied around her wrist were colors of a different sort. Keldon's colors of blue and green, the sky and the grass, showed starkly against the knight-lord's hues. He had taken on the sky and grass as a tribute to his late father, a shepherd by the name of Mica.

Edwin had remembered when Mica had died and Lady Berna had been red eyed for weeks. Keldon had joined their family late in their lives, and while the baby boy was a blessing, Mica's death was a legitimate hardship for their small family. Desperate for a reliable source of income, Lady Berna had come to work for the castle and had helped to raise Edwin in these very walls.

Seeing Edwin, she gasped and reached out to him for embrace.

"But I'm covered in sweat, milady." Edwin said.

"Sweat, mud, shit, when have I ever not hugged you anyway, Master Edwin?" Lady Berna replied, seriousness written all across her face. Edwin let his smile come back and embraced the old woman; she nearly disappeared in his arms.

"It's good to see you, Anna," Edwin said. He could smell a touch of alcohol on her skin, despite the perfume she used to mask it. It was not a surprise to Edwin that she had been comforting herself as best she could, but this was coming through her pores. "How are you doing these days?" Edwin asked, worry showing on his face.

"As best as can be expected," she answered, her eyes taking in the concern on Edwin's face. "Well, not good," she added in sudden admission. "Not very good at all."

She looked down for a moment before continuing, "But that's nothing to say for the man who was thrown into his father's dungeons for all those long years." Tears suddenly welled up in her eyes, some small part of shame rising to the surface. "My word, Edwin. I wanted so badly to go visit you, knowing that you were suffering down there. But your father—"

But Edwin cut her off with another embrace. "Think nothing of it. In truth, it wasn't that bad, no different than the many times I was locked away as a youth for forgetting my table manners."

Lady Berna shook her head, knowing very well he was lying for her comfort, but she was grateful for the chance to lift that particular burden off her shoulders.

"But I'm here now and you must tell me what I can do to help."

He had been so caught up in his own problems that he'd forgotten about Keldon's death just a few days ago.

How many mothers must be in her state of mind these days.

His hands kneaded the sides of her shoulders as he took in every wrinkle of sadness on her face. This was a woman on the verge of a breakdown, despite Edwin having only really known her as someone strong, capable of handling the direst of dilemmas. Even when her husband had been attacked by those wolves out in the field, he had never seen any sign of Lady Berna's drinking. And to have to wander these halls every day in the service of the man who had ordered Keldon's death, he couldn't even imagine how that felt. Surely the men were still coming to her for advice, and to bear that weight on top of it all, he figured he would probably start drinking as well, perhaps enough to put the bard to shame.

"Just speak of it, whatever you need," Edwin said. While the bard's betrayal and his father's plotting had left him feeling helpless, this was something that he could feel good about, like he possessed some semblance of control over his life again.

"Just talk to me a while," Lady Berna said. "Every time I can help one of my boys unload his woes, it makes mine feel lighter somehow."

"Surely not. I should rather listen to yours, milady."

"Ridiculous," Lady Berna said. "Some other time perhaps. You have a daughter in the dungeons. A younger brother hells-bent to prove himself to your father. And now, now you're just expected to resume your duties as if nothing had ever happened," she sighed. "My poor boy, what must be running through your head."

She peeked around his side and saw the dummy on the floor. She also spotted the broken sword and decided her worries were confirmed. "Come on and sit," she said, motioning them to the floor. Edwin looked into her eyes once more and realized that he didn't have a choice. The strong, singular woman was still there, he could see it, just as he could see he didn't have any say in the matter.

As they both sat down, Edwin regarded the overbearing silence. Neither felt sure as to where they should start, so they spent a few moments without speaking.

Lady Berna took in the plainness of the room and tried to admire it for its simplicity. She could see why Edwin had spent so much time in here when he was younger. These complicated times were hard for him, she knew that, but she also knew it was time that he started taking notes from his father.

"You know this isn't the world anymore, Edwin," she said, gesturing to the room in its entirety. "The plainness of it all is gone."

Edwin barely heard her against the pressing hush. Her voice seemed to sneak in through his ears like a thief through a crack in the wall. He wanted to stay there, in the simple silence, but it was a battle he wasn't just losing—he was being torn away from it.

"Perhaps, but I'm just not ready to accept it yet. That much I know," he whispered, barely hearing his own voice escaping his mouth.

"The time for acceptance has passed you by, my boy," Lady Berna said. "You don't have that luxury anymore. None of us have it."

She resisted the impulse to talk about how the war with the Gravewalkers had left them feeling spiritually adrift, their loved ones burned and charred like one would dispose of common rubbish. Being unable to bury their dead, it weighed heavily on all of them, whether one had partaken in the Gravewalkers' services or not. Her thoughts drifted back to her son like she saw him every day, trapped up against the castle gates, beating back the clawing Untoten. Her own mind hardly left its own comfortable place, despite the pain. There she could wish vengeance on those who had wronged her son. There she could feel anger with the sadness, an emotion that had been growing stronger by the day.

As she turned back to Edwin, she wasn't sure how much he was thinking or how hard he was trying to ignore her, trapped in her own reveries.

"You're right. You've always been right with such matters," Edwin said. His head never moved as he kept it looking straight forward. "How often I'd dreamt of doing something, anything, while I was trapped in my cell. How often I'd wanted vengeance but couldn't decide on who or what. This anger, this frustration, it always holds itself in my limbs and I feel it bursting. Then my mind reaches out and grasps it, drowns it all in the wish of wanting to crawl into a corner and accept the simplicity of the stone walls around me."

"Fell a bit in love with that cell, did we?" Lady Berna asked. She knew the answer and feared it as she stared at Edwin.

"A bit, I suppose. You can't fail in your ideas when you're trapped and unable to act upon them," Edwin said. "And here I am, betrayed again, losing my daughter again, and all I can do is thrash about in my cell." He suddenly found himself wanting to be alone, his eyes darting around the confines of the training room, feeling tears trying to build in his eyes. They wouldn't come forth, because he wouldn't let them.

"You're a man of action, Edwin," Lady Berna insisted. "We all know it. Your father is a bit afraid of it. You didn't stand by and let love pass you by." Edwin felt Evelina begin to envelop his mind. "Your father feared it and discouraged it, but that didn't stop you, did it?"

"No," was all Edwin could say.

"That love is still there," Lady Berna said, resting a hand on Edwin's arm. "That fight is still there, both in your heart and in that poor girl down in the dungeons. She may seem to have lost it, but as a parent, I know there is no possible way that you have lost it for her." Her eyes stung as her tears began to well up again. Her son was in the dirt again, being thrashed and ripped apart. Her love drove her anger forward, drove her need to drive Edwin toward what he needed to do. For her own gain, for both of theirs. She knew it was selfish, but she didn't care. They both needed this. "She just needs to know it, Edwin."

"I don't even know what that means anymore," Edwin said, his eyes to the ground. "I've wandered this land again and found nothing but dark despair. My daughter brought that about, my father has enforced it, and I'm here beating a dummy."

"Oh, will you shut up already?" Lady Berna said, wanting to beat some sense into the boy she used to look after. "Sitting here, whining in your new cell. We have all lost, Edwin!"

"And how many hours have you wasted away in your cups?" Edwin said, striking back. The anger he felt startled him, but Lady Berna had struck a nerve.

"And what if I have?" Lady Berna asked. "What if I sit in the dark, inviting the spins of spirits? My son is dead." She let the bitterness sit heavy in her tone. "Your daughter is alive; despite what she has done, you still have her walking about. Not for long if your father has anything to say about it."

She was missing the confines of her drink right now. It wasn't the time for wishes, though, and she needed Edwin to see that. If she wasn't pushing in the same direction, then he would fall back into his own darkness.

"And what have I to offer her?" he asked.

"All you have is you," Lady Berna said. "That's all we ever have. Ourselves and what we do." Even as she said it, she wasn't sure she believed it. The importance of it rested on whether or not Edwin believed it, so she kept at it. "What can you do besides sitting around wishing for a frozen moment?"

Edwin had been wishing for that for some time now. He had lived in frozen moments for the past fifteen years now.

"Nothing is still any longer," Edwin said. "There's no way around that, no way around the movement." Evelina flooded his thoughts. He could see her face in front of him, Mela's face as well. Bloodied and beaten down they both were, where they found themselves. There was time still to act, even desperately, but without hesitation.

"Love, whether right or wrong, is a motivation worth following." He surprised himself with his own words.

Lady Berna could see the confusion ebbing away and being replaced by a single drive.

"Right or wrong," she said.

"Right or wrong," Edwin repeated back.

"Now help an old lady up," she told Edwin. "Help these bones creak back into a position more suitable for making an exit." Edwin smiled as he stood up himself and then reached out a helping hand. Lady Berna was as good as her word; her bones did seem to creak with every movement. Edwin couldn't help but realize just how old she had become. Her burdens weighed down on her heavier than most, on shoulders that were beginning to cripple beneath the weight.

He held her hand as he escorted her to the doorway, and she gave it a knowing squeeze before she took her leave of him. He walked back slowly to reset the dummy in its proper position. After the dummy stood, he looked it over for a while. The ghosts were no longer there—not in the dummy, not watching him in the room, nowhere in sight or mind. He smiled again and made his way to the practice swords. As he took one up and felt the grip, he felt his mind harden. It was in a better place now, for the moment. *It's a good place to be.*

Then, in three short strides, he crossed from the wall to the dummy and slashed down. All of it strung together, one sweeping, smooth motion. Splinters filled the air and danced downward to the floor, coming to a rest next to the two halves of the dummy. Cleaved in half, defeated, an illustration of the power of a single driving thought.

CHAPTER 16

The Fine Line between Plotting and Planning

"Sire?"

Alain looked up from his desk to see Jonas standing before him, his posture straight, his armor oiled and polished to a mirror shine.

"At ease, Jonas," he said. "And there's no need for the 'sire'; I'm not my father."

Jonas nodded, with no real intention of being at ease, especially in the presence of the knight-lord's son.

Alain sighed, now knowing why his father had grown so enamored with the young knight. *That,* he mused, *and his uncanny resemblance to Edwin.*

"Take a seat."

Jonas panicked for a moment, not sure if he was hearing Alain right. This was the first time he had ever been asked to sit with a superior. "A seat, sire?"

"Yes, Jonas. A seat. Take it," Alain said with some impatience. "And what did I say about the sire thing?"

Jonas stiffened slightly and then did as he was commanded.

Alain gestured to a glass carafe of brandied wine, the lone display of color in the bare chamber of wood and stone. "Care for a drink?"

For the second time, Jonas had a flash of anxiety. "I must pass, my lord. I'm to report back to duty after your lordship no longer has need of my presence."

Alain nodded and filled a glass for himself. "Of course, Jonas. You're a credit to our ranks, a real 'Knight Proper,' as the commoners are so fond of saying."

At that, Jonas brightened a bit, his deference to Alain's higher rank showing right through. "You do me much honor, my lord."

"Do you know why I called you?" Alain asked as he sipped from the glass.

Jonas gave a slight shrug of his armored shoulders. "I confess that I do not, my lord."

Alain shook his head, as he got out of his seat with drink in hand. "Enough with the formalities. We're brothers here, Jonas."

Rather than muster up the courage to address him as anything other than *sire* or *my lord*, Jonas gave Alain a cautious nod.

Circling the chamber, Alain lazily made his way toward the front. "I'd like you to be my guest, Jonas. At tomorrow's honor dinner."

The excitement in Jonas's voice betrayed his poise. "Your . . . your guest, sire?"

Alain gave him a pointed glance.

"Alain," Jonas stammered out.

Having reached Jonas's chair, Alain smiled. "Well?"

"Surely there are other knights more deserving than I. My brother Luther, for instance . . ."

"Your brother will already be present as a member of the knight-lord's personal guard. No, there's a very specific component to your attendance, Jonas." Alain took one last drink and set his glass upon the desk. "Will you accept?"

Jonas stood up, unable to contain himself any longer. "It would be my duty and my privilege."

"Excellent. Let us go, then," Alain said, as he headed toward the door.

Jonas looked on in confusion. "May I ask where?"

Alain came to a halt and turned around. "To see my father, of course. Did you think I could just invite anyone on a whim?"

Alain made to leave again, his steel-plated boots echoing down the hallway as he called back to Jonas. "Oh, might be best to forget about that 'Alain' nonsense for now."

Jonas swallowed, then hurried to catch up. "Yes . . . sire."

***

As a rule, Castle Riesenstadt was austere to a fault. A stern grey stronghold, with rows of oily torches keeping the lurking shadows at bay, cobblestone and timber seeming to be the only materials one was able to come by in these lands.

The grand chamber, however, was the lone exception. A vast stretch of polished stone surrounded by circular walls that stretched high above and ended in arched rafters that allowed glimpses of the stars just beyond.

At the head of the hall, just above the largest of the great hearths, hung the great banner of the Konig Protectorate. As tall as three men and almost as wide, it held a commanding presence. It shined brightly in sky blue with a great tree woven into it. The tree's branches stretched forth to the edges of the banner, many of them still bare. Tangled in the branches were leaves here and there, bearing the color and name of each knight-lord passed. There was, of course, forest green, but there was also radiant orange, dullest brown, and some who blended into the sky.

Standing alone was Renton's, the only knight-lord to adopt a shade of crimson, one that others would say resembled spilled blood, as his color and his legacy. At the trunk, the two strongest branches reached out and helped to hold the man crucified to its core. The man was nothing but a skeleton, his hands and feet disappearing into the wood of the tree. Being absorbed by the tree itself, becoming a part of all the gathered knowledge of the Brotherhood. Having given himself up wholly, without question—not as a sacrifice but as a virtue piece of their history. The roots reached nearly to the bottom but were halted by their motto curved upward, as if a smile of pride—"The Pieces of the Whole."

Jonas's gaze then drifted to the smaller banners of all colors and distinctions as each current member's emblem hung about the collective flag of the Brotherhood. His gaze climbed to his brother Luther's banner. Blood red like the knight-lord's, it stood out among most. A great shield embroidered in gold flashed brighter than the red, the only one of its kind. It was a broad diamond with two gold corners and two red, the four corners of the land. Luther's symbol was unique, for he was the only knight to choose the art of the shield. Broad and heavy, this piece of weaponry was rarely pursued by anyone for its inability to be carried or swung easily. Luther had dedicated a great deal of his life to a weapon used to protect others, although many looked at the shield as a weapon suited for cowards, nothing more than a place to hide behind. Such talk vanished, however, when the knight-lord Renton saw fit to place the great honor of being his personal guard to Luther, a show of faith and respect toward his unpopular choice of fighting skill. He also had bestowed upon Luther a dirk, commissioned from the best blacksmith in the land. Luther had yet to draw it from its sheath in combat, but the knight-lord had insisted that it was always better to be prepared, for even the strongest walls eventually crumble.

Of course, just below Luther's banner hung Jonas's, blue like the great banner, but he hoped soon it would be changed to bear the blood color of the knight-lord. Each knight of the personal guard adopted the color of their knight-lord. Only five banners carried this honor, including Renton's sergeant and right-hand protector, Vintas. A golden boar was embroidered upon his banner, a rather self-explanatory symbol to all who knew the man.

Like Jonas's gaze and all men's upon entering the grand chamber, Alain's line of sight rose up to the wall of banners as well. But the height of his gaze did not travel far, as his eyes fell to his own banner. There it hung, at the bottommost left corner. Grey and dull all about, except for the bright-white horse's head, the word *Son* embroidered in its bridle. Alain had never shown any exceptional skill except for that of horseback riding. His patience with the men was not very high, and therefore, the position of teacher was never granted to him. But his horsemanship was recognized nonetheless. The word *Son* had been his father's idea. A small memento to the one thing Alain had to be proud of.

Alain stopped for a moment to take in the last banner, a razor-sharp broadsword splitting a decrepit skull in two . . . the sigil of House Talmaris, the bane of Gravewalkers. He reflected upon his father's grand legacy, then gave thought to his own destiny. Was his fate to be merely another notch in his father's tapestry or would he weave his own future? His own legacy?

For now, it was only a fleeting thought as Alain heard his father's voice from the other side of the chamber, directing his servants this way and that. He could sense Jonas stiffening right beside him, coming out of his reverie, and Alain realized that the boy was smarter than he had thought.

From Jonas's perspective, this jaunt had the sense of being in the right place for the wrong reason, where he could fall out of favor with the knight-lord just as quickly as he had fallen into it.

"Should I wait here, sire?" he asked Alain.

Alain smiled and motioned him forward. "Of course not."

As they approached, Renton looked up for a moment and locked eyes with Jonas before returning to the seating chart spread out over the table. Despite their previous afternoon, Jonas felt his blood go cold, his respect for the knight-lord still mixed in with the fear of the man himself. Not that Jonas worried for his life, but there was something that ran through his veins that couldn't be explained. There was a presence about Renton, that he was a man to be feared as well as respected and it was Jonas's duty to recognize that. He continued forward stiffly but with recognition of the honor he was being afforded. He wasn't quite sure how to act yet in front of Alain, but he was determined to stay within the good graces he had recently earned with his father.

Renton carried on with the minutia of who would be seated and where. The honor dinner, celebrating Edwin's return, his redemption, was all too important in restoring the people's faith in the Protectorate and nothing would be left to chance. It was very important to Renton to refer to this whole ordeal as a dinner rather than a feast or a banquet or anything else insinuating appropriated privilege. His family was to be here to attend the rejoining of a son with his brothers, rather than a host of others flouting their self-perceived importance. Extra food had been distributed throughout the castle so that everyone would feel that they were joined in the celebration, but here, at this table, would sit the lifeblood of the Brotherhood.

As they reached the table, Alain came to a snapping halt, quickly followed by Jonas. "Father," Alain called out. "I've come to seek your consent."

Renton simply continued to dole out orders to his staff, emphatically jabbing the seating chart with a finger to make his wishes known.

Alain waited a few moments more, politely smiling at Jonas in reassurance. But as he turned back toward his father, his cheeks turned red with embarrassment.

"Father," he said again, feeling the heat on his face, trying to will it away.

"What?" Renton said, still not bothering to look up from the table.

Feeling a small measure of affirmation that the knight-lord had actually acknowledged him, Alain took a step to the side, to showcase Jonas, as if he were some prize buck. "I thought that Jonas here would be a suitable guest, and I thought to seek your approval in inviting him to the honor dinner."

Renton fixed an eye on Alain, then his gaze moved toward Jonas.

"What makes you think you were invited in the first place?" A question Alain knew very well was for him, even though Jonas was the subject of his father's attention.

Alain closed his eyes, trying to will himself forward. "I'd thought that—"

"Yes, you did, and you were correct. Jonas will make an excellent addition, a fine example of the Brotherhood." He nodded to Jonas in approval.

Alain relaxed slightly, seeing that he still might just win his father's favor yet.

"You will join us, won't you, Jonas?" Renton asked. As with most things, this was a statement more than a question. To hear a real question come from Renton's lips was a rarity, and someone of Jonas's rank and stature did not warrant such an inclination.

Incredibly, Jonas paused before responding. He was young and perhaps inexperienced, but he knew when he was being bounced between two opposing forces, to what ends exactly he could not quite figure out, but he was wary about answering immediately all the same. A pawn in some game that he'd never stopped to think was capable of being played by these men of distinction, but he couldn't shake the nagging feeling worming its way into his gut.

"Of course, milord," he said finally, without any sign of emotion.

Slightly irritated by Jonas's delay, Renton turned back to the table and to the seating chart. "Very well, then."

Jonas immediately turned about and marched away, but Alain wasn't about to completely lose face to Jonas just yet. "Hold, Jonas."

Still loyal to a fault, Jonas did as commanded, but he found it hard to contain his growing anger.

Satisfied, Alain faced his father once more, unable to let it go just yet, not wanting to leave without absolute confirmation.

Renton's jaw twitched, his son's impertinence adding to the many other items demanding his attention. "If you wish to join us so badly, then convince the witch to reveal the location of her army," Renton said, knowing full well what kind of approval Alain had been hoping for. In truth, Renton was happy to have Jonas around tonight and Alain had provided Renton with the opportunity to save a look of favoritism. But blood alone wasn't a guarantee of anything, in this life or the next.

Renton waved a hand of dismissal toward Alain. "Earn your seat at the table, if you think yourself capable of leaving your cups. Now leave us."

Alain squirmed under his father's command, but there was no trifling with the knight-lord after such a dismissal. He snapped a salute, then turned to leave.

***

On the walk back, both men kept their thoughts to themselves, a heated stew of betrayal and embarrassment. After some time, Alain finally spoke up and Jonas was glad for it, thinking that such thoughts would only lead to ruin.

"You served well, Jonas, and I thank you for your loyalty."

Jonas nodded, grateful to put the day's events behind them. "Of course, milord," he answered, more comfortably than he had intended.

They fell back into silence as they continued down the narrow corridor, but Jonas now found himself desperate to know more about the character of the man he walked next to. Would Alain really sink so low as to use another knight for his own personal gain? And was the knight-lord perhaps using Jonas in turn, to provoke his son for some unknown cause? Jonas could still smell the spirits lingering in Alain's breath, and it wasn't unreasonable to think that Renton simply desired for his son to turn away from such vices.

"What will you do, sire? With the witch?" Jonas asked him, testing the waters, feeling more and more confident around the man.

Alain briefly closed his eyes, as if he was imagining some grisly sequence playing out before him. "Everything that I can, Jonas. Everything that I can."

Jonas gave a curt nod in response, but Alain's tone disturbed him. Down the endless stretch of stone and mortar they went as Jonas considered that it was one thing to affect suffering for the sake of saving lives . . . but it was entirely another to enjoy it.

CHAPTER 17

Blonde Is Not Always Better

From the moment Mela disappeared in a sudden pillar of fog and sparks, Acacia knew that the knights were somehow involved. In secret, it gladdened her, because this was just the thing her sisters needed.

First, however, was the issue of proving it.

The initial suspicion was that in a fit of anger, Mela had simply teleported to a cemetery or a graveyard above, tired of hearing Elaine and Acacia's never-ending argument. Given that the Gravewalkers could only teleport from one place of death to another, her travel options were limited to begin with and Mela herself was hardly a wandering spirit. So there wasn't much bother about her disappearance despite Acacia's arguments otherwise. So they waited. And they waited.

And still nothing.

Days passed and the sisters grew restless. Apart from being their leader, Mela was also the most gifted of their kind. The thought of having to engage the knights without her at their side was an unsettling one. Thus, sisters were sent to search each and every conceivable graveyard, cemetery, mausoleum, and burial ground that they could think of. All done in secrecy, all done under the cover of night, and yet, despite all their searching, there were no clues or any shreds of evidence as to what had befallen their leader.

And this is when Acacia had noticed Elaine's unusual silence.

Always, Acacia thought, *always that witch was endlessly complaining about one matter or another, spelling out the inevitable doom that war would bring to them, hoping instead for some return to their former days of glory, an existence as docile sheep just waiting for the butcher's axe.*

But now, strangely enough, ever since Mela's absence . . . she hadn't uttered a single word.

Acacia knew she was hiding something, and she was determined to find out exactly what it was. After searching for the better part of the day, she finally found her on the surface, sitting under placid skies. Nestled beside the remnants of a campfire, its charred embers smoldering into oblivion.

"Why, what a lovely little scene this is," she called out to Elaine.

"As if you would recognize one," Elaine taunted back. "Go back to your charnel house below; I've no use for it."

As ever, Acacia found more delight in the pauses, the spaces in between. The moments of awkwardness. That is where she lived, where she had learned to ply her trade among her dark-haired sisters who would fret and stare at the sight of her golden locks. And in this moment of silence, as she took in Elaine's weary, furtive glances, she knew her guess had been correct.

"You know where Mela is, don't you?"

Elaine shifted a few embers with a stick, but said nothing.

"So it's true. What will the others say when they find out you've been keeping this to yourself?"

"And you'd be the first to pass that along, wouldn't you?"

"Not if you tell me first, dear sister."

Elaine shook her head, a bittersweet smile upon her lips. "Of course."

"Well?" Acacia asked, getting tired of their usual cat-and-mouse game.

"In truth, I don't know."

"But you have an idea. And you've been keeping it to yourself because this gives the reprieve you've been hoping for. That without Mela, there's no way that we would dare engage the Protectorate, yes?"

Elaine looked up to Acacia's sly grin, then slowly rose to her feet. *The brat knows me too damn well.*

***

Back in the earthen tunnels below, Acacia leaned in closer to the skeletal hand, its crystalline composition shimmering in the dim torchlight. "The Knoch-en-what? What does it do again?"

Elaine closed her eyes, trying to retain her composure. "You know what this is, Acacia. Stop playing the fool."

Acacia smiled, conceding the round to her counterpart.

Acacia watched as slight trails of electricity wormed their way through the crystal ridges of the skeletal hand. "So you had this hidden down here for all this time?"

"We had no direct need for it," Elaine answered back.

"Oh, yes, we did. Perhaps we could've rallied more sisters here to our cause, something you knew I'd want." Acacia smiled as she watched Elaine. The old sister had been found out and they both knew it.

"Assuming there were other sisters out there, we'd what? Drag them into this fine mess we've found ourselves in? I think not, sister."

Acacia let it go for the time being. She had lost that battle without even knowing it had started so many years ago. There was no doubt that she wasn't trusted, and here was the overwhelming truth. The question hung inside her head . . .

Did Mela know about all of this?

"We could use it to bring her back," Acacia suggested, trying to turn the tide toward the present predicament.

"If we had her father with us, yes, but they've no doubt hidden him away somewhere in Castle Riesenstadt."

Acacia pulled herself away from the skeletal hand and faced Elaine. "You'll travel with me, then. To the other safe houses, to gather evidence, to prove this to the others."

"To what end? To rally them for war? For a direct attack against Riesenstadt?"

Acacia knew why the old witch had been desperate to keep this to herself, but this was borderline treason. Yet, for Acacia to play that hand now would smack of desperation and would result in even more sisters joining Elaine's side. *No, this will require a delicate touch,* she mused.

"Come with me, Elaine. Let us put our differences aside, let us make amends in this time of troubles."

"Just the two of us?"

Acacia nodded with a smile.

Elaine laughed. "And I'm sure you would be the very picture of sorrow, returning alone, my corpse cooling somewhere else. No, I'm afraid, my dear, that if you're so insistent on discovering the truth, you'll have to do it without me."

Acacia knew her game was up and tipped her head in respect. *That old hag knows me too damn well.*

CHAPTER 18

How Not to Play an Instrument

Mela hung limp against a filthy wooden board, strung up by her hands and her feet. The ropes burned, but not so much as the coals that glowed before her. She was exhausted, and the day wouldn't stop.

In front of her was Alain, a tight-lipped smile on his face informing Mela that his patience was quickly running out. He had come to collect her a few hours before, ordering two large knights and a vile, toothless old man to take her down below to the dungeons. The knights had done the stringing while the old man prepared instruments upon a table. They shined and glistened in the firelight. He had prodded the coals from time to time and looked them over as closely as he looked over his tools.

Now he stood behind Alain and waited.

"I'm going to introduce you to someone, Mela," Alain said, his smile never fading. "This here is Fiddler, and he's going to be helping you and me with our conversation tonight."

Mela tried to laugh, but only worked out a few shallow breaths, the ropes digging deeper into her skin, her ribs feeling as if they were trying to escape her body.

"Fiddler," she finally got out.

"Do you know why we call him that?" Alain asked.

Mela looked over to the man, his emaciated chest seeming to give everything it had to keep him breathing. He fondled a set of tongs with a softness most men would reserve for their lovers. Mela stayed silent this time, knowing full well Alain would tell her, whether she liked it or not. She was sure it wasn't something she was going to like, but that had been her day so far.

"You see, they call him that because he can play a man's guts so well, he'll sing anything in just the pitch and tone we want him to."

Fiddler chuckled, barely capable of containing his excitement.

Alain grabbed Mela's hair and pulled her head up to face his.

"As much as I would like to hear that music, it is possible for you to skip all of it."

Mela knew a deal was coming and she didn't care. Her hair was pulling loose from her scalp; she could hear it slowly ripping away from her skin in Alain's tight grip.

"You can simply tell us where you have your forces, and my father, the great knight-lord himself, will grant you mercy." Alain only waited a single heartbeat before continuing. "But personally I hope you continue to act like the self-righteous little bitch that you are so that I can see that real justice is paid forward."

Mela forced herself to let out a shallow laugh, intermittent with coughs and gasps for air.

"You . . . ," she said. "You impudent little knights. You can feel it, am I right? You know it, deep down inside your fancy little suits of armor." Her raspy voice wormed its way through Alain's ears. Her own eagerness was growing now, embracing the futility of her fate. "Death. She's coming for you."

"Fiddler!" Alain yelled, his heart pounding. "Start the music."

He released his grip and let Mela's head slump back down. The skin of her head tingled with release as the rest of it lulled itself back and forth. She could hear Fiddler set the tongs down on the bench and shuffle himself toward the fire. The coals hissed and spit into the air. The sound alone was enough to make her tremble, but she held her ground. There was nothing to be done about it now, and she knew that her suffering was inevitable.

The hot stone came closer, hissing as each drop of saliva from the shrunken toothless man splattered upon it. His excitement filled the air; he lived for this, nothing else for him to yearn for besides pain and suffering.

As the coal touched Mela's skin, there was a sizzling whisper that filled the room, snaking its way into Alain's ears. Fiddler was slow at first, allowing the coal to kiss Mela's abdomen and then aggressively pushing it harder into her as if it would burrow straight through her. She let out a scream for the first time since she could remember. Harsher than the hissing coal upon flesh, Alain's ears felt they would bleed to the sound of Mela's pain. Fiddler twisted the coal to a side with more heat and Mela let out another echoing scream into the chamber.

"Where . . . ," Alain started as he lost his breath. This was not as he had imagined it. Alain thought of Keldon and the screaming men at the gates. Revenge in this manner was not sitting well, and he knew there would be more than he could stand.

Where am I? Alain thought. His mind was lost as if he had just been struck in the head.

"You heard him, dear," Fiddler said. "Where are your armies?" he asked as he continued to twist the coal tighter into her flesh.

It smells sweet, Mela thought to herself as the aroma of her own burning flesh reached her nose. *Why is it sweet?*

Fiddler pulled the coal out and walked back to the fire. Alain came back to himself as Fiddler stoked the flames. *How to convince her?* Alain thought. *Get her to talk.* He watched Mela's body heave as she tried to catch her breath. He stepped closer and brought his face to hers.

"If you don't speak, if you let this go on, do you know what will happen to you?" Alain asked her. Mela's eyes slid sideways to take in the sight of her interrogator, her chest still heaving, her skin doused in sweat.

"Do you know . . . what will happen to you if I ever get free?" she rasped.

Alain couldn't help but laugh a bit at this.

"You will never be free again."

"Don't be so sure. I've done and seen things far worse than you can think," Mela continued. "I see you sweating this out worse than I am, you ball-less wonder. The Trauergast and I will take special pleasures with you," she finished with a grin.

"You! You're going to face the People's Affliction, you malicious bitch!" Alain shouted, losing the patience he possessed just a moment ago. He would not take insult from someone he had been trying to help. *An enemy that I actually felt sorry for,* he thought. "I'm going to watch your head slowly pop like a melon," Alain added. "A pity we won't be able to place your pretty face on the castle wall after they make such a mess of it."

"You like my pretty face, don't you?" Mela said, leaning into Alain against her chains. Alain chuckled, caught off guard and uncertain what to do with the situation. But Mela saved him the trouble and spit in his face.

CHAPTER 19

The Better Lesson

"Of course. When there's the prospect of food and drink to fill your miserable gullet, lo and behold you magically appear, eager to be led like a sheep to pasture," Cass said, her voice ringing out in the starless night, followed by the clip-clop of roughshod hooves over packed dirt.

The bard looked back to see the beast happily trailing along, not quite caring that their relationship of mutual convenience seemed to continually favor horse over rider. Cass shrugged and kept on walking. Though the horse was far from anything resembling a loyal steed, Cass was still secretly glad to see the old nag again, regardless of its ulterior motivations. Perhaps, Cass thought, perhaps they were really just kindred spirits, two rogues willing to do whatever it took to see they had a full belly and a soft bed. Even if it wasn't true, the thought certainly brought Cass a small measure of momentary peace.

She looked down the stretch of road to see the fortified walls of Riesenstadt, bathed in a soft haze of orange light. If there was one thing that Riesenstadt never seemed to be in short supply of lately, it was the many torches lining its parapets and towers, a bulwark against the threat of the Gravewalkers. But what struck Cass as odd was that the towering gates were still open at this late hour. Not enough to suggest a yawning portal of access, but just slightly ajar, the steel portcullis raised up high.

As she drew closer to the gate with her horse in tow, she was even more amazed to see the spectacle of villagers drunkenly cavorting about in the streets. Spilling out of their homes and their huts, dancing, drinking, yelling, and laughing, as if an enormous weight had been lifted from their shoulders.

And hasn't it? The witch was now locked down in the depths of the castle, hidden from the people in a place where they knew she was no longer a threat. *While her enraged sisters plot our demise in their own dark holes, beginning with me.*

Finally reaching the sentries on duty, Cass gestured over to the townspeople dancing wildly about. "Excellent, then. Will the Untoten be joining us for drinks later this evening?" she asked.

A thick-jowled sentry barely regarded her as he leaned back against the wall. "Bah, they'll be closing soon enough," he answered back.

"So you mean to say they've already joined us, then?" Cass asked half in jest, half in anger at the sentry's laziness.

To Cass's eyes, this one didn't even appear to be one of the Knights Proper—perhaps a failed squire who had grown fat and indolent. *Those loose leathers can't even hide that gut he's grown over too many helpings of mead and worse.*

Looking up high, Cass caught the faintest flash of golden armor patrolling the walls and was reassured to think that Renton, or at least those in command of this stretch, hadn't totally lost their minds. Still, this was alarming, this sudden shift in priorities. At the furthest reaches of her mind, she knew that her actions were directly responsible for whatever she was witnessing, but she decided that there was no good in dwelling over it, as a loud cheer that reverberated from the Castle took her attention elsewhere.

Cass looked up to the lighted windows and balconies in confusion, but the sentry answered the question before she could ask. "They're putting the witch in the press on the morrow, they are. Doin' a bit o' merrymaking, I suppose," he added with a lecherous grin for extra emphasis.

"The press?" Cass asked softly, her teeth grinding with irritation at the lazy bastard's grammar and tone, but she already knew exactly what the man spoke of.

"Aye, the People's Affliction. Hoping to get a fair turn myself after one of my cousin-kin got done up by her dead ones." The guard nodded in affirmation, as if he wanted a personal consensus to the brand of justice that he'd be wielding.

"How delightful," Cass said, her own head beginning to hurt with the growing frustration of this sorry excuse of a man. *Who should we be judging, really?*

The sentry didn't seem to catch Cass's jibe and shifted his attention to the lute strapped across the bard's back. "Playing the lute tonight, bard? You'd figure to make a pretty coin at the Pig tonight if yer doing so."

Then he leaned in a bit closer, his eyes widening. "Hells, you're a bloody woman!"

With a practiced air, Cass nodded in confirmation. "Incredible, isn't it?"

The sentry then had another thought, looking her over with renewed appreciation. "Perhaps you'll be plying another trade?"

Cass narrowed her eyes, but was cut off by the arrival of two knights, their intent of duty plain to see. For whatever lapse Cass may have witnessed, she knew that even on a night such as this, it was nothing more than a temporary dalliance.

"Inside with you, now," one of the knights called out to Cass.

The sentry made an attempt to straighten up, but the other knight saw right through it. "I don't believe that consorting with travelers was one of your many duties," he said, not showing him any particular kindness.

"I was just pointing out to the *lady* here where she might make a bit of coin," the sentry said, his tone snapping to the attention of one who knew it needed to be shown.

"A bit of coin, you say . . . ," the knight repeated, his finger gesturing to the sentry to step forward. "Come here."

The fat man slowly walked over to him, his head hung low but never taking his eyes off the knight. As soon as he reached arm's length, the knight's gauntlet struck out hard and fast across his face. The man's skin blossomed with blood and raised with heat.

"You sorry wastrels finally get a chance to help out and I catch you making time with some woman," the knight scolded. "Come here, come back over here," he called after the cowering man. The sentry did as he was told and paid for it twice as badly when the knight cuffed him again. "Lazy and stupid to boot," he said, looking the sentry over. "Stand up, will you? Have some respect for yourself. You err, you learn, but you never cower!"

Cass could respect the knight's attempt at a lesson, but she was afraid that this poor fellow just wasn't up to the task. Sometimes there was a meekness that just couldn't be helped.

As the knights set to cranking the gates shut, Cass gave her steed's reins a tug and proceeded to walk in, turning to the sentry as she did so. "Appreciation for the suggestions regarding my livelihood, but thankfully, I've enough coin to spare me from the tedious drinking songs that you louts seem to prefer. Or from whoring myself out, which you also seem to prefer."

The sentry lifted his spear off the ground and puffed out his chest, giving him the unseemly appearance of an overripe piece of fruit. He was already agitated at the knight's rebuke, and Cass's words rekindled aspirations that had died a long time ago. "Careful, bard, lest I throw you in with the witch 'erself!"

Cass's horse snorted in amusement as she offered the sentry a stately bow in passing. "Of course, good man. Of course." She watched as the knight reached back and pulled the spear from the man.

"Don't you ever shut up?" he asked.

"But I—" the man began to argue.

"As I thought," the knight said in disappointment. He leaned the great spear up against the wall and turned back to closing the gate.

With that, Cass walked past the entrance and into the city, a metallic slam signaling the portcullis being lowered behind her, along with the poor sentry's feet shuffling about in despair.

***

In the cavernous expanse of the grand chamber, the festivities were already well underway. Servants hustled to keep ivory plates occupied and gilded goblets fully stocked, a daunting task given the length of the table and the number of guests, a colorful hedgerow of laughing citizens of distinction and formally attired knights.

His mighty shield shined to a polish and resting at his side, Luther took it all in with some reservation, thinking that there were better things for him to be doing with his time than smiling politely for an endless array of well-to-do civilians. Still, he hadn't risen through the ranks because of wayward thoughts, but because of his steadfast loyalty to Renton, who was seated just adjacent to him. And it was also because of that loyalty that Luther found himself pained with what was coming next.

For now, the knight-lord made amiable conversation with those sitting next to him, but Luther had come to recognize the creases of distraction in his brow, as Renton kept looking over to the only empty seat at the table, the one where Edwin was supposed to be seated. Beside Renton it sat, full of air, a place normally sequestered for his sergeant, Vintas, who now sat to the knight-lord's left just one more over. And Luther knew that Edwin would not be showing himself, regardless of whatever hopes that the knight-lord had been holding on to.

Despite the fact that Edwin served the people, as any knight did, he would not have approved of them in the Brotherhood's sanctum. Adding to the fact that the poor man's daughter, traitor or not, was currently being tortured by his own brother on orders from his father. *No,* Luther thought, *the seat will remain empty and there's nothing that can be done to suggest otherwise.*

Even with the embarrassment it had caused his liege, Luther found himself not caring either way. He had known Edwin as a young man. He had served with him before that fateful night occurred, and as did many other knights, he still respected the man. No, what concerned him now that Edwin had been freed from his father's prison was something else altogether. He'd come to notice that Edwin shared a weakness with his father: pride.

Though they both went about it in different ways, they were both stubborn men—Renton's faults with power and Edwin's blind allegiance to tradition. Both of them saw the Protectorate as better than the normal folk, but where Renton let people in to have a taste of what they weren't, Edwin had preferred to keep them at an arm's length. Poor Alain just wanted a piece of it but would see none of it shared by his family, adopted or blood.

Still, Luther knew Edwin to be a man of honor and wasn't shy about saying so, despite what others might've thought. There was a reason why the knight-lord had fought so hard for so many years to bring Edwin back into the fold, instead of just killing him outright or submitting him to the Trial by Swords. He had even gone so far as to stage an elaborate ruse to show Edwin the depths of his folly in thinking that the witch could be reasoned with.

Luther let all of these thoughts sift about inside his head as he sat there and watched the rush of everyone's mouths. All speaking at once and few truly listening.

A celebration was at hand and there was plenty of scheming and plotting to be had, given that the Gravewalkers' threats had been greatly diminished by the capture of their leader. Or so they thought. Luther had no patience for politics or false pretenses, although he understood them. For that reason only, he desperately wished for Edwin to be here, to have someone else around to endure this endless gawking about. He thought to dispatch his younger brother Jonas to search for him, but Renton wouldn't have any of it. Edwin, he said, would show. And if he didn't, sending a knight who had been given the honor of attending would've been an insult to the creed of what united all of them together in the first place.

Indeed, Jonas sat just one seat away from Renton, directly opposite Edwin's empty seat, an incredible honor and a testament that when the knight-lord gave his word, he meant it.

***

Jonas remained quiet and watched just as his older brother did. Luther had taught him the importance of listening instead of speaking. Everyone wondered about you out loud, yet you were free to learn about them in silence. Above all, it was polite, a quality the knight-lord valued very highly from what Jonas could tell. One could always show respect in silence. You were there to answer questions when asked and it was seen that you weren't just hearing what your superiors were saying but rightly paying attention to them, truly listening.

Unfortunately, Alain—who, Jonas noted, was a man who rarely, if ever, listened—was nowhere to be seen, apparently having failed in his appointed task. Even now, Jonas swore that he could hear the witch's screams reverberate in the very stones themselves. Alain undoubtedly doing everything in his power to win his father's favor before the night came to an end.

***

The tavern was warm and its patrons' spirits were high. Bawdy revelers were drinking away amid ale-stained tables and sputtering candles, dancing jigs to the lively tune of a flutist. A straw-filled effigy of Mela swung wildly about from the ceiling, its head doused in goat's blood that dripped down to the floor. The sight of such had kept the people's spirits up throughout the day. Every time their sorrows had gotten the better of them, the tragedy and destruction of all the past years, they would look up to the bloodied effigy and feel their hearts fill with hope again, followed by the filling of their mugs. Clearly, there was quite a lot to celebrate this evening and there would be even more to celebrate after tomorrow.

Perhaps tomorrow the effigy would be replaced, and the rafters would hold the Gravewalker's body in its place. The innkeeper hoped very much that the knight-lord would bestow such an honor on him and in turn bring him riches enough to support himself quite well for the foreseeable future. The

Whistling Pig was just a name, and one that could be changed to suit the whims of whatever his heart desired. Or his pockets. But the truth was the witch's body would most likely hang from the front gates for everyone to see, including her sisters, who would look on from afar, from their hiding places among the distant trees.

Cass sat among them, as dull as she'd ever felt. She couldn't find numbness in drink, only an upset stomach. The fires and the press of bodies couldn't make her warm, although she found that she didn't really care. Her quill hung above a page stained with mead instead of ink. There were no words marching in her brain any longer, no words that she wished to share.

The hustle and bustle of the room used to be intoxicating, especially to men and women like the bard. But on this night, guilt was the only thing running through her veins, as much as she tried to put it behind her. Her heartbeat had slowed to a point where she could no longer feel it, and she wasn't entirely sure she wanted to anyway. Trying to shake herself out of it, Cass forced her quill to the paper for the first time that evening. She let it scratch about the parchment and draw black ink all about, circling it around and around. The cycles repeated over and over, just like her thoughts.

I am a poor player, she thought, *a poor player paid with a king's ransom and none the happier for it.* She considered that perhaps another cup would do the trick. She gripped her drink tightly and watched the contents stir about with her unease.

The serving lass from her last escapade at the Pig sauntered up to her table, dodging pinches and slaps to her rear.

"And I thought you might never show your face again," she said as she set down a wooden tankard, splashing even more mead onto the yellow pages of Cass's book. "Oh, that won't do. Here, let me clean that right up, love."

She lifted up the frilly hem of her dress to clean it, revealing a shapely leg in the process of doing so.

As she wiped the pages clean, delicate to a fault, Cass sat back in her seat and raised an eyebrow, some life finally returning to her. "How could I not?" she replied, taking in the blank pages, then the barmaid's tanned leg.

The barmaid smiled back at Cass, amused by this turn of events. "Will you be playing tonight, my lady?"

Cass turned a distasteful eye to the flutist's antics of dancing and hopping around and shrugged it off. "I'm not quite sure if I'm worthy of sharing the stage with such . . . talent."

The barmaid turned from the flutist, then to Cass's book. After a moment of deliberation, she flashed Cass a smile, a different smile. "Well? What *will* you be doing tonight then?"

Cass closed the book's cover and put the quill back into the inkpot. "Trying to forget," she said, the defeat in her voice suggesting that whatever promise the night may have had, it was beyond her grasp for the moment.

The barmaid shrugged, then turned to leave, the grabbing hands of the others patrons already jostling for her attention. "You'll let me know if you change your mind, won't you?" The look in her eyes suggested that she already knew what the answer was to be.

Cass watched her go, then turned her attention back to her tankard. She picked it up but, after a moment later, set it right back down.

It struck her then that the words she didn't want, she needed. There was no better story than the truth, especially when there was no one who would believe it anyway. Her confession could be that story that sparked a hundred lessons. Campfire warnings to those who had a mind for gold and ignored their hearts. Yes, she decided. It wasn't what she wanted, but perhaps it was what she needed. It certainly was what the world needed as there never should be a lack of lessons to be ignored.

Cass flipped her parchment and dipped her quill for fresh ink. As the feather touched parchment, she felt a strong breeze rush over her body. She paused and let the ink pool in its place as she looked over her shoulder.

And there stood Edwin. No armor, no weapons, just a hard stare.

"You," he said to Cass.

Perhaps there was one other option, Cass thought to herself as the ink continued to pool about her fingers. Another way to earn forgiveness or, even yet, serve a better lesson.

CHAPTER 20

A Most Pressing Matter

Mela lay sprawled on the floor facedown, as if she'd been thrown there, rather than placed. Seeping out from her prone form was a slow-moving rivulet of blood, crawling its way through an expanse of filth and debris. Her dress was ripped and caked with red scabs, the gaping holes revealing deep purple bruises. Her hair, once soft and fine, was now a disheveled mess. She appeared now as a stain upon the floor, left as a forgotten display of misbehavior.

Outside her cell, two knights stood guard, stiff and nervous. Both men possessed a very serious understanding of just what the Gravewalkers were capable of, especially Mela, as they had both fought and lost brothers in skirmishes with the Untoten. Still, seeing the handiwork of Alain's assault had shaken them to the core, and they now expected some summary retribution to rise forth and crush them all. The witches could never be underestimated and rising up from nowhere seemed to be their specialty.

But perhaps it wasn't for the fear of what Alain had done to the witch—but, rather, what Alain had done to the Brotherhood. They were men of honor, of duty, not men who tortured women for the favor of their father. What added horrors might this bring down further upon everyone's heads?

Thus, when they first heard the sound of footsteps coming down the hallway, they clasped the hilts of their swords tight, sensing perhaps that retribution was closer than previously thought. The knight closest to the sound stepped into the corridor, keeping an eye fixed on Mela at the same time.

"Who goes there?" he cried out, but there was no immediate response, only the continuing echo of the footsteps, rising in volume.

The other knight cursed under his breath and joined his brother, a bulwark of armor in the narrow corridor as they stood side by side.

"I said, who goes there?" the other called out once again.

With that, the footsteps came to a sudden halt. Exchanging grim glances, the knights unsheathed their swords, prepared to do what they'd been sworn to do, what they'd been fearing they'd have to do, from the moment they drew lots for this watch. As the footsteps picked up again, they raised their blades—

Only to snap to attention as they saw Renton round the corner.

The knight-lord raised his eyebrows at the scene that was laid out before him. But just as much, he seemed to be pleased with their loyalty, as if it was an indicator that all was right with the world.

He gave the red-faced men a wave to return to their posts, then approached Mela's cell.

The knight-lord took his time and let his eyes probe over every inch of the witch's body. Looking down to his steel-plated boots, he spied the small tributary of blood creeping its way toward him, but he made no effort to move out of the way.

The boy certainly wasn't pressed for anger, but I'd hoped he'd learn a thing or two of precision. A senseless beating was not the way to go with this creature.

"Your last chance," he said quietly.

Mela stayed silent, oblivious to his presence.

"Where is the burial ground? The rest of your kind? If you want to receive anything the like of mercy, you'll answer me."

But there was nothing even remotely resembling a response, the faint rise and fall of her back being the only indication that she was still even alive.

"They're looking for you, you know. Your sisters. Right this very moment, they're turning over every grave and tomb, trying to find you."

Seeing that she wasn't going to respond, Renton turned to the knights. "Wake her up."

Immediately, the two of them set to unlocking her prison cell, then entered inside. They didn't roughly haul her up, however, instead gingerly lifting her arms, as if to somehow atone for Alain's recklessness.

"We haven't all day," Renton said, not quite feeling the same restraint.

As they turned her around, Renton reached out and held her by the chin. "No, the truth is we've set aside the whole day, just for you. The People's Affliction will hold you and twist you for hours to come, hours for you to think about how you could've ended this right now, at this very moment."

Stirred into some type of fluttering consciousness, Mela swayed in the arms of the knights, her face one large angry welt of blood and bruises. Renton lingered on the excesses of Alain's efforts. *What a waste of his efforts, his time. That stupid, thoughtless boy.* Her suffering was nothing compared to the countless numbers of those who had lost their loved ones to the Gravewalkers' depredations, and his sole purpose was to prevent more of the same from happening. Thus, Renton couldn't help but try again.

"Where . . . are they?"

But Mela couldn't even hold herself upright, let alone answer the knight-lord's questions.

Renton stood for a moment longer, then made his way back down the corridor. "Send my regards to your mother."

***

The excited chatter of the gathered crowd rose to a roar when the two knights carried Mela out from the castle and toward the grand platform looming before them. It was all she could do to stay conscious, her thoughts broiling in a hazy red cloud of throbbing pain, each agonizing step sending reverberations throughout her whole body. The knight-lord's son had delivered on his promises, and she had no doubt that whatever further suffering lay in wait for her, it would be delivered as well. Tugging at the edges of her consciousness was Riesenstadt Cemetery and its solemn rows of molded stone, but it was simply too far away to be of any practical value. It was the only feeling of home she could find locked away in her mind; it was the only place of comfort or power that she had left.

As they ascended the wooden steps, it stood before her, the great and heavy wooden chair . . . the Affliction. Its seat was still thick with the dried feces of its former victims and their brains still embedded into the wood of the press. Large leather straps adorned the arms and legs of the contraption, having held many victims down, just as they were to now hold Mela in her place. The crowd's jeers were muddled in her ears as she approached the device. Her focus was only on the gore of her future and the sheer certainty of her fate.

There were no hooded executioners around to place the blows upon Mela. There was simply a line of citizens that ran down from the stage and through the streets, all those who had somehow suffered a loss or an injustice through her actions. The contraption itself was a rather simple crank, each rotation bringing the two halves of the press closer, inch by excruciating inch. Each citizen would have their own turn at vengeance. Each turn would be at the hands of someone else, taking as much time as they wanted, while the victim would beg for deliverance, for yet another turn of the crank to end their suffering.

For the first time since Mela could remember, she could feel her hands shaking. Her body felt light, as if it were ready to float up and away. The cheers grew louder and her mouth went dry as she searched for the words to curse them all, but nothing came. It wasn't that she couldn't think of anything to say. Years of hatred had given her volumes, but fear was ruling her actions now and they dictated that her mouth remain silent. The shaking was beginning to grow inside of her; the floating sensation was starting to wane as she felt herself being shaken back down. The two men escorting her came to a stop, a look of something akin to contrition on their faces. Just as much, for Alain walked up the steps and onto the platform with two other knights who appeared to share no such regrets.

Her new escorts forced her down into the seat and removed her restraints. They raised her hands to the straps and tightened them down, harsher than the heavy chains they had removed. The blood seemed to stop flowing to her extremities completely as they tightened the straps around her ankles and her wrists. Instead, it all rushed to her head. The knights seemed eager to make as big a pop as they could when it came time to that. Mela's head was eased back against the chair and lightly tied down. There was no need for it at the moment, as the vice would take several turns before the sides even reached her temple.

And it was then that the true significance of the Affliction grasped at her heart. There was as much torture in waiting for the pain, as there was in the pain itself. *How long will I have to wait? How long then will the pause be before my death?*

As if sensing her deliberations, Alain leaned over to whisper in her ears, "You had your chance, witch. You had your chance."

Alain and the knights then stood back from their prisoner, for it was time to begin . . . and then, just then, did Mela spy the glint of polished steel in the crowd, of her father and grandfather standing side by side. Just as her mother had died before them so many years ago, she was now to do the same.

***

Edwin stared straight ahead, taking in every detail of his daughter's bloodied and bruised face. Her hair, tangled and clotted with filth, purple and yellow smudges of suffering blotted across her cheeks. And yet, as Edwin kept on looking, he imagined that he could see his little Mela, with her cherubic, dimpled smile, her eyes, sparkling with love and laughter . . .

"She'd kill you now if she could. Just as she tried to before. Remember that."

At hearing his father's voice, Edwin snapped out of his trance. Looking back to Mela seated in the Affliction, the illusion of his little girl was revealed to be simply that . . . nothing more than a memory left about to confuse him. She glowered at him, undoubtedly blaming him yet again for what was about to happen. And by all estimations, Edwin reasoned that she was right.

He looked to his father and nodded. "I know."

Renton carefully studied Edwin's face. "You do?"

Edwin nodded again.

And then, the first turn of the crank came. From a small child no less, no more than perhaps five winters of age.

Wiping the wisps of blonde hair from her face, she nervously walked up to the crank, gawking at Mela with utter trepidation. With prompting from Alain, she then placed both hands on the steel wheel shaft and pulled it downward to the roar of the crowd's approval.

Somehow, the metallic screech cut through the crowd's wild cheers, through their cries of "witch" and "murderer," to ring clearly within Edwin's ears. While the two halves of the press had just barely budged, to him, it seemed like they had covered an endless span with one turn. Even now, a wizened old grandmother hobbled as quickly as she could to take her place at the wheel shaft.

Once the Affliction had seized Mela's head within its grasp, Edwin had no doubt that then, and only then, would the pace slow.

"Was it your intention to make a fool out of me last night, Edwin? Or the Brotherhood itself? A feast in your honor, yet you apparently had something more important to attend to."

Edwin opened his mouth to speak, but the shriek of rusted metal once again reached his ears. Looking back to the Affliction, the halves of the press had inched in even closer, his daughter's eyes blinking wide open in some unknown mixture of rage and terror.

"I know it's been much to consider. Your return, the prospects of your reinstatement. It's not been an easy responsibility to bear, but it has to be yours," Renton said, his eyes fixed on Alain as he spoke.

The wheel shaft cranked over again as Edwin cast his eyes to the ground. "I gave it some thought."

Edwin's words seemed to have been the appeasement that Renton had been seeking, so he quietly nodded and turned back to watch the spectacle taking place before them, as yet one more turn of the crank rang out over the castle grounds.

The Affliction's halves had now closed in on Mela's temples, and as such, the din of the crowd had risen in volume. A fight broke out back toward the end of the line, someone undoubtedly worried that they would not get their turn, but it was quickly quelled by Luther's arrival, his imposing figure putting an end to the fray as he continued to patrol the line.

Edwin watched as another villager leisurely strolled upon the stage, an older man, the soot and stain of his frock showing him to be a metalworker of some sort. The man took his time, even pausing to leer at the crowd before he took his place before the wheel shaft. With much procession, he slowly turned the crank and then, without warning, turned it yet again and again as if it were some jest. The crowd jeered, for the metalworker had violated the unspoken tenet that the criminal's suffering must be prolonged as long as possible. Even now, the halves of the press were exerting a considerable amount of pressure upon Mela's temples, her face blossoming a bright red as she gritted her teeth.

The metalworker's ploy set in motion exactly the opposite of the principle that the Affliction operated upon. Instead of being willing to wait their turn patiently while the victim suffered, the other citizens in line now feared that they wouldn't get their due entitlement at exacting vengeance. Thus, with much haste, supplicant after supplicant moved quickly to the wheel shaft, turn after turn, hoping to get their chance before Mela's head exploded in a shower of gore.

Tighter yet did the halves of the press draw together, Mela's face pinched impossibly tight in a rictus of pain and anguish.

Renton looked over to his son to gauge his reaction, but his attention was drawn back to the line of citizens awaiting their turn. Yet another fight had broken out, a woman screaming out her frustration that she would be robbed of the retribution that she was due. Things were quickly descending into chaos, and Luther and the knights were having to work hard at keeping things in order. Seeing this, Alain quickly waved the next citizen forth—

And the crowd went silent, for a beauty upon beauties stepped onto the stage.

Dressed in a gossamer gown that revealed winsome shoulders, topped by waves of hazel-brown hair. Smoky eyes, rouged lips, and a brilliant smile, it was a few moments before the gathered assembly remembered what they were there for.

It was also a few moments before a faint trace of recognition dawned in Alain's eyes. "Bard?" being all that he could croak out for the moment.

Cass floated him a wan smile and sauntered right by. Alain took an initial step after her but then contemplated that removing the bard would've possibly caused complete bedlam if the surging line thought justice was being denied. Instead, he gritted his teeth and motioned for Cass to take her place at the wheel shaft. Cass offered him a slight twirl as a way of thanks, then with a delicate cough, ambled her way up to the mechanical device, gingerly grasping its curved handles.

"Oh, I've got my hands on you now, don't I, my lady?" she said, grinning at Mela's expense as she continued to suffer. From the line, several shouts came for her to hurry up with it. Cass shrugged it off and grasped the wheel shaft tighter, but she didn't turn it. Instead, she spun around, and skipped to the front of the stage, offering the cheering crowd a practiced bow.

Alain, barely able to contain himself, growled his anger. "What . . . are you doing, woman?"

Cass looked back and smiled. "Why, giving them what they want!"

Indeed, as Alain looked down to the crowd, their desire to see Mela's prolonged suffering along with more of the gracious beauty that stood before them, it seemed to vastly outweigh the venomous stares from the citizens still waiting in line. Calling out in a singsongy voice across the crowd, Cass focused her sights on Renton. "To your magniloquent magnificence . . . I come to deliver an ode, a paean to this glorious moment! Will you not hear what I have to say?"

Embedded in a sea of bodies, Renton remained neutral as the crowd shouted their support, while Edwin stood still. Thinking the better of it, the knight-lord made a motion for his knights to seize her, but was immediately answered by a chorus of boos. Even for the supplicants waiting in line, they sensed a fair bit of entertainment coming their way, and while they didn't quite join the chorus of boos, they kept to themselves, waiting to see how it would all play out.

Not wanting to miss the opportunity given to her, Cass gave a flourish worthy of the highest of noble courts and called out to the crowd, "And to you, the good people of Riesenstadt, you who have suffered so much . . . surely you deserve a just and proper accounting of the witch's crimes, do you not?"

As Mela continued to silently suffer in the Affliction's grip, the crowd roared again and Cass doubled up on her momentum, raising her fist in the air. "Should we not send her wretched soul screaming into whatever hells await her with her heinous acts fresh upon her conscience? Let me hear you, good citizens of Riesenstadt! Yes!"

Not yet understanding or even really caring where the silky-tongued beauty was going with it, yet caught in the throes of her speech, their approval was deafening, an avalanche of cheers, whistles, and applause . . . just as the knights seized Cass, dragging her toward the exit.

The cries of outrage started off very slowly, legitimate worry on many faces. But it wasn't for long, however, given the catharsis that they'd been promised after enduring so much for so long. They were due this, this moment to see their years of fear and suffering finally acknowledged.

The knights hauling off Cass paused, hearing the chorus of angry dissent. They looked to Renton for his consent to continue, and after a moment, he waved them off.

Hearing the crowd's summary roar of approval, Renton turned to Edwin. "We'll gut her afterwards for her insolence."

Edwin didn't say anything, his eyes intently focused on Mela's suffering face instead.

Atop the platform, Cass exhaled in relief, then dusted off her dress in a most unladylike manner. "Quite a steaming load of shit you've gotten yourself into now, Cassandra," she cursed under her breath. She shook herself once more, then took in a deep breath.

With the sureness of a master orator, she marched back to the very front of the stage and raised her hand on high, poised to deliver the greatest sermon that Riesenstadt had ever seen . . .

Until she lowered her arms and reached into her bodice for a silver flask. "Ha! Really, you curs? Good citizens indeed," she said to no one in particular. Renton raised his eyebrows as Cass pulled one back, followed by another drink.

Wiping her lips, she put the flask away and turned back to the crowd. "But there is no doubt that, indeed, a terrible injustice has been visited upon you!" she cried out. "An injustice even more foul than the stench of your unwashed bodies!"

There was a smattering of ribald laughter, along with a few jeers, but no one really knew what to make of it just yet. The witch still continued to writhe in pain, her breaths coming much faster now, and the crowd was content to watch and listen for the time being. Cass paused for a moment as she heard someone shout in the back, a plump noble with more hair on his face than his head.

"Cassandra, is that you, girl? What in the pits are you doing up on that stage?"

Alain gripped the hilt of his sword, waiting for his father's command to intervene, but none came as Renton continued to watch in silence.

"This one, however," Cass said, as she pointed to Mela, "this one is not to blame, no!" The crowd drew silent; there was no shuffling of feet or even whispers. "The true perpetrators of this war are right here in your midst . . . these so-called noble knights! Hardly proper, I tell you!"

Aware of the consideration that they were embedded deep into the crowd, Renton gave himself a bit more space as a trio of knights instinctively made their way over to him and Edwin to lend their support.

"They murdered women and children in cold blood . . . innocents! They are the ones who brought the Gravewalkers' wrath down upon your lice-riddled heads! And you let them!"

With the crowd now starting to mutter in confusion, Renton finally nodded approval to Alain.

"Indeed, you sorry lot," she continued. "Need I remind you that this so-called witch, this poor soul before you today . . . is the knight-lord's very own flesh and blood?"

A gasp rang out over the crowd, proof that perhaps the reminder was needed after all. Given this, even some of the citizens lined up for their turn at the Affliction fell out to better hear what the bard was saying.

Alain, however, did not care what the bard had to say at the moment. He drew his sword and strode straight across the stage, his blade to her chest. "You've had your little moment. Get off the stage before I gut you in front of your beloved audience."

In the crowd, Edwin tore his gaze away from Mela, who was still in too much pain to consider in earnest what the bard was saying. Instead, he glanced toward Renton, gauging his reaction in turn. But the knight-lord, surrounded by a handful of knights, simply stood in place. No fits of rage, no emotion whatsoever. If Cass's treacherous words were upsetting to him, he didn't care to show it.

Atop the stage, Cass momentarily regarded Alain's blade before returning to the crowd, as great a dismissal as any could give.

"And consider this!" she cried out. "What sort of man would imprison his own son? Torture and condemn his own granddaughter to death?"

As Alain fumed at the brush-off, Cass took another swill from her flask, chuckling as if she knew her imminent demise was coming one way or another.

Edwin suddenly straightened and looked to his father. "I'm going to end this. Every bit of treason from her mouth is another eternity that my daughter has to suffer."

Almost as if she had heard Edwin's words, Cass wiped her lips and turned her head in Edwin's direction. "And tell me, are we not to be judged by our actions . . . by our good deeds?" she shouted out, her eyes locked on Edwin and his father.

Wrestling with the variable outcomes of slaying Cass in front of the crowd, Alain took a step closer. "Your last chance, woman!"

But Cass continued to ignore him and stabbed a finger in Renton's direction for extra emphasis. "If so, then I ask you . . . who is the real villain here?"

The crowd was quickly approaching pandemonium, some shouting for the Affliction to resume, while others shouted for answers. Seeing this, Edwin grasped the hilt of his blade and made a straight path for Cass. "Enough. This ends now!"

Edwin took a step forward, but was suddenly blocked by Renton's sergeant, Vintas, with three others flanking his rear and his sides. "I'm afraid you're right, Son," Renton said, circling around Edwin. "It does end now."

Edwin's eyes quickly shifted to Cass, but Alain now had her in his grasp, while she squirmed and flailed about. As for Mela, she was either unconscious or dead, Edwin could not tell which.

He made another start for the stage, but was quickly seized by the other knights as Renton slowly approached. "You really think I wouldn't anticipate this? Yet another betrayal?"

"What betrayal, Father? That insufferable twat is stretching this out for far too long!" Edwin screamed.

"You'll forgive me, Son, if I don't take you at your word." Renton answered back. With genuine regret, he looked Edwin directly in the eyes. "But I promise you this . . . this time, you won't rot away in some cell. You'll die a noble death, even if you couldn't lead a noble life."

At that, Edwin fought with everything he had to escape, but the other knights had his arms pinned to the side and he couldn't reach his weapon. Vintas landed a fierce, armored thrust into Edwin's gut, knocking the wind out of him. Sheer panic settling in across his reddened face, he looked up to the stage to see if Cass had been able to escape her captor's grasp, but she too was held fast, the both of them certainly soon to follow in Mela's footsteps.

With that, Edwin realized that for all their planning, their grand scheme had come to an end.

***

Cass bucked and kicked like a woman possessed of every evil spirit imaginable, but still Alain and the other knights held her fast, just as Renton and his troops had Edwin trapped.

Renton had triumphed and Mela was most likely already dead by the looks of her, but that's not what bothered Cass the most. She could see the defeat in Edwin's eyes and it gutted her. Trusted again, a failure once more. Despite her earlier betrayal, he'd believed that there was still something in her worthy of being redeemed and she had disappointed him yet again.

She waited for Alain's blade to finish her off, hoping it would come soon. She'd noticed that her father was nowhere to be seen or heard after his earlier shout, but she wasn't surprised in the least. The crowd was wildly stirring about and had lost interest in the questions she'd posed. Now, they just wanted answers, and they certainly didn't need her for that anymore.

***

Luther had almost wished that he was battling against an army of Untoten minions rather than what lay before him now. The line of citizens awaiting their turn at the Affliction had completely devolved into absolute chaos, and the crowd facing the platform had become a medley of screaming and yelling. Using his shield to push back the citizens who were liable to harm others or themselves, he worked his way to Renton and the handful of knights that had Edwin restrained. Luther wasn't sure why they had the knight-lord's son held fast, but he guessed that it had something to do with a last-ditch attempt to save his daughter, and for that, Luther couldn't fault the man. Despite his loyalty to Renton and to the Brotherhood, he could sympathize with the affections that one had for their kin.

And that is why he stood in complete shock when he saw his brother Jonas walking out onto the stage with grim intent in his eyes.

***

As Jonas walked onto the wooden platform, the other knights initially nodded to him, but paused as they took in the stance of his body, instantly suspecting that something was amiss. And they were right, for Jonas did not consider himself to be an actor or a performer like the bard they held captive. He wasn't some courtly fop, and he wasn't capable of hiding his true feelings as he passed Alain and made his way to the wheel shaft. He considered himself a man of principle, not some puppet, and this, what Alain had done with the witch, the backstabbing and the intrigue that he had seen play out at the highest levels in the Brotherhood, it had to stop. And it was going to stop, with him. Now.

***

As if the machinations of time had slowed to a complete crawl, Cass watched the young knight seize the wheel shaft and twist it in the opposite direction, turn upon turn. The halves released Mela's head, which immediately slumped to her shoulder, her facial features slack and pale. The young knight then unsheathed both of his swords. Alain hesitated as one of the other knights stepped in front of Jonas, challenging him. Before he could strike, however, the knight was put to the floor by Jonas's elbow. His old comrade Aras began to take a step forward but was warded off by one of Jonas's blades pointed at him—the other keeping Alain frozen in place.

"Don't even try it, Aras; we both know you haven't the skill." Jonas kept his eyes on the knight until he saw his muscles relax. "No one has to die today!" he cried out, and in a singular motion, he cut Mela's bonds with one blade while the other kept its place holding Alain at bay.

Somewhere behind her, Cass heard Alain scream with rage, and then she was quickly shoved away so that he could deal with the new specter of betrayal that had risen up before the Brotherhood. Cass could also see Renton doing the same with Edwin, as it seemed the entire combined might of Renton's army was now marching upon the stage.

Cass quickly hauled out her rapier, which was tied to her thigh underneath her dress. She gathered up the garment's many folds with one hand and slashed the hem right off. Satisfied, she reasoned that there was only one thing left to do, and that was to simply whistle as loud as she could for all she was worth.

***

If the crowd had previously been considered unruly, it had now dissolved into absolute and complete mayhem as villagers shrieked in terror at the sight of the Gravewalker being freed from her bonds. But then, they had a more immediate threat to deal with.

Parting the crowd with ease, Cass's horse rampaged its way toward the stage, bucking, head-butting, and trampling everything in sight as it continued forward. Even the knights nearby didn't dare to stand in its path, for it seemed to be a creature possessed of the very hells themselves as it spat and frothed with reckless abandon.

The nag finally reached the stage and disappeared for a moment . . . before it barreled right back out, with Cass and a barely conscious Mela on top. Bowling over a cluster of knights in the process, they charged back toward the open gates. The screams of the crowd rose to a fever pitch, not knowing whether the horse or the Gravewalker was more of an immediate threat.

With their escape in their own hands, Jonas slammed both of his blades deep into the wood of the stage and knelt between them.

Alain looked down at the young knight's surrender, shaking his head in disgust. "I haven't the time for you," he rumbled, as he signaled the other knights to seize him.

***

Suddenly left alone, while his father and the others charged the stage, Edwin made it count as he withdrew his blade and turned to slow the tide of knights making their way to recapture Mela. He had seen Cass moving toward her, but he didn't have the luxury of waiting to see what happened, nor could he get there in time to stop the others. All he could do was clear a path as best as he could and hope that Cass's horse would see them through the crowd and out the gates.

With a solid kick, one knight went flying backward while he turned to parry another knight's thrust with a loud clang, finishing the man off with a clout to the head. Another knight lunged directly at him, but Edwin dodged to the side and angled his blade into the man's greaves, striking solid flesh. The wound wouldn't kill him, but he wouldn't be walking on his own anytime soon.

Turning around, he heard his father scream, his true emotions now showing as he pointed his sword at Cass's departing horse with Cass and Mela seated on top. Then, the blade turned toward Edwin. His father locked eyes with him, the spittle flying from his mouth. He also saw Alain sprinting toward a stable full of horses with a group of knights in tow, but there was nothing more he could do to help.

Taking advantage of the pandemonium, Edwin took his cue to leave, slipping into the sea of bodies that ran every which way across the grounds of Castle Riesenstadt, angling his way toward the back alleys and an uncertain future.

CHAPTER 21

Whereupon the Lady Leaves Us

Up the winding cemetery road, Cass goaded her horse onward with every curse and profanity that she could think of. They were already galloping at a breakneck pace, foam flying from the creature's mouth, while Mela barely held on, slipping in and out of consciousness.

Dead trees whizzing by, Cass looked back to see if the knight-lord's son was still in pursuit—a wistful hope, because she already knew what the answer would be. Atop a magnificent white charger, Alain was edging ever closer, along with a handful of other knights also giving furious chase.

Cass quickly turned back around and, in doing so, almost knocked Mela off her precarious perch. Switching one hand to hold the reins, she steadied the Gravewalker with the other as they continued on.

"No need to fall for me just yet, my lady! Ha!" she cried out, not quite feeling as confident as she let on.

A crossbow bolt zinged right by her ear, taking a few locks of hair with it. Cass muttered under her breath, until a gleaming sword sliced deep into her arm—the knight had caught up to her. She howled out in pain as Alain pointed his bloodied blade directly at her.

"Give her up or you'll suffer the same fate!"

But Cass knew that was already a forgone conclusion. Mela's fate was now hers, whether she wanted it or not. She snarled the agony away, then tugged on the bloodsoaked reins, veering the ragged horse away from Alain. The knight's steed certainly had no problems with staying the pace, however, as it closed once more to allow Alain another shot.

Cass ducked as Alain's blade whooshed over her head. "Surrender the witch! Now!" he shouted out over the din of thunderous hoof beats. Cass tugged the reins even harder, but the nag was at its breaking point, its eyes wild with madness. Ahead, the gates of the cemetery loomed even closer, but not yet close enough for the bard's liking.

Sensing Cass's desperation but also feeling no small measure of dread himself for what might happen if the Gravewalker reached the cemetery grounds, Alain came in yet again, raising his sword up high to end the chase once and for all.

Cass heard the white stallion's shriek, then saw Alain drawing near. Unable to muster anything more from her steed, she suddenly switched the reins into her bloodied hand and reached for her rapier, wedged underneath the saddlebag. "Ha! Prepare to eat cold steel, dog!"

Alain disregarded her taunt entirely and brought down his heavy blade, giving Cass no chance to do anything other than to raise her rapier in defense. The two weapons collided, but only for a fraction of a moment as Cass's thin blade snapped in half with a loud crack.

Cass grimaced as she stared at the jagged edge of what used to be her rapier. "Oh," being all that she could muster as a retort.

***

Edwin sprinted down a narrow cobblestone street, hemmed in on both sides by rustic houses and shops. Still wearing his full armor from the morning's ceremonial proceedings, Edwin's appearance was that of a steel juggernaut, one that didn't allow any real kindness to those sharing the same narrow walkways. Clanking his way past chickens, goats, and street merchants, Edwin left a stream of feathers and angry curses trailing behind him. Given that these were villagers who hadn't been present for the morning's festivities, when they heard the shouts of the other knights on his trail, their curses quickly became gasps of astonishment.

Edwin looked back for a moment. While he couldn't see the other knights just yet, he could hear them. With the commotion he was causing, he had no doubt that they could hear him as well. He had a notion of where he could possibly take cover until things died down, but it wasn't a certainty. Many years had passed since he had last visited, but it was his only chance.

If she lets me in, that is.

Turning back around, he found his path blocked by a meandering wagon led by a team of oxen. Instinctively, he knew that there was no way that he could maneuver in his armor without considerably slowing down, so he committed himself to an open passage at his side. He skidded into a wooden wall, rattling the entire frame of a cottage with a loud bang, then continued down the alleyway.

***

Cass desperately held on to the reins with the one good arm left to her—the only arm left to her, as she felt like her other appendage was due to fall off at any moment. Behind her, Mela swayed from side to side as she weakly clutched at Cass's waist. Still, the bard noticed that the Gravewalker's grip was subtly tightening as they drew closer to the cemetery.

Good, we'll need it soon enough, she thought.

Just ahead, the familiar sight of the lofty gates filled her vision—but so did Alain as he drew ahead, then swerved over to run them down once again. Cass threw her rapier away, its edge now nothing more than an impotent stub. As Alain drew near, she looked down to her horse, not knowing quite what else to do—until the creature matched a bloodshot eye with her, drawing its lips back with what could only be perceived as the insane grin of a deranged beast.

Whatever it was, Cass got the message and suddenly leapt from her saddle, letting go of the reins to clutch at Mela instead. They hit the dirt hard, rolling several times, mud and dirt flying in all directions. Cass took the brunt of the impact, but kept Mela pinched tight within her arms and her legs as they came to a stop.

Alain cursed from atop his charger, but was soon presented with a much more immediate problem, as Cass's steed suddenly cut off the shrieking charger, throwing its body right in the charger's thunderous path. Down they both went in a wild, thrashing tumble of hooves and sweat-slicked horseflesh. Alain was thrown from the saddle, flying straight into the dirt. The other knights behind them pulled up hard on their steeds, not wanting to trample the knight-lord's son nor collide with the two horses still trying to untangle themselves, the bard's horse weakly kicking for all it was worth.

Alain fumbled to his feet, trying to shake his head clear. When his vision finally returned, what he saw sent a shudder of fear running through his body. Not because of the Gravewalker, but for what his father would do to him if he let her escape.

"Seize them!" he screamed, then limped his way forward.

***

Cass dragged herself and Mela toward the gate, the Gravewalker's arm draped across her shoulder. Favoring her right leg over the other, the bard grunted with each step, her face scrunched in pain. She subconsciously reached up to push her hair back, but her appearance was beyond saving at the present moment. Blood streaming down her face from a gash on her forehead, she pressed on, one desperate lunge after another until they reached the heavy iron bars, only to find them locked with two thick chains of linked steel.

Cass swung her head over to see a rough wooden sign nearby: "Closed—By Order of the Knight-Lord."

"Mother of all!" she cried out, almost dropping Mela in the process. She looked behind them, only to see that Alain was on his feet now, running toward them, the other knights dismounting from their steeds and drawing their blades as well.

Cass turned back to the gate and shook the chains in frustration, cursing with every epithet that she could muster, which was no small feat in itself.

***

Quickly losing steam within the maze of intersecting alleyways, Edwin turned again and stepped into a puddle of filthy water, the splash alighting along both of the narrow walls that confined him. He turned a corner and then another, taking what felt like the longest path ever imagined. His pace slowed ever more, given his bulk in an unwelcome, tight space. Another turn, then he stopped to listen, even if it was really just to catch his breath. He didn't have to wait long, as the shouts of the pursuing knights echoed from just a few alleyways over. Edwin considered drawing his blade and fighting them off, but there were simply too many. Plus, he knew that they still ultimately followed his father's orders, regardless of however they planned to deal with him.

Edwin started off again, running raggedly down a narrow passageway, dodging piles of trash and refuse. There were no citizens mulling about, as all of the abodes lining the alleyway were facing outward—most likely to a wider, more welcoming avenue, the rear of their homes being where they discarded their rubbish and worse. He could never really understand why they had made the streets this way, but today, he was extra thankful for the decision. Despite the racket he was making, no one had spied him just yet and no one had alerted his pursuers to his presence. And ahead, it looked as if his luck was taking an even brighter turn, but it turned out to be just the opposite.

Grabbing a metal post, he brought himself to a complete stop, because there really wasn't a need for him to go any further. What appeared to have been an alcove opening was actually a dead end, and the only way out was to run the indeterminable length that it had taken to get here. He thought again to draw his blade, but only for a moment. No more lives would be taken, and even if that meant his own death, Edwin was at peace with his decision.

***

She had to try. After all that had transpired, with being given another chance thanks to the young knight's help, Cass couldn't let the curtains close just yet. There was more to this story, and by all hells, it wasn't going to end with her being spit on that fop of a knight's blade. She faced the gates and tested the slack of the chains—there was a gap, but it wasn't much.

Setting Mela to collapse against the iron bars, Cass awkwardly wedged herself in between the two gates, with her one good leg and her one good arm straining to force them even wider. To her relief, it worked, as she dragged her slender frame through, then reached back out for Mela.

The Gravewalker, however, wasn't of mind yet to contort her body to slip through. Hearing Alain's shrill cry, Cass quickly slid back out and propped herself up once more, in between the narrow space of the gates. She pushed with all her might and the space widened, the chains stretching taut as she reached out and dragged Mela in. Once the Gravewalker was through, Cass turned to slip herself back in, but not before a bolt slammed into her side with a dull thud.

Unable to will away the pain this time, Cass screamed, but they were clear—just as Alain's blade came down where she had been only a moment ago. Hearing the winch of a knight's crossbow being drawn back for another round, Cass somehow found the strength to stand up and hurriedly drag the both of them away from the gate. She gingerly tested the edge of the bolt jutting out from her side, but soon decided it wasn't even worth the time.

Behind them, the knights tried the same tactic with wedging the gates open, but these were broad-shouldered men enclosed in bulky plate mail, not slender women with nary a shred of armor to obstruct their passage.

Realizing the futility of trying to slip through, they instead hefted their swords and began to hammer away at the metal links, sending sparks flying with each thunderous blow. Each swing spelled disaster for their weapons, but at the present moment, that seemed to be the least of their concerns.

***

The heavy footsteps of the approaching knights echoed all around Edwin, who was still gasping for air. They were possibly just a few streets over, lost just as much as he was. But he had no doubt that they would find him, unless he suddenly designed to sprout wings to take him aloft and into the sky. Edwin chuckled at that one, thinking that the bard would've appreciated his attempt at humor. While his end was drawing near, he sincerely hoped that Cass had escaped along with his daughter. The sting of her betrayal was still fresh in his mind, but the bard had redeemed herself. More than anyone else, Edwin deeply understood the notion of having another chance to make things right.

As for Jonas, Edwin could only hope for the boy's safety, taking a small bit of consolation in knowing that Luther would be there to look after him. But it was, indeed, a small consolation. Jonas's intervention came as a complete surprise to everyone, and Edwin knew that his father, after having congratulated himself for seeing through Edwin's plans, would be enraged beyond all meaning.

With that, Edwin leaned back against the wall and waited for the inevitable end. That was, until he heard the rustle of a wooden door sliding open. Turning around in surprise, he could see Lady Berna peering into the alleyway from the rear entrance of her home. She paused, cocking her ear to the clamor of the knights' near arrival. Edwin remained frozen as she waited a moment longer, not sure yet how to process this unexpected grace, and more so, he did not want to enter unless she expressly permitted it.

After what had seemed like a stretch of eternity, she shook her head in silent resignation and motioned for him to come inside. Catching his heartbeat in his throat, Edwin quickly moved into the house as Lady Berna shut the door behind him.

***

Cass gritted her teeth in pain as she took Mela deeper into the cemetery. As they passed moldy tombstones and chipped mausoleums, Cass noticed that Mela's eyes were starting to widen now, like someone emerging from a comatose state. Her steps became more pronounced, relying upon Cass less and less.

Behind them, the bard could hear the continued assault of steel crashing down on steel. She looked back for a moment to see that the gate had widened slightly, the shouts of the knights matching in volume.

Turning back, she desperately tried to take another step but almost stumbled. "Come on, damn you . . . ," she muttered, trying to will her feet forward, despite the loss of blood that had created a trail of crimson behind her. She took one more step before she finally collapsed.

But Mela remained standing.

Cass watched the Gravewalker rise to her full height and noticed that her bruises and gashes were not as visible as they were before, as if being in the immediate proximity of the cemetery was somehow healing her.

For the bard, however, there was no such luck. Blood dribbling from her lips, Cass coughed, then feebly wiped her mouth with the back of her hand. "Heh. Not . . . not bad for a mere pretender, eh?"

Mela opened her mouth to speak, but just then, a loud crash reached their ears. They looked over to see the gates now wide open and the knights sprinting directly toward them.

There were a million thoughts running through Cass's mind, of what her legacy would be, of who would remember her, of what she wanted Edwin to know, of what would possibly await her in the afterlife. Instead, it all came down to one simple question to scratch her curiosity, for above all things, she was a lover of mysteries. A breath, more than a question, she asked the Gravewalker what was burning the most in her mind . . .

"Where are you off to now, my lady?"

Mela stared down the fast-approaching knights, then turned back to Cass, a small trace of pity on her face. She leaned down to whisper in the bard's ear . . . and Cass started to laugh—each chuckle causing her to wince in pain, but it didn't matter.

Mela gave her an impromptu kiss of thanks on her dirtied cheek, and with a loud rush of air, disappeared in an implosion of white fog. A moment later, Alain's sword cleaved the very space that she'd just occupied.

"No! Damn it all, no!" he screamed, his face tight with the imagined price of failure that he inevitably would be facing.

Furious, he leveled his sword at the bard, but Cassandra Lethellon's time had already passed; she lay in a spreading pool of her own blood, still and quiet. What infuriated Alain even more was the woman still had the same insufferable smirk on her face, even in death.

Alain nudged the bard with his blade, just to be sure, the edge biting into her flesh, but there was nothing.

Or perhaps there was something.

One of his knights walked over, the glint of a gilded metal tube in his mailed fist. "From the bard's saddlebags, sire," he said as he placed it into Alain's waiting hands. Alain gave one last glance at the bard, then nudged open the lid to get a better look.

Slowly, a smile crept across his face as Alain examined the yellowed parchment before him. While his father would undoubtedly be quite upset at the Gravewalker's escape, Alain reasoned that he may have just found the very thing they'd been searching for all along.

CHAPTER 22

The Best Laid Plans

The council chamber's air hung thick with the knight-lord's disapproval. Renton stormed back and forth across the floor of the great room, his stride growing wider with every pass. His feet landed like thunder and rumbled fear throughout the bodies of his advisors. His face burned crimson as his thoughts ravaged each other in frustration inside his head.

Among the shaking advisors stood a handful of knights, their scars plainly showing their ranks as veterans of battle. Though the knights could feel the rage of their leader as strongly as his advisors did, they held themselves still and strong, like stone visages, in his presence.

"Would any of you care to explain . . . ," Renton finally spoke. "How my traitor of a son, and a bard—no less a *woman* . . ." His head sank at the words he had to speak out loud. "How they managed to escape an entire cavalry of the Protectorate?"

His voice echoed about the chamber as the group of men, veterans and sheep alike, kept silent.

"And this . . . ," Renton said as he motioned toward the chamber door. "This treachery above all others!"

Two knights escorted Jonas through the great oak doors and across the chamber floor, but apart from a few scratches, he was unharmed. He marched of his own free will, unbound and unbroken. His brother Luther stood nearby, a mix of emotions dancing behind his eyes.

"How does this sort of behavior come about?" Renton asked of all who stood in the chamber. "Are we not all brothers?" The knights tightened their stances and raised their heads higher in respect.

"And yet one of our own, yes, one of your brothers, he saw fit to defy my orders. Despite the blood that has been spilled by that witch, he saw fit to stand with her instead of us!"

The knights each stomped their right foot down in unison, sending an enormous weight of consensus into the air.

Jonas felt the wave of thunder in his chest and knew his fate was sealed. He looked up to Luther, for Jonas knew what was coming, what his fate was to be, and he embraced it in its entirety.

There were no words between them, just a glance of understanding. That matters would be settled as they'd always been. Luther lowered his head, one last acknowledgment of their brotherly bonds. Jonas had made his choice, Luther reckoned. Whether it was right or wrong, he couldn't say, but to intervene now would be to dishonor the very essence of what Jonas was trying to say about the state of the Brotherhood itself.

Renton stepped close to Jonas and raised his hand, cradling the boy's head in his gauntlet. "You will now face the swords, Jonas," he said, tears beginning to roll down his face as the pain of this new betrayal grew in his chest. "On your knees, son. And we will see if you can redeem yourself."

If Jonas was surprised to see the tears, he didn't show it. Instead, he nodded and quietly descended to the floor, his knees settling atop the hard wood.

Hiltiger, one of the knights who'd escorted Jonas in, signaled his brother to draw his sword. The broadswords slid slowly from their scabbards as Jonas closed his eyes and gathered himself. The brothers brought the points of their swords down on Jonas's shoulders. He could feel the sharp steel already piercing the skin of his collarbone. The brothers raised their own shoulders, ready to plunge the cold steel down straight into the floor as Jonas opened his eyes and threw his head back. He let out a great battle cry, a charge toward the heavens—as he began to rise. Out of pure will, the young man forced his own body upward, pushing the blades slowly into his own body.

Renton, along with Luther, watched silently as Jonas continued to rise, higher and higher. The brothers held their blades fast, preparing for the final strike. When Jonas's body began to give way and it felt more as if he were hanging upon the blades, only then did he feel the final strike—and the satisfaction of knowing that he had redeemed his honor in these last dying moments.

The two brothers pushed downward with all of their might, their blades breaking free at the young man's pelvis. His blood drained out and onto the floor as he let out a final dying gasp, his strength and his life finally leaving him.

Renton nodded his assent and turned back to his veterans. They were each standing silently behind an advisor, their armed presence a reminder to the nervous gathering of old men and sages to watch the ritual in full, that all eyes would pay witness to this redemption of the spirit.

As Renton faced them, they stomped their feet once more in unison. A long silence followed, interrupted only by the faint sound of Jonas's body slowly sliding back down the sword blades toward the floor.

"The Gravewalkers!" a voice suddenly cried out, interrupting the morbid silence as Alain marched triumphantly into the chamber. "I know where they are!"

Soaked in mud that dripped upon the floor, Alain strode to the great circular table in the middle of the room and slammed down a tattered map. Renton gazed at him dubiously while the rest of the room held their collective breath.

Before turning his attention to the map, Renton gestured to Hiltiger and his brother. "Take him outside and burn him. Not like some common chattel, but as a knight," Renton ordered the brothers in regards to Jonas. He glanced over to Luther, who gave a silent nod of appreciation.

"We found this in the bard's possession. Look . . . ," Alain said, pushing forward with his discovery. Renton kept his eye on his son while he motioned for his veterans and advisors to come over to the table.

Alain pointed an excited finger toward the map and rested it on the discolored depiction of a skull. "It has to be."

Renton's eldest advisor, Vanthar, leaned forward and began to study the map closely.

"Possibly," Renton offered.

Vanthar's coarse, silvery beard suggested a hut-dwelling hermit, but his blue eyes were as sharp as any of theirs. He traced his finger in between the depictions of the two mountains, settling atop a valley that lay in between them, where the skull was directly centered. "Legends speak of a great and terrible battle waged upon those plains, milord," he said, a reckoning rather than a statement. "One that left the battlefield bleached white with the bones of the fallen."

"Yes, a fortune of soldiers," Renton said. "And not that far removed from Riesenstadt. This could very well be it."

"Milord, I counsel you to practice restraint in deciding the best course of action," Vanthar warned. Renton fixed him with an icy stare, but the advisor didn't budge on his opinion. He turned to the other sages, who nodded in agreement. "If this is truly what I and the rest of us believe it to be, then we should best consider another form of engagement, one that finds us holding the advantage, not the Trauergast."

"Irrelevant," Renton answered. "We'll send a small force to survey the area, suited for mobility but strong enough to defend themselves if the enemy engages. Even if what you say is true, they'd never be able to anticipate our sudden arrival." He turned away from his advisor and addressed Alain. "The bard. Tell me you delivered the final blow to that traitorous bitch."

"She died just as we found her . . . she'll trouble you no more, Father." He worked hard to contain his emotions, to show that he was worth his rank for the first time.

Renton's stare lingered a moment, as if he were indeed sizing him up, before he turned back to the map.

"It's decided then." He looked back to Alain. "You'll take a mounted contingent of our forces there—without delay."

"Milord, forgive my impudence," Vanthar interrupted as the other sages shrank back in surprise, "but I would beg you to heed my words. It would be a terrible, terrible province upon which to encounter a Trauergast . . ."

For the first time since his excited arrival, Vanthar's admonishments finally reached Alain, apprehension now showing on his colorless face. Even among the veterans, for Vanthar to press the knight-lord so, the significance was not lost and they too considered their own fate.

"I'll hear no more of it," Renton said, making it a moot point. "If he's now to inherit my position, he should earn it," he said, without actually addressing Alain.

***

A few hours later saw Alain at the head of his men, ready to depart. He mounted carefully and slowly while his mind struggled to catch up with what lay ahead of him. After the rush of battle had left him, such a mission now felt foolhardy and wasn't what he wanted. If the advisors thought this to be a mission of suicide, he could not help but think the same.

He sat down in the saddle, hesitant at first, but reminded himself that his father had trusted him enough to lead these men. To hells with the advisors—they had never fought a war, never shed blood, but the knight-lord had done that and more. If Alain was to rise higher than those cowards, then he would have to trust in his father's delegation of authority. He wasn't there yet, but looking down from his white charger, he at least felt the part. Alain's heels stabbed back against his horse, and they began their slow march out of the castle as the city looked on.

CHAPTER 23

Lost, and Not Found

I'll be back in a moment," Lady Berna said as she left the room, moving toward the cellar.

The room was dim with candlelight. As before, the hearth flickered warmth but never grew bright. Even through his steel boots, Edwin could feel the softness of rugs all about the floor. The dancing flames revealed each of their many colors one at a time in the cozy embrace of the small chamber.

"The knight-lord's rightful heir, a guest in my humble home," Lady Berna said as she walked back in. "I should be thankful, hm?"

She set down a wooden tray of food on the table, then offered Edwin a cup of mead. She looked him over, especially the mud and grime that was splattered across his lower half.

"You're going to change out of the armor sometime soon, I hope . . . ," she said with a slight smile.

"Perhaps you should've left me in the alley," he said, as he accepted his mead with more enthusiasm than his voice was showing. Lady Berna sat down and took her own mug, watching him lap down his drink as if it were medicine.

"How could I? You made enough of a racket that the entirety of Riesenstadt was soon to come looking for you. Luckily for you, many of them were still recovering from the chaos of your daughter's escape."

Edwin froze, his mug lifted to his lips. "You were there?"

"Nana! Nana!" a young girl squealed. A precious waif of a girl came stampeding into the room, her long blonde hair trailing behind her. Edwin stood up with a start, recognizing her for the girl who was the first to take a turn at cranking the Affliction's wheel shaft.

Lady Berna looked at Edwin, her eyes leveled with his. "We were only needed for a short while."

Edwin stammered, trying to discern her true motives, but then it came to him. "Keldon's daughter," he sighed.

"Who is this, Nana?" the girl asked. "One of Papa's friends?"

Lady Berna patted the young child on the head. "Now then, you know better. Where are your manners?"

The child stepped closer to Edwin and curtsied. "Lissa Berna, milord. Pleased to meet you."

Despite the revelation of who she was and her role in Mela's torture, Edwin couldn't even consider the idea of being angry with her—or with Lady Berna for that matter. She had every right to turn the wheel, every right to have had her moment of justice.

"Well met, my fair lady. You may call me Edwin," he said, with a formal bow in return.

Lissa grinned and reached out to touch Edwin's shoulder plates. "You're a knight?" she asked. "Did you know my papa? They made me turn that terrible wheel for him."

"Now, now, Lissa," Lady Berna cut in, trying to avoid the subject for the moment. "Hurry off to your room and give us some time to talk, won't you?"

Lissa leaned in close to her Nana and was rewarded with a kiss on the top of her head. She turned around to give one last glance at Edwin before leaving the room.

"She knows what happened to him?" Edwin asked.

"I wish that she didn't, Edwin."

Edwin paled at the revelation, then swiftly took another drink. "By all the spirits . . ."

"Your father demanded that she'd be the first at the wheel. And despite many reasons to say otherwise, I agreed," Lady Berna replied.

Edwin was only able to offer a nod of understanding in the awkward silence that followed.

"I must leave," Edwin said. "Every moment I stay here puts you and her in danger."

Lady Berna suddenly got up from the table, never taking her eyes off of Edwin.

"Nonsense." One of her eyebrows rose as she tried to hide the bit of amusement she'd found in breaking the rules, this sense of kinship that she felt with Edwin. "You're welcome to stay as long as you need."

Then she left, taking her mug with her.

Edwin turned toward the fire and poured himself another helping of mead. He could remember respecting those who were straightforward with him, those who spoke plainly of what they needed. He'd never seen the need to seek warmth or softness until Evelina—and until now. And in truth, he now considered himself perhaps a better man for having done so. With that in mind and the fate of his daughter and the bard cast to the wind, his thoughts now turned to his brother Alain.

There'd been many days of his youth that Edwin could remember his father playing games with him, much like how Edwin himself had played with Mela—but these were games of swordsmanship, of wrestling, of physical prowess. The joy of spending time with a child had been lost on Edwin's youth and forgotten in Alain's. He could remember the effort their father had gone to in ignoring his younger brother.

Edwin himself had tired of it all, wanting more time to himself to train with the other knights, but his father would have none of it. He'd always insisted on wrestling with Edwin but letting him win, some small expression of patriarchal pride, something that frustrated Edwin to no end. He wondered if the same would've been true for Alain, but Edwin knew, in all honesty, that Alain would've been beaten into submission each time.

The mead coursed its way through Edwin's body, its current growing stronger by the heat of the fireplace. He remembered warm fires much like this, where he had sat with his father pouring over maps of past battles while Alain would sit and watch but never be allowed to participate. Memories were all Edwin had in his cell, but they were all born of regret. Now he sat and learned from them, having watched himself act the part of a spoiled brat, watched poor Alain struggle to find a place in this world.

He reminisced that his brother had sought and found some comfort here as well, in this small house. Lady Berna had helped, but a boy near Alain's own age had helped much more, and that boy was Keldon. Years later, while they both struggled through their trials into the Protectorate, they'd separated—Keldon keen on escaping the reputation that came with being friends with the knight-lord's son and Alain determined to show that he was every bit as good as Edwin had been at that age. Of course, he wasn't. Everyone knew that, but it wasn't for a lack of trying.

A tear ran down Edwin's face, catching the light of the fire and glowing upon his skin. He knew Alain's strength was in trying and knew better than most that it had meant nearly nothing. If he hadn't tried as hard as he did, Edwin was sure their father would have forgotten Alain altogether. Thinking back now, despite what he'd done to torture Mela, the reasons were one and the same, Edwin thought. To earn his father's love and attention.

"That poor boy," Edwin muttered to himself, now fully realizing for the first time that before he had failed his daughter and his wife, he had failed his brother. The pitiable bastard just floated about in this existence, never bad or good, never much at all, but indeed a bastard. More tears began to follow the first as Edwin continued to sit and stare into the fire.

All of this was doomed. None of it was in his hands—not that he had known what to do with something when it was.

Edwin was finding himself very lost in the comfort of Lady Berna's home, very lost indeed.

CHAPTER 24

The Fields of Sorrow, Once More

Elaine seethed with an anger that she didn't think was possible. *Yes, this is how it begins. This is what it takes to create the Toten-Geist,* she reflected, thinking to the now-crushed fragments of what had been Mela's former lover. The memory of the disembodied skull and its hollow recitations chilled the fires of her fury and brought her back to herself, even if her golden-haired counterpart hoped to stoke the flames once more.

"And what will you do, Elaine? Throw them offerings of flowers, perfumed scents . . . concoctions to ease their bowel movements? Do you really think they're showing Mela the same kind of affection at this very moment?" Acacia cried out, stalking the gathering chamber where the other Gravewalkers had convened.

Mela's capture had thrown the sisters into complete disarray, as they had quickly aligned themselves into either Acacia's camp or Elaine's, with no real distinction in between. Acacia had indeed gone with a troop of sisters to where the other Knochenbau had been destroyed, Mela's blood still wet and sticky upon the floor, the guardians of the chamber smashed to dust.

Given this outrage, Acacia had argued that now was the time to march upon Castle Riesenstadt. To rescue Mela (or avenge her death) and to ultimately rid themselves of the despot knight-lord that had harried them for so long. Elaine, of course, had reasoned that even if Mela was dead or soon to be dead, it wasn't worth opening themselves up to a counterattack for just one sister. Other sisters had felt the same, that they simply didn't have the numbers to sustain the aggressive campaign that Acacia was fighting for.

It wasn't that they didn't want to make a genuine effort to save her. The plan through which the Protectorate had summoned Mela into the ambush was ingenious for recognizing that Mela no longer had any living kin other than her father to utilize the apparatus. It was as useless to the Trauergast as it was instrumental to their enemy. A short siege against Castle Riesenstadt was also considered, but Mela and Acacia were the only Trauergasts with real experience in directing the Untoten warriors at their command, and Elaine wasn't about to cede total control of their forces over to her fiery counterpart. The others sisters had seen a fair share of practice, but only in the service of menial tasks or to animate the dead and then set them loose in the countryside, where they would create chaos for the knight-lord and his forces.

Amid the shouting of her sisters clamoring for their respective sides, Elaine closed her eyes and took a deep breath before continuing. "Mela is almost certainly dead at this point and throwing ourselves into some bloody campaign serves no purpose whatsoever to her memory. For now, we're safe, protected, and I really don't see that changing anytime soon."

Several cries of agreement rang out in support of Elaine's argument, but she wasn't done just yet. "And with all this talk of war and revenge, there should be only one focus: to recover her body and give her the peaceful repose that she's due. That we're all due, that everyone . . . is due."

"Oh, yes. Peaceful repose. Of course. That will certainly help with convincing the knight-lord to stop murdering us, that he'll let us just walk about in plain sight. You're as naive as you are long in tooth, sister."

Despite her desire to avenge Acacia's insult, Elaine knew that she wasn't going to win any battles arguing face-to-face with the woman, so she turned to her sisters sitting atop benches of hard stone. "Look what we've become. We've forsaken our traditions, and in doing so, we've forsaken who we are." Elaine noted the murmurs of approval before she continued on. "This, this is our chance to move past this meaningless talk of revenge. We all know the knight-lord won't live forever . . . and we know that there are men who exist within Protectorate ranks, men with compassion and understanding. We know this because one of our very own took such a knight for her beloved and we found the courage to accept it. Perhaps one day they'll do the same for us."

A quiet whisper of assent spread throughout the chamber, and Elaine nodded in turn. She had said her piece, and it seemed that many of the others shared similar thoughts—or, at least, they did now.

Acacia glanced around, not liking what was transpiring before her very eyes. She had never felt the threat of losing the loyalty of the sisters on her side, but now she was seeing that loyalty severely tested as many of them looked on with uncertainty wavering across their faces. She was going to have to take action soon—no, right this very moment, she suspected, if she was to have any hope of winning them back.

But Mela's reappearance solved that problem for her as a great vortex of mist rose up from the ground like a storm coalescing in their very midst. The sisters in the room broke out into anxious chatter, for it was considered poor form to spontaneously appear at such a meeting, but Acacia shared no such concerns as a wild grin broke out across her face. From the height of the column . . . well, Acacia knew of only one sister who could make such an impressive appearance. Once the mist had dissolved and the loud rushing of air had ceased, she was proven correct.

Mela stood before them, her face still lined with the faint traces of bruises and bloodshed that she had endured during her imprisonment, her dress a mockery of its former self . . . but it was her.

Their leader.

And the fire in her eyes was such that Elaine immediately knew that she had lost, that war was coming, and that there would be no such further indecisions as to what she'd been able to stave off just a few moments earlier.

***

Atop his white charger, Alain took a long look around. The others marched in formation behind him, bearing the standard of his father and of the Brotherhood itself. Yet in the strange ochre light that passed for daylight in this region, the standards seemed to shrink as they hung limply in the listless breeze. They'd marched hard and it had taken its toll upon them, their steps less and less certain as they carried on.

Or perhaps it was something else, Alain considered.

As they had traveled, he found himself harboring a suspicion that there was no truth to the Fields of Sorrow. That it was a glorified myth at best, a tale for the delight of old spinsters and addled sages to keep them occupied in the waning years of their lives. Additionally, he considered that there was even less truth to the idea that the Gravewalkers would be found in such a place. Years had passed and his father had duly scoured every inch of the realms in search of the witches and their ilk. Nations and city-states acquiesced to his intrusions, fearing the knight-lord's reach and, more importantly, his anger. But even after every stone had been turned, they were no closer to discovering their enemy's whereabouts than when they had begun.

No, this was just perhaps nothing more than a very public and substantial response to a disastrous series of events. Given that the witch had escaped back to her sisters, the citizens of Riesenstadt were suitably nervous. Sending a force out immediately with the supposed knowledge of where to find them, it was the only real move that his father had available to him.

And Alain could claim some small measure of responsibility for it.

Perhaps it was trivial, but he'd had to seize the moment, some small claim of redemption after the witch had been stolen from right under his watch. Finding the bard's map after a long list of failures and disappointments gave him a chance to look his father in the eye and feel as if he were a greater part of the sum rather than just the knight-lord's runt.

Ahead, two mountain ranges rose up from the earth, facing each other like colossal guardians standing watch. Beyond them, the horizon flattened out, a contrast to the sloping plains they currently marched across now. Alain knew that they were drawing close to their destination, and perhaps it was for the better, as their march was beginning to wear them down both physically and mentally. Some of the men were skittish, like they sensed that they might be marching to their deaths . . . even though Alain knew that to be a virtual impossibility, for his father wasn't one to underestimate what kind of threat the Gravewalkers presented. Time and time again, the knight-lord had proven himself to be a master tactician, and it didn't make any sense that he would needlessly send a significant portion of his forces to be slaughtered, even if there was any real suspicion that the map proved to be correct.

And yet, thinking upon it, where was his father now? Where was Luther? The Master Sergeant Vintas? Why did they have no real veterans in their ranks?

What real loss would Riesenstadt suffer if they were slaughtered to a man?

Alain cast such dour thoughts away. The size of the legion he traveled with was enough to make most invading armies give pause, and it was certainly enough to handle a few unruly Gravewalkers and whatever piles of bones they could conjure up. There was also the notion that after resting, come nightfall, they would reach their destination in plain daylight. There was a reason why the Gravewalkers staged their campaigns under the cover of night as they had done so many times in their attacks against Castle Riesenstadt. There would be no hiding, no marching about blindly in the darkness.

He urged his charger forward, the conviction upon his face prompting his men to do the same. After so long, after so many disappointments, this . . . this was to be his day. His moment of triumph. Even if it was nothing more than a mere stratagem, for the first time, he was leading this army—not his brother or anyone else. He had marched forth from Riesenstadt in command and he would return the same.

***

The chamber as a whole held its collective breath as Mela stood before them. Elaine didn't say a word, already knowing the battle was lost. Acacia also remained silent, for there was simply no need to speak. The other sisters who had previously sided with Elaine now felt the heavy weight of the glares from the sisters on Acacia's side. Their leader had returned; she was alive. Yet only moments ago, they had advocated her death so that they could live.

Mela waited another moment, taking in the countenance of each and every sister in the room.

"Whatever debate may have just ensued, know this, sisters: I don't hold any reservations as to what you had or had not intended. I would've told you myself to forsake any such foolish endeavors to rescue me or to challenge the Brotherhood in their seat of power."

At her words, Elaine mentally breathed a sigh of relief. She could see the sense of validation in the eyes of the sisters who had vouched for the same.

"But for those of you who would say that these knights, these warmongers, that they could be trusted or that their murderous ways could be redeemed . . ."

Acacia grinned, sensing the change in temperament. *Here it comes . . .*

After coming so close, Elaine found that she couldn't just let it go. She summoned her courage, calling upon the wisdom of their ancestors to confront their leader thus. "Don't," she said, a single word that spoke of immeasurable defiance—but for her, this was a battle for the very existence of their kind.

Acacia whipped around, her cheeks flushed red with the disrespect that Elaine had just shown Mela, especially in front of the other sisters. She reached for the blade hidden underneath her robes, but a hand from Mela stayed her wrath.

Instead, Mela walked over to Elaine. Slowly and immeasurably in control.

"Don't what?" she asked.

"Don't set down this path. Don't plunge us into unchecked war. Let us live, let us bide our time, and let us forgive."

Mela considered her words, then turned to face the other sisters.

"There is wisdom in what she says . . . but it's the wisdom of one who has failed to see the knights for what they truly are. Men who would murder. Torture. Imprison their own brethren. All of it for the sake of political gain, to retain power, status, wealth." Mela closed her eyes for a moment, not wanting to remember what she'd endured. But she forced herself to bring it all back so that her words wouldn't ring hollow in the hearts of those who needed to hear it the most.

"These . . . these are men who would subject their prisoners to unspeakable acts of suffering and degradation. I know this because I endured it myself."

She took a step closer to the gathered crowd and to their hushed whispers.

"In the spirit of our sister Elaine's words, I want you to know that I no longer hold my father to blame. No, this is an evil that is rooted deep within the very soul of the Brotherhood itself and it is one that we can no longer allow to exist. We alone are possessed of this sacred duty to put an end to their machinations; we alone have the power to do what must be done."

Despite the blow to her cause, Elaine found herself incredibly proud of the young woman standing before her. She thought back to when Mela was a little girl, alone and heartbroken. She remembered reaching out, gently wiping away her tears and promising her of a day when she would find the resolve to forge her own path, to find in her heart the power of forgiveness, to make her mother's sacrifice a worthy one. And she had. Elaine herself was even convinced by Mela's words and her resolve . . . but she still meant to go to war.

"The cause may be just, but it is not our place to right wrongs and it is not our place to wage wars. That is not who we are, Mela," Elaine said, with no small measure of deference to the woman who had truly earned her place as their leader.

Mela nodded with understanding. "Then you are free to leave, Elaine."

Elaine gasped, as did the other sisters, but Mela turned to face them as well. "And anyone else who shares her convictions . . . you too are free to make your way elsewhere."

The sisters in question did a poor job at disguising their anxiety, given their thoughts of being separated from their sisterhood, of trying to survive in a world that despised them. Elaine waited for them to join her, but after many moments, she still found herself standing alone. *So be it,* she thought.

She readied herself to leave, but the joyful sneer on Acacia's face was too much to bear. "You know this will mean the end of us. Of our kind," she said, one last bitter pronouncement for all to hear. "They'll never be beaten in their stronghold; they'll learn of our whereabouts and they'll march directly here, upon our doorstep, with every intent to see us driven into extinction."

Mela turned back to Elaine. "That, dear Elaine, is exactly what I'm counting on."

***

Cutting through the dense morning fog was a host of flickering torches carried by the knights and their footmen. Sweat across their brows, their faces stained with exhaustion, they marched forth, tendrils of white vapor swirling in their wake. Alain cursed their luck, for while they were marching by daylight, as soon as they had crossed into the flat plains, they were beset with a thick miasma that made it near impossible to see.

Occasionally, the fog would disperse; when it did, they were able to glimpse the barren soil all about them, occasionally spotted with tufts of dead grass. The withered trees, their lifeless branches bereft of leaves or foliage. In fact, the only real sign of life that they'd seen or heard since entering these desolate plains was the harsh squawking of crows. An army of them it seemed, judging by their incessant cries.

After some time, however, the fog did indeed lessen and the spirits of the men seemed to improve as a result. Sensing perhaps their time of wandering about was coming an end, Alain fell back to confer with Randrok, one of the only knights who could rightfully be called a veteran in this outfit. The older knight was currently preoccupied with trying to keep his horse at a steady trot, muttering quiet curses under his breath.

"Ho, Randrok. Trouble afoot?" Alain asked lightheartedly, also feeling the encouraging effects of finally escaping the thick soup of fog.

At his approach, the dour-faced knight tightened his grip on the reins and shook his head. "Damnable beast is being fidgety, milord. To think she was steady as could be in that cursed murk we just left behind."

Indeed, Alain could sense that his charger was being tentative as well, but when he pressed his knees inward, the steed seemed to shake it off. These horses that were bred for fighting in close quarters, the kind of fighting that could also be construed for butchery, with much screaming and yelling as one could tolerate. They were trained to charge even through the most challenging of conditions, this being no different.

"Fear not, brother. They just haven't had a good march in some time, fattening up in their stables while we repelled the witch's attacks."

Randrok seemed placated by Alain's suggestion, and soon his steed fell in line as well.

"Randrok, I'd have your counsel."

"Speak your mind, milord."

Alain glanced around. Now that their visibility had improved, he could truly see that there was indeed nothing that lived nor grew here, other than the insufferable crows that would occasionally taunt them from dead tree limbs.

"I appreciate your candor, brother, and I fear I'll have need of it."

"Why, milord?"

"Because I believe we're lost," Alain said as he looked around once more. "There's nothing here but misery and desolation. And those damn crows."

Randrok shook his shaggy white mane. "Nay, young master. Look about us," he said, referencing the mountain ranges on both sides, lined with crags of white snow. "There's no mistake. We are where we're supposed to be."

Alain nodded, relieved at the older knight's assurance.

"But that's not what worries me."

Alain looked over in surprise as Randrok continued.

"You're right about what you're feeling."

"And why does that worry you?" Alain asked.

Randrok sighed. "I've been fighting these battles with your father for far too long, milord. And there's one thing that I've come to understand. These feelings, the sense of sadness all about you, milord . . . that's what makes these witches what they are."

"And?"

"And at this very moment, we're bloody knee-deep in it all."

The fog was beginning to creep back in now and with it came the grumblings of the men. Alain gave the old man an uncertain nod of thanks, then galloped ahead to the front. His heart racing, he peered about the barren earth until a metallic glint caught his eye.

"Yah!" he cried, spurring his horse toward the object. As he got closer, he could see it now for what it was . . . an old, dented helmet.

"Hold!" he shouted out, and as one, the troops came to a halt. He dismounted from his horse and dropped to a knee. He picked up the helm and carefully turned it over a few times in his hands. Once a respectable piece of proper armor, it was now nothing more than a rusted skullcap. Red flakes fell off at Alain's touch.

He looked a bit farther ahead to see a rusted, broken sword, half-buried in the dirt. The feeling of desperation only grew in his gut as he set the ancient helmet aside and walked over to the blade.

Halfway there, he heard a footman cry out, "Sire! I found a shield here!"

Then, another foot soldier called out as well. "Aye! And a breastplate here!"

All around him shouts continued to ring out as Alain continued toward the sword, not so much exhilaration in their voices as it was mounting terror. *The rumors might be true.*

Finally reaching the blade, he crouched down to retrieve it . . . but it wouldn't budge. Fear churned in his gut. He muttered under his breath, trying to restore his courage. "Up with you now." He pulled even harder.

Around him, the men's murmurs of confusion got louder, but Alain meant to have the blade in his hands, even if it meant looking like a fool.

He planted his feet and pulled as hard as he could until it finally broke free with a loud snap.

The murmurs and nervous chatter stopped, as they all saw what Alain was holding in his hands. Alain paled as he also noticed what was still clutched around the hilt of the dirtied blade . . . calcified, skeletal fingers.

"No . . . ," he breathed aloud.

The sight of it brought him out of his stupor, as he immediately flung it away and turned to his forces.

"Close together . . . now!"

Even though these were mostly new recruits and footmen training to become Knights Proper, each one of them had already seen enough drills to last a lifetime. Thus, at Alain's command, they quickly drew their ranks in, tightening up their formations.

Alain jumped back onto his horse and wheeled around, searching for any sign of their sworn enemies. But there was nothing. Not even the cries of the crows that had tormented them their entire way here.

The men behind him looked warily about, waiting. Their blades were drawn, their lines pulled taut.

Alain's heart continued to race for several moments, but still he could see nothing. No camp, no tents, no structures . . . nothing.

He found his breath coming a bit slower now, for while perhaps they had indeed found the legendary Fields of Sorrow, the witches were not here—or, if they had been here, they were now gone.

But that moment of respite only lasted a fleeting moment before Alain's horse suddenly reared in the air, its front hooves lashing about at some imaginary foe.

In the distance, the telltale rush of air reached their ears first, followed by a white shroud of mist, rising from the carpet of fog that lapped at their boots. Emerging from the shroud was a Gravewalker, her face hidden by a grey hood.

Then another, and yet another . . . a multitude of white pillars encircled them, more Gravewalkers stepping forth from the mist.

Alain found himself frozen in the saddle as the last Gravewalker teleported directly in front of him. She threw her hood back and Alain grimaced and pulled his blade forth, for if anything, he was assured that *this* particular witch wasn't here to broker a peace treaty.

Mela locked eyes with the man who had tortured and beaten her . . . and she grinned. She grinned at him, then at all of the collective knights and footmen assembled, even while they cursed her under their breaths.

The rest of the Gravewalkers removed their hoods, including Acacia, her long golden locks unfurling. As one they spread their arms out, their eyes pulsing with white heat.

Alain shook his fear off, for the lives of his men depended upon it. Just then, Randrok charged up from the rear and called out to Alain, "We have to attack them now, while we still can!"

Alain considered his words, then turned to the others. "Hold, damn you! They want us to spread ourselves thin, remain in place!"

A knight and a loyalist to the end, Randrok gritted his teeth and remained silent. Instead of arguing with the young noble, he unsheathed his blade and gripped it tight.

"'Tis a good day as any to die, milord. May we do so with courage and with conviction."

But Alain wasn't ready to die just yet. "They have nothing. They're simply trying to force us into some ambush."

Randrok laughed and wheeled his steed around. "Milord, we're already in the ambush."

Alain opened his mouth to order Randrok back, until he realized that the fog was receding now, like water being sucked away by an incoming tidal wave. This spooked the horses to no end, and the knights fought wildly to retain control of their steeds.

Then the earth itself began to quake. Tremors rippled throughout their ranks, throwing the knights and footmen to their knees with startled cries. While most of the knights fought immediately to their feet, some of the footmen began to beg for mercy.

Alain shouted orders atop his steed, but his cries were drowned out by a booming, guttural moan that rolled out over the plains. It seemed to be everywhere, yet Alain couldn't spy anyone else besides the Gravewalkers, who were still locked in their trance.

He kicked his horse in the flanks and made a move to charge Mela. *If I can finally put an end to that witch, we might still have a chance . . .*

Then a skeletal hand seized his steed by the leg. The charger quickly broke free, but that wasn't the immediate problem anymore.

All around him, in every direction, rising from the ground, clawing their way free of the graves that held them for so long . . . ancient corpses, composed of grey, sinewy flesh and discolored bone. Bearing broken, jagged swords and chipped axes. Remnants of rusted armor, hanging about their wretched forms . . . an army of the dead.

And they had Alain and his men surrounded.

He looked back to Mela, to the other Gravewalkers, but they were gone. In their place stood a legion of Untoten warriors, and they were closing in on them like a noose drawing tight. He looked about for a possible escape route, but there was none to be had.

And then, in that very instance, Alain had a moment of perfect clarity. It was one of truth, and in that truth, he realized that he was finally free. It was a realization of knowing that his father, despite whatever words he may have shared or grand gestures he may have shown . . . that he simply didn't care.

Alain readied himself for battle and trotted his loyal steed to the head of the ranks. He would be the first to attack and he would be the first to die. But before he galloped forth, there was still one final utterance that he had left for this mortal plane.

"Damn you, Father."

CHAPTER 25

Betrayal of the Family Bones

How is it that we always draw the bad weather?" George asked, standing at his watch. The young knight didn't mind this particular shift atop the battlements, but it seemed as if they would never be free of the gloom that had attached itself to Castle Riesenstadt and its surrounding lands as of late.

"We're just the lucky ones," Donovan replied. He shivered, sending tiny droplets of cold water from his armor. The rain hadn't come yet, the moisture hanging in the air for long moments before it would slowly descend. There was no sky in the late afternoon, just the growing grey of the settling storm clouds. The two guards stood atop the battlements and kept a steady watch on the horizon, the weather only allowing them to see a few hundred feet from the castle walls.

"Doesn't seem lucky to me," George said.

"I'll tell you about unlucky. I ever tell you about the barmaid whose wet was like the first touch of winter?"

"Yes, of course you have. Every time the weather drizzles like this, the memory of that poor girl comes to your mind."

"I can't help that it keeps becoming relevant," Donovan said with a sly grin.

"What I don't understand is why you need to constantly bring it up, though."

"Well, that's because you're a clumsy oaf," Donovan said.

George looked down at his gardbrace and gave a moment's stare at the golden arrow emblazoned upon it.

"And you're a motherless bastard," George said. He gave a halfhearted swing and clanked his gauntlet against his friend's own blank gardbrace. "I just find it crude," he said with distaste, slightly jealous that he didn't have any such stories to share himself.

"Well, better a bastard than an oaf," Donovan said quieter this time. He had caught the point his friend was throwing at him, but he wasn't going to let it go completely. "Look at that swing, will you? What a sorry sad thing that was."

"I'm sure that's what the barmaid said." George laughed. "And I'm saving my strength," he said, shaking the water from his long beard like a shaggy dog. The dew had been collecting for an hour and had finally started seeping down to his skin through the layers of cloth padding underneath his armor. His friend gave another quick shudder, the droplets flying from his armor like a small mist.

"I suppose we'll probably need it. Don't think that Alain will bring much luck with him on his hunt."

"That boy definitely knows the difference between luck and none if he knows anything." George said with certainty. "Never seen his luck rise his entire life. And he's a dandy shit atop it all."

The wet mist grew heavier and raindrops began to fall down around them.

"Here we go!" George said. "Finally made up its mind to start acting like a real storm." Their armor began to ring as the water fell harder and harder upon the steel. They stood quiet now, listening to the rain and standing straighter than they had all afternoon. It was good to stand tall in a storm and the taller it was, the taller you had to be.

George breathed it in, relishing the sudden downpour. So much that he almost missed the figures emerging from the wet gloom.

At first there was just one, riding high upon a horse. It moved slow and steady, as if it was enjoying the downpour and hadn't a second thought for a warm fire. Then more figures followed in a tight formation, marching in unison, trudging through the rain-soaked mud, like shadows in the heavy mist.

"I think maybe that dandy shit may have just proven us wrong," George said as his friend squinted through the rain to get a better look.

"Eh. I've never seen the witch's forces move that tightly," he said. "Maybe that uptight prince really has done us all a favor." The forces grew nearer and George called down to the gate, "Oi, let's pull it up, fellas!"

"Can't mistake that white horse," Donovan pointed out. The rain poured down harder than ever before and thundered atop the gathering knights' armor. Word was spreading like quick-fire that Alain had returned. The courtyard was already half-full by the time the front gate had completely opened. Quietly they all stood, suddenly possessed of a newfound respect for the knight-lord's son. Their minds raced with the questions that the rain saw fit to drum out of their voices.

The gate slammed to a halt as it reached its topmost catch. Alain then marched in astride his horse, streaks of blood running down its sides and to the ground. His armor was rent and torn—long, terrible gashes that spanned the length of his breastplate. The force behind him was significantly smaller than the one he had left with. So many men missing and the ones still left looking exhausted and worn down, their eyes cast down upon the ground.

***

Just like everyone else, Edwin had heard the news only minutes after Alain's forces had been spotted. Given the sudden commotion, he figured this would be the best chance he'd have to sneak out, while everyone else was preoccupied with his brother's return. He wasn't sure where his travels would take him, but he knew that he could no longer call Castle Riesenstadt home.

With that, he said his farewells to Lady Berna and set on his way. She wasn't pleased with his decision, but she also couldn't argue for any other course of action. She'd passed on the news that despite the bard's death his daughter had indeed escaped, and he had no doubt that she would soon return for her revenge. Thus, with the all too certain likelihood that both his father and his daughter would attempt to kill him on sight or, worse, throw him back into some prison to rot, Edwin knew the time had come. He considered that if Cass were still alive, together they could've possibly engineered some strategy, some plan . . . but such was fate. He found himself unable and unwilling to process her loss just yet, but there would be time for that later.

Garbed in leathers and a heavy cloak, a bittersweet gift from the keepsakes of Lady Berna's son, Edwin rambled through the alleyways and made his way to the top of the courtyard to see his brother's return. The knights hadn't given up their search for him, but Edwin figured they would be much more distracted by Alain's arrival than his skulking through the alleyways.

He gazed down at all of the men already gathered below him, thinking that Alain had finally earned some real recognition. The knights stared forward in the rain, never minding their footing, but keeping a steady eye on Alain atop his horse. After his earlier musings by the fire, Edwin was proud of him, finally battle-tested and poised for praise. Every knight wished to prove himself in combat, and here Alain was, ready to receive his due.

Given all that, Edwin could not help thinking how lucky Alain had been to escape Mela's wrath. The more he considered it, the harder it was to accept. She sat in his mind as well and plagued his fatherly apprehension with the worry of her well-being. Was she truly defeated? Was she lying dead in the mud of the distant battlefield where she had met his brother? Was her head in one of Alain's saddlebags as a present to their father? Edwin's muscles tensed up and he could feel his stomach tightening. All of the pride and excitement he had for his brother just moments ago had been washed away with the worry for his daughter.

Where could she be?

***

Alain's forces cleared the gate and came to a halt in the middle of the courtyard. The men were silent, on both sides, and there was only the sound of the falling rain. The knights' armor rang throughout the courtyard like bells of chiming victory. A young squire began to weave himself through the crowd. He slinked around the suits of armor, ducked beneath massive arms, while he kept his eyes on Alain. The boy's hair was stuck to his face with the wet, but he didn't seem to care. He smiled as he noticed he was the first to arrive at Alain's side.

"Master Alain," the boy said, looking up. "Might I take your horse? Or serve you in any way?" This would be his chance, a real chance to rise and show everyone he was capable of joining their ranks.

Glancing at Alain's horse, however, he suddenly noticed just how bad off the beast was, amazed that it had even managed to make it home. One eye was replaced by a grisly, gaping hole, and through its blood-soaked flanks, he could spot ivory fragments of bone. But what really shook him was the complete absence of hot air bellowing out from its wide nostrils. As if it was frozen in time, the creature simply just stood there, still as the very stone around them.

The boy gasped as Alain's head turned from the rest of his body, the movement stiff and sure. His gaze, hollow and empty. The boy's thoughts went blank, and for the first time since he had run outside, he could feel the raindrops smashing against his skin.

***

Edwin watched the young squire stand at attention by Alain's side. And like the boy, he suddenly felt the weight of the rain. His tension was fading now, traded for the encumbrance of the moment frozen before him. Alain still had not spoken. No speeches or proclamations of bravery. Edwin saw the stillness of the boy in the downpour and recognized the fear in his stance. He looked past his brother and his men, something in the back of his head making him glance outward.

Beyond the gate, just down the road, he could make out a figure. A woman in black who drew his vision to her, quickly over the distance of rain-soaked mud, to a leer that spoke of vengeance. Any remaining doubts that he had, they melted away and were replaced instantly with dread. The full reality of this moment and the one before it were clear now, that death was standing before them. The unwelcome guest was just beyond their doorstep.

***

Even a boy knows a man's eyes. Children, like all of the wild beasts of the forest, trust first with their fear. The man who sat high upon his horse, soaked in blood and showered by the cold, hard rain, was to be feared. But unlike the wild beasts of the forest, a young boy's reactions were not as nimble or as quick. So when Alain's blade came down upon him, the child's mind barely had the time to recognize that he was to die in this moment before the steel crashed its way through his forehead.

***

"The gate!" Edwin yelled across the courtyard before the boy's body had even crumbled to the ground. "The bloody gate, you fools!" he yelled again, all thoughts for his safety gone.

Most of the knights stood still in confusion; a few turned to see who was yelling orders. But none made toward the gate. Two knights who hadn't noticed Edwin sneak by realized who he was and reached out to seize him.

Below, Alain's men ambled their way into combat positions to face the knights surrounding them. The knights reacted on instinct and mirrored Alain's men. Swords were drawn and spears held high, but no one moved. The shock of the situation was still running its course through their bodies.

***

George had watched the young squire's head collapse under the weight of Alain's blade and unconsciously notched an arrow in his bow. As the men below snapped into stances with their weapons, he loosed his first arrow. It streaked through air, cutting through the rain to sink deeply into Alain's collarbone—but it had no effect. No cry of pain, no reaction whatsoever. George already had his next arrow notched and ready as he watched Alain's figure simply sit still, blade still in hand, but otherwise oblivious that he had just slaughtered an innocent child. George's blood pumped harder than ever, his heart shuddering with adrenaline.

"What was that for?" Donovan asked, unsure himself as to whether he was asking about George's actions or Alain's.

"Murderous wretch," was all George could say as he loosed his second arrow. As the second shaft embedded itself even deeper than the first into Alain's collarbone, the Protectorate finally began to move. The stillness had vanished and the warriors struck forward with a will. All of the confusion was gone, and there was no doubt as to whom—or what—they were facing.

***

"Let go of me, you fools!" Edwin ordered the knights trying to subdue him. "The enemy is right below us!"

In response, one of the knights reached over and unsheathed Edwin's sword, and threw it to the alleyway below. Edwin grimaced. It was one thing to be held up by these two, but without a weapon, he was assuredly helpless against what was coming.

He kept his eyes forward, watching the battle before him, trying to find Mela in the fray, but it appeared as if the Gravewalkers were still waiting just beyond the gate. Everything was jumbling in his brain, so many things happening that it was testing his composure beyond measure. There wasn't any time for this—he needed to get free and they needed to close that gate.

***

George unleashed arrows with tremendous accuracy. Each shaft crashed through an Untoten skull of his choosing.

"Pierce their skulls, you soggy twat!" he yelled at Donovan in frustration. The young knight was shaking at the elbow with each pull of his bowstring. George watched from the corner of his eye. "Slow and easy," he added flatly.

Donovan loosed his next arrow and caught one at the base of its skull. Stunned, the Untoten knight stumbled for a moment and allowed his attacker to cut him down.

"Better," George said.

But it was a short-lived victory as the Untoten continued to push the knights back to the corners of the great courtyard. Fighting in such close quarters, they had a difficult time separating between friend and foe.

As he continued to seek out targets, George noted that these dead knights were the strongest they had faced yet. The skills and muscle memory of a Knight Proper without the pain or the stress of battle weighing down upon them. A far cry from the long-dead corpses that they were used to fighting—and it was taking its toll. Worse yet, out of the corner of his eye, he saw that those same long-dead corpses were now just down the road. An entire legion of them, mindlessly trudging toward the gate to join their newly minted comrades.

George heard a battle cry in the distance and looked up from the courtyard to see Renton riding hard with more men at his back. His crimson cloak flowed behind him like a war banner, the tip of a bloody spear.

***

Edwin heard the war cry of his father and knew that the knight-lord and his personal guard would be here soon. He, however, was still being held down by the pair of guards who were focused on him rather than the fighting at hand. With his father on the way, Edwin knew the tide of the battle could change, but he needed to secure that gate before any more Untoten soldiers could get through.

As for the Gravewalkers, they still lingered behind the bulk of the Untoten legion outside the gate, but even then, Edwin couldn't fathom why they would leave themselves unprotected without any cemeteries or graveyards nearby to fuel their magics. Still, Edwin figured that they were safe enough, hiding behind scores upon scores of their minions. The real threat was the Untoten knights. With any luck, the Protectorate would be able to rid themselves of their former brothers and hold off the legion marching toward them.

He dropped to a knee and threw each knight off balance—one too high, one too low. He twisted hard at the hip and knocked each of them down in a different direction, his eyes still focused on the main gate.

"Get up and fight! Your brothers need you!" he commanded as he sprinted away toward the opposite side of the courtyard.

***

As Renton approached at a full gallop, he could see his men falling too fast to count. He leapt his horse from the top of the stone stairs to the next level. He swept off of his saddle and leapt himself down the next two levels. He reached the courtyard floor with a bended knee and unclasped his cloak. He bent farther forward and gripped the hilt of the sword at the back of his head. He let the earth pull the weight of the great claymore downward, all five feet of steel flowing out of its sheath like a raging river. He stood up, both hands wrapped white-knuckled around the oversized grip of his sword.

Sergeant Vintas clamored down beside him as the rest of his men could be heard leaping down the stone levels to join them. Vintas reached up to his breastplate, where a golden heart shined. It bled ten golden drops and he expected it would be bleeding heavier by the end of day.

Then there was a thundering bellow felt across the entire battlefield as Luther's great shield crashed to the ground, its point cracking deep into the cobblestone at the sergeant's side. Luther knelt behind it, turned his head to Vintas and Renton and nodded in grim approval. They charged into the fray and joined their brothers, weapons drawn and faces contorted in battle cries.

***

Edwin pushed his way through the battle. He was at full stride and ignoring everyone and everything in front of him. He could hear his father joining the skirmish behind him, the metallic ring of his claymore unmistakable over the din of the others. Edwin crashed his forearm against a charging dead knight, cracking his jaw, sending him sprawling. His goal was in sight as he reached down for a forgotten axe. It was heavy in his hand, throwing him off balance. He stumbled for a moment before grabbing control of the axe with his other hand.

With his weapon held high, he continued his charge for the gate's rope, but then something rose up before him, a nightmarish appropriation of blood, bone, and horseflesh. His brother Alain, now an Untoten, standing directly between him and the gate. Edwin paused a moment, horrified by the sight, but then quickly marshalled his courage.

He ran toward Alain on a collision course—until he was suddenly cut off by a small mob of Untoten foot soldiers. The axe in his hand was a poor substitute for the reach of his blade, and Edwin found himself having to wildly swing it back and forth just to give himself some space. Dodging their grasping hands and thrusting blades, Edwin risked a glance to the gates, seeing the might of the Gravewalkers' Untoten army about to surge through.

"No!" he cried out.

Desperate, he renewed the fight against his opponents, whirling, slashing, and cleaving, taking each one out in an awesome display of methodical butchery. But it wasn't without toll—bereft of his armor, scores of bloody gashes and tears ran down his arms and chest.

Looking over the head of the last Untoten foot soldier between him and Alain, he spotted his gore-soaked brother, still mounted atop the rotted remnants of his white charger as if he were just waiting for Edwin to finish. Not wanting to delay him, Edwin buried the axe into his opponent's skull with a wet smack—and not a moment too soon, as Alain charged in, swinging away on horseback. Edwin rolled, barely avoiding Alain's blade as the Untoten horse tried to bite and trample him underneath.

His axe still in his last adversary's skull, Edwin scrambled to his feet and snatched a short sword from the cold hands of another foot soldier. Barely blocking a downward swing from Alain, Edwin grunted as the horse forced him to break off once again. Edwin backed off, frantically trying to think of a way to separate Alain from his mount, but the nightmare horse wouldn't allow him the luxury.

Rearing in the air, the creature thundered back down as it charged in again. Edwin gave himself over to instinct and charged as well, head-on. At the last second, he slid on the rain- and blood-slicked cobblestone, right underneath the horse's legs, with his blade raised high.

Edwin could feel the creature's shriek of rage in his bones, followed by the sound of its wet innards smacking the stone. Edwin turned around to watch the beast stumble in the stew of its own guts, his brother about to topple from his saddle. The thing that used to be Alain seemed momentarily confused, not able to understand the shift in balance.

"Rest in peace, Brother," Edwin breathed, a blessing just as much as it was an atonement. With that, Edwin got a running start and vaulted atop the horse in one leap, impaling both Alain and the horse in the same breath. The monstrous steed screamed one last time, as they fell, pinned together by Edwin's blade. A fire raged in Alain's eyes for a moment longer, then faded to nothingness and to true death.

Edwin shook himself off, then recovered his axe from the foot soldier's skull. Sprinting over to the gate, he threw his whole weight forward and crashed against the wall. The axe's hefty blade made short work of the thick gate rope, and the iron gate broke loose and came crashing down. The ground shook hard enough to bring Edwin all the way down to the cobblestones.

He turned toward the battle to see that his father's men had made quick work of the Untoten horde, rallying the men who had been waning. Despite the heavy losses incurred, the battle had been won and the Gravewalkers and their skeletal legions were no longer a threat inside the heavily fortified walls of Castle Riesenstadt now that the gate was in place.

***

Renton knelt next to Vintas, who was lying at his side, bleeding out. He had been caught midswing and pierced through the armpit. He had nearly been dead when he had reached the ground, but not before his knight-lord had caught him. There were no words. Renton's arms strained underneath the full weight as he held his friend, the sounds of battle dying down all around them.

As the sergeant faded, Renton caught sight of movement in front of him. He looked up to see the final corpse standing before him. He was fresh except for the hundreds of little cuts and gashes accenting his body. The Untoten knight didn't raise its sword; he simply lunged forward, his blade as sharp as they came. Renton hefted the body of his friend up as a shield. As the Untoten's blade rebounded off of the sergeant's armor, a bolt came crashing through its skull. An explosion of bone rained down on Renton. He turned up to see George atop the battlements, bow still in hand, quiver empty, and breathing a sigh of relief. His pulling arm shaking and bloody, cut all the way down his bicep, his friend Donovan slumped at his side.

***

There was a calm that came as the last corpse fell. The surviving men were breathing heavy, the civilians who had taken up arms doubly so. Hands wrenched the handles of pitchforks and hammers. Everyone was gathered in exasperation and relief. The enemy had sent men through the gates and caught everyone by surprise as they realized just how close they had been struck.

A lone figure made her way through the crowd of people, weaving forward in a hesitant manner. Brushing her soaked garments aside, she stepped lightly over the bodies at her feet, even slower than she had through the living. As the woman reached the center of the carnage, she stopped and studied the body of the young squire, his mangled face mercifully pressed against the bloodied cobblestone.

As she knelt down beside him and her knees crashed into the stone, never minding the pain it caused, an entirely different exasperation overwhelmed her. At first there were no tears from her eyes, the very same blue eyes of the boy before her. Struggling to understand what had just happened, there simply wasn't a true emotion she could place forward. Then they attacked, her tears bursting forth with no control amid the heavy raindrops. Her chest heaved silently, as everything about her was drenched in grief. All around her, others joined as each began to find their own among the dead. Their anguish seemed to fill the air as the sky appeared to join in the deluge of sorrow. The rain became so thick they would have hardly seen in front of them if they had been looking anywhere but down at their loved kin.

It sank in slowly, the deeper feeling. The feeling that one had in a place of the dead. A certain heaviness one was burdened with in a place of veneration and sorrow in the confines of a graveyard.

***

Edwin felt it in his chest just as he saw that his father felt it too. The presence of such grief was palpable, and men of their season felt these things stronger than most people. The calculations ticked away in both of their heads as they began to put the pieces together. Edwin stayed transfixed by the woman hunched over her dead child.

The downpour was so overwhelming that he had barely made out the presence of the fog behind her. A figure enshrouded in golden hair appeared from thin air, as if she had been stalking the woman as an invisible phantom, a manic smile stretched across her face. A slender, curved blade was clutched in her hands. The raindrops changed pitch as they bombarded the sharp steel of her newly present weapon. The water seemed to be singing now, high and clear as the Gravewalker grabbed a handful of the grief-stricken woman's hair. There was nothing Edwin could do, and his father barely budged in the corner of his sight. The grieving woman's head was lifted skyward, neck extended, and her hair pulled taught. The rain continued to sing upon the blade as it swept across the air. It appeared to kiss her flesh at first and then sank deep like a rabid dog having its meal. It cut across her and carved out a canyon of split meat, its red river pouring forth, rushing down the woman's front and into the crevices of the cobblestones. A few spurts spouted into the air and caught the Gravewalker in the face, staining strands of her pale hair. She beamed brighter and grinned wider as she let go of the woman's head.

The woman slumped and began to fall downward, but before her face reached the ground, her arms reached out, flexing tightly under the strain as they stopped her descent and raised her back to her knees. Her legs straightened and she rose up, as if she were learning to walk again.

Then, fog columns began to rise up all around them and terror once again returned to the men.

***

The bodies began to rise from the cobblestone streets. People watched in horror as their loved ones came back from the dead at the will of the witch they had always feared and now another whom they feared even more. Acacia's wild golden hair whipped in the wind as she looked on in excitement. Her eyes darted about to the dance of her minions and sparkled in their armor's reflective light. The time was here and they would all pay—they would pay with the crunching of their bones and the spilling of their blood. She could see the future as great gushes of crimson rushed their way throughout the small canyons in the cobblestones.

Renton caught everything in stride as his vision was engulfed by the Untoten bodies of his comrades. The Gravewalkers' plan was readily apparent to him now; the lack of compassion with which he sent Alain off to a certain death was being revisited upon him in turn. Their home was now consecrated by grief and sorrow, led by the Untoten forces under his son's command. But that attack was never the true threat. They were merely pawns, an instrument to create an arena that would allow the Gravewalkers to call upon their powers.

No, Renton thought, *these witches desire to strike more than fear into my people.* Here, there was true terror. Even the trained soldiers were starting to freeze in their own tracks as their friends came back to life. There was no decomposition, no mutilated faces—everything was clear and haunting. The men looked as they did just minutes before. Sporting mortal wounds across their bodies but moving none the worse for wear. An army of loved ones now stood for battle, damning their own families, prepared to cut down the ones they once cared for without remorse, without knowing.

***

From across the courtyard, holding an iron-capped staff, Mela looked on just as her grandfather did. These men marched to the morbid beat of her broken heart, and she found herself having second thoughts. *Is there justice here? Is this the way it should be won?*

A knight came down on her with his axe but met nothing but air. She transported herself all over the battlefield. She could sense the tangible threads of grief and sorrow, the ground before them sanctified with each additional teardrop. Now her sisters could travel about them at will. Swords and axes swung through air and met nothing. The witches seemed untouchable as they commanded a fresh army against the rest of the living.

A great boulder of a man charged his former commander, and Renton's feet began to loosen. Here was his old friend, the man that Renton had just laid down moments ago. Vintas made no battle cry or grimacing look. He simply charged at full speed with a blank expression on his face and a fog in his eyes. The knight-lord shifted in place and brought his claymore to bear. As the sergeant came on top of him, with no hesitation, no doubt, Renton split his belly across the middle, nearly cleaving him in half. The charging corpse splintered into two and was dispatched as he fell.

Renton severed his head from his body, his spine exploding with a mighty snap.

"They are your brothers no longer!" Renton yelled aloud. The other knights looked toward their commander, still frozen in their places. "Kill these puppets! Kill these abominations of your brethren! And do them justice!"

The other knights rallied and gripped their weapons tight. Their leader was back in their midst and they accepted him wholeheartedly. Battle cries rent the air as each man found his courage once more and prepared to do battle and give their comrades one last proper and bloody farewell.

CHAPTER 26

The Knight Proper

Everything seemed to blend into itself. The battle raged stronger than it had before at the power of Renton's words. His knights were renewed in spirit and vigor, which only seemed to spur the Gravewalkers on even more. Corpses of loved ones; armored knights; pitchfork-swinging farmers; and biting, gnashing children all swarmed about in a violent frenzy. Their masters popped in and out of combat, assisting their puppets as best they could, whenever and wherever they felt it was necessary. The Brotherhood reverted to their training and combat experience. They accepted the change and adapted to these new battle tactics as best they could, but knew that little would change unless the raven-haired beauty and her fiery counterpart were brought to heel.

***

Mela had stayed out of the way and watched like a general from afar. If a knight grew close to her, she simply relocated, a rapid cloud of fog wrapping around her and transporting her to a safer location. Her fingers never seemed to stop moving as she directed several of her Untoten at once with the fluid precision of an artist. Her sister, on the other hand, felt at home in the thick of it.

Acacia held great curved blades in both her hands and guided her corpses in front of her like a shield. She would simply move them from side to side as she needed them, taking each opening as an opportunity to plunge one of her blades through the flesh of the enemy. She seemed more interested in seeing just how many men she could harm rather than taking them out of the picture. The kill wasn't the thing; the simple pleasure of the hurt was. Most of the time, she would only maim a poor soul and then let the Untoten have at him. As each knight would begin to recover from the sting of her blades, they then would be struck by several bodies, their flesh torn apart and ravaged by Acacia's hate. Every Untoten at her command attacked with viciousness, more often ripping apart skin with their teeth and nails than their weapons, which were now thrown aside or nearly forgotten.

Edwin was still on the floor against the wall. He watched Mela with both the intensity of a soldier watching his enemy and with the relief a father feels for his daughter's safety. The mix did not suit the situation and he knew it. He could feel it rising in his chest as the two notions tore at each other. As each man he had known fell and rose back up again as one of her puppets, he could sense the fatherly trust ebbing away, slowly losing its battle with the soldier. He gripped the axe tighter in his hand as the fight raged on all around him. But his eyes stayed transfixed on his daughter. Her hair clung tightly to her body. Her eyes never met his or even glanced in his direction.

She kept the battle in front of her and never let it go. He had to admire that—his daughter the leader—but his own grip never shifted from his weapon.

It had to end.

***

Luther's first charge dispatched more than ten of the Untoten, smashing through them and scattering them to the side. He heard their bodies crumble against his shield as they slowly brought him to a standstill. He had kept the sides of his shield sharp since the rise of the Gravewalkers' armies years ago, and it served him well now. As he deflected each blow, he was also landing one somewhere else. The blades would slide against the polished exterior, and at just the right moment, he would lean and twist and sever.

Above all of the commotion, he found himself drawn to the lustful cry of Acacia across the battlefield. She was washed in crimson, soaked in blood from the wounds she had inflicted, set apart from her sisters not only by the color of her hair but also by her lust for bloodshed. Luther reasoned that putting her out of the fight would perhaps give them a chance at survival.

He started to make his way toward her, but an armored corpse lunged at him with a great broadsword just past the edge of his shield. He lifted his arm and trapped the enemy's forearm by pinching it between his own arm and side. He held it tightly against him as he heaved the face of his shield against the Untoten's head. He pushed forward all the while, bashing the enemy's face inward, each blow crushing more and more bone. The creature he held seemed to realize its defeat and began to kick at him, missing the knight and instead hacking its own foot off with the sharp edges of the shield. Just as Luther let go of the defeated corpse and renewed his march toward the blonde witch, he heard another cry—this one a bloodcurdling, pitiful scream of death. It wrenched through the air and caused everyone a moment's frozen hesitation.

Renton stood with his claymore buried halfway through a young Gravewalker. The blade had started at her shoulder and worked its way through her ribcage. It was now stuck at her hip. The Gravewalker's body was still in shock; what was left of her chest still heaved while it begged for air. The knight-lord lifted his foot and pushed squarely into the girl's hip to free his sword. The force was so harsh the girl split in half as the blade wrenched free from her body. Her useless corpse joined the rest in the blood-soaked cobblestones, the look of shock still on her face, and the pause faded.

Luther turned back to Acacia. She was surrounded by four corpses and her blades no longer glinted; too heavily covered in blood, they simply dripped in anticipation.

With barely a flinch, he dropped her first bodyguard. It fell to the ground and Luther crushed its pelvis with the bottom of his shield. He lifted hard and used the top to cut off the second one's face. Its head still attached, brains looking out in front of it, it leapt forward. Luther planted his foot into its knee and brought it to the ground. He wrapped his steel hand around its throat and ripped its faceless head, spine still attached, from the rest of its body.

"You have come to the end, witch," Luther said, the Untoten's skull and spine still gripped tightly in his hand. Her other guards seemed to have been ordered off as they charged outward and away from Acacia to join the rest of the battle. She just smiled through her blood-drenched locks and spun her blades in her hands, showering Luther in his brothers' blood.

She made a start, then disappeared. The fog seemed to have attacked her more than anything else, but the next instant, she was at his side. The witch was close enough for Luther to feel her breath on his face. He struck her with her own dead soldier, the spine splitting the skin on her shoulder as its expressionless head cracked against her own.

She fell to the ground and laughed, realizing her mistake. She disappeared again.

Luther loosened his grip on the skull and let it fall. Before it could strike the stone below, he caught the end of the spine.

Acacia's fog column appeared on his other side, her scythes still held low near her hips. Luther swung at her with the bones in his hand like a great mace. The gore flew through the air at immense speed from the power of his arms. Acacia's arm matched the speed of the flying skull and met it with her blade. The scythe cut straight through the bone and finally severed the head from its spine.

More female screams began to rent the air as Acacia and Luther took in each other's stares. The deaths of her sisters didn't seem to faze Acacia. Her mind was too focused on the knight in front of her, her blood flowing with the gleeful thought of his defeat.

Luther, calm and attentive, could see that the Gravewalkers' numbers were dwindling fast around them, but this one was his. This witch could not, would not, find herself free from this battle; she had to fall here. She spun forward in attack, and her blades caught only Luther's plated armor as he lunged forward in defense. The next moment, cleverly enough, she appeared just inside his shield. His outreached arm exposed, all of his body now open to attack. Her blades rose and fell quickly, deep into his armor at the collarbone. He pulled his shield toward him and caught her in the back of the head. Her eyes rolled back for a moment as she smiled so wide that it froze Luther in his place. Her eyes then rolled forward into focus and she pulled down on her scythes with all her strength.

As they wrenched his chest plate away from his body, the tips of the blades dug into his skin, carving into his ribs. He let out a painful scream and her smile grew unnaturally wider. He brought his head downward and crashed hard into her forehead. Acacia felt a silent crack in her skull and then a shattering ring in her ears. As the ring hit its highest pitch, the world turned black and she fell, her blades pulling from Luther's body before they crashed onto the cobblestones.

She lay there, unconscious for the moment, while Luther gathered his wits. He had no strength left and let his shield drop to the ground. He bent down on one knee and unlocked his dirk from its scabbard. The well-oiled steel glinted, even among the dark storm falling down all around them. His grip wasn't strong as he rested the blade upon the Gravewalker's throat, his arm extended fully. He would simply put his weight into it and bury it into her neck, just lean downward and thrust. He felt his eyelids fighting against his stare. Then there was a touch of wind at his side as Mela raised her staff toward the sky, then brought the iron-capped end down like a hammer. A blinding pain ravaged Luther's mind as he watched his elbow explode before him. She reversed her grip, leading with the pointed end of her staff toward his head but was suddenly tackled by Edwin. Before she could reach the ground, she disappeared and her father found himself face down on the cobblestones.

Quickly rising to his feet, Edwin eyed a sword just a few paces away. There would be time to reach it before Mela could get to him. She was fast, but he would be able to arm himself faster than that. His eyes hung on the glint of the sword for a long moment, but his limbs wouldn't follow their gaze. There was no need for weapons here. Edwin's hands flexed open and closed, feeling the raindrops slide over his skin. This is how it would be, wits and flesh. He continued to let himself feel the water roll over his body, through his hair, under his clothes, and into his eyes. Edwin felt the moment as if the storm were drowning him.

The moment passed and he turned to Mela.

Her body ached as she reappeared in the center of the courtyard. Mela felt her pulse in every bruise, like a barrage of beating hearts throughout her body. Overwhelming at first, she let them attack her until they began to fade away. As the pain dulled, she could feel movement all around her. The knights were gathering around her and Edwin. They had come to force the issue, as even she knew this moment would have to run its course. Acacia was the only sister left alive; Mela knew that Elaine had been right. She shrugged off her regrets and gripped her staff with both hands.

This would be the finish to it all, one way or another.

Edwin watched her disappear, the column of fog running up her body in one swift motion against the falling rain. He could see it all happen step by step. It was all slower than the blonde witch's movement and yet he found Mela more impossible to move against. The young girl who used to play hide-and-seek was a predator now. He wasn't going to be able to find and catch her while he was being stalked. There was no sound of the fog returning, just the sting of Mela's pointed staff gouging his flesh. She was gone before he even reacted, before his voice found the ability to recognize the pain in his arm and announce it.

Out of instinct, thanks to his many years of combat training, he turned to face the empty air where the pain had been delivered from. She reappeared in front of him and he lunged at her. The fatherly instinct to simply reach out to his daughter and grab her was overwhelming. His mind was foggy and fighting itself; everything was just as he had ever feared. Even if she hadn't been faster than him, and even if he wasn't he too tired to be fighting anymore, she was his daughter and there was a natural order of things. Even animals didn't strike out at their children, not with death on their minds, never with anything as horrid as that running through their heads. He fell in front of her as she was just enough out of his reach to have his commitment work against him. Mela landed a kick to his face. Her bare foot caught him squarely in the cheek. It lifted his head from the ground, the sting of her attack reaching him only after it had evaporated from the air.

"Fight, old man!" Mela yelled at Edwin from somewhere behind him. Her anger caught in her throat as she heard her own words. *What did I just say?*

Edwin pushed himself up slowly from the ground, his face red-hot and still stinging from Mela's kick. He could see the poor farmer in his mind's eye. That poor bastard burning his family for his own safety. She had done that—his own daughter had driven men to destroy their loved ones in fear. He thought of Keldon. And Alain.

The flame was set inside and his body ached with it. He set himself in a defensive stance, sturdy, strong, and ready to receive attack. Mela disappeared again. He heard her appear just off to his right; there had been a pop just before the fog had brought her forth. He jabbed quickly down into her thigh. She vanished instantly only to strike at his left, where he rabbit-punched her in the ribs. She let out a gasp as his fist struck her. Mela stumbled back a bit before letting the fog take her again. She materialized out of thin air behind him and swung out with her staff, the jagged tip raking a deep furrow across his chest. She drew a heavy amount of blood and disappeared again.

Edwin's body didn't let him falter; the adrenaline was running too high. Heat continued to course its way through his body as his muscles tensed tighter with every second. Mela suddenly seemed to attack at every side at once, lashing out with both ends of her staff. Edwin's leathers fell in strips, exposing him from the waist up, his mind a fog once again, unable to keep up with his daughter's speed.

The onslaught ended as she appeared right in front of him and, with both hands gripping her staff, broke his nose with one loud crack. He let out a great roar of anguish, a sudden gush of blood running down his face. He pushed her away with what strength the pain would allow him. She flew across the cobblestones and collided with Luther's great shield. The clang of her body against the steel rang out nearly as loud as Edwin's shout.

Mela was breathing heavy, the magic draining her as if she had run all of those invisible miles' worth of jumping to and fro. Her head throbbed with the echo of Luther's shield while the rest of her body ached just as much, as if in competition with her bruised skull.

Edwin's own tiredness was wearing on him, his chest heaving for breath only as far as Mela's wounds would let it. His anxiety met with it head-on and made his body slump. Water streaked down, thicker than the crowd that surrounded them.

Luther raised his shield with what little strength remained in his arm. He lifted it just a few inches and let it fall. His face grimaced as he lifted it again, letting it descend once more onto the hard cobblestone. He tried yet again and the knight to his side lifted his foot and let it fall in unison with Luther's shield. Soon each knight followed suit and joined in Luther's reinforcement. The Brotherhood shook the ground like the thunder of an invisible lightning strike. It was time this ended and they needed Edwin to see it through.

Edwin felt the initial temptation to rally around their chorus of assent, to charge his daughter and finish the matter once and for all—

But he could clearly see now, why that had failed him so many times before. He'd been shown wisdom on many different occasions by many different teachers . . . and there was only one person who needed to see that he had indeed learned the lesson at hand.

"This . . . this won't bring her back," he said to Mela, taking in the destruction all around them.

The gathered knights looked on in confusion, not yet understanding Edwin's hesitation or his words.

Given the moment of respite, Mela lifted herself up from the water and stone. The fog rose gently up with her, softly propping her to her feet. She flexed her grip on her staff, her father's blood splattered on both sides . . . but said nothing.

Edwin looked her squarely in the eyes. Despite his fatigue, there was a certain relief, a sense of weight that had been lifted from his shoulders. The spiritual acknowledgment of a man who had arrived at some inkling of understanding about the world around him.

"I loved her, Mela. Dearly. And I love you too. I want you to know that."

There was an uproar from the crowd, but Edwin didn't care. Time had slowed to a standstill. He let his arms hang limply at his side.

Mela hesitated, not believing the words coming out of his mouth.

"But you can't continue to destroy the lives of innocent people," he said, the weariness returning to his face, the capstone to what she'd been expecting.

And with that, Edwin closed his eyes in silent resignation, awaiting the inevitable.

Mela's expression quickly hardened as she considered her father's pathetic attempt at reconciliation. *A coward to the end.* Her hands clenched as she dug her nails into her own flesh.

The waiting and the planning was all a memory now. She was here, where she knew she wanted to be, where she knew she needed to be.

She lunged forward for just a moment, and in the next breath, she was just a foot from her father, the first time she had repeated an attack.

This time, however, Edwin reached out in sudden anticipation, their connection not as far away as he had so recently feared.

Before she could bring her staff to bear, he clenched his hands around her throat and began to squeeze. Without time to really react, Mela dropped her weapon to the ground, instinctively reaching up to pry her father's arms from around her neck. Her leg struck out and caught him in the groin. Edwin didn't flinch, his mind completely set on the task at hand.

Her eyes began to well up as his hands squeezed tighter. He could feel her trying desperately to breathe. Mela's neck began to spasm, great singular throbbing bursts charging through her veins as she struggled for air. Edwin saw himself reflected in her eyes. He saw his mental struggle in his face as he desperately tried to subdue his daughter. Her nails began to loosen their grasp of his forearms. The tension they once held was weakening but remained stuck inside his flesh. There seemed to be no more blood to give, his skin growing pale as all his strength surged toward his hands.

Mela's face was flushed and matched her father's arms, but she felt the rage leaving her. She could see blinking stars growing out of his face as her thoughts began to fade. Growing as black as her vision, she could see the end now. The spasms lessened and Mela's eyes rolled back into her head. Edwin could feel the life leaving her as her whole body collapsed. He let his hands loosen and watched her drop straight to the ground.

***

"Finish it, Son!" Renton commanded.

Edwin's vision slid over to Luther's dirk on the ground.

"Slice that bitch open!" Renton screamed in a maddening rage. "Her armies are still outside our walls—we must be sure!"

Edwin turned away from the blade and looked up at his father.

"No."

"By all of the vast hells," Renton growled. "I will see a piece of her in every one of them." He pushed forward through the surrounding knights. "And if you aren't willing to do it, then your brothers will."

"No, they won't," Edwin said in defiance.

Renton shook his head, the outrage of this day seeming to never end. He pointed to Luther and the other knights. "Put an end to this madness."

Luther tensed, but in that very moment, he felt the bonds of his loyalty dissolve in their entirety.

He thought back to his brother's sacrifice, his lone voice of dissent against the Protectorate's slide into corruption and ruin, this endless politicking of a king. Given the reason of why and how their Brotherhood was formed in the first place, to check the overreach of a despot tyrant, it was just as profound.

No other knight dared to move, waiting to see what Luther would do instead. And what he did . . . was nothing.

Renton fumed at this new betrayal as he brought his massive claymore to bear. He would handle the witch himself, then the matter of this insurrection.

"You will not stand in my way again, boy!" he cried out, his blade raised high above his head. Edwin knelt, his eyes to the ground, waiting for his father's footsteps to thunder inside him. When the thunder hit its peak, Edwin rose up and squarely placed his shoulder into Renton's breastplate. The knight-lord was brought to a sudden halt, his blade dropping in shock as he fell to his back.

Renton scrambled to gather himself up and Edwin gave him the time to do so. "So that's how it's going to be?" the knight-lord said with a low chuckle, finally giving up on fighting the inevitable himself. Deep down, he knew that he could never best his son in a fight, armed or unarmed. He thought of all their wrestling matches, realizing that the lines had been forever blurred.

At that, Edwin suddenly strode forward, his legs carrying him with the same surprising speed as his daughter. Renton rose up, still ever the warrior, his fists ready to receive Edwin. There was a battle roar as both men shared in the cry of conflict, but Renton didn't have a chance to blink as Edwin reached out and grabbed his breastplate, pulled him close, and cracked his skull with the might of his own. Renton dropped to his knees unable to comprehend what was happening or to remember where he was. His son reached out and gripped the knight-lord's blade with his bare hand, bathing it in his own blood.

Edwin pulled Renton's head back by his hair, the knight-lord's eyes rolling around in their sockets as his jaw slacked and his body submitted to complete defeat. He raised his father's sword, the blade still cutting deep into his flesh. At the full height of Edwin's reach, the tip of the blade kissed Renton's bottom lip in coldness as Edwin plunged the steel downward. He felt the blade sever the inside of his father's throat until his own hand crashed into Renton's jaw. He paused then for just a moment, to watch the knight-lord's eyes widen before he grasped at the sword's grip and rammed it straight down to the hilt.

Renton's body went completely limp and rested against his own blade. On his knees, his back prodded straight by the claymore, his face looking up into the sky while the rain ran over his body and his wounds. There was a singular crash of steel as the Brotherhood signaled their approval. Edwin stepped back from the growing pool of blood and cleansing rainwater and collapsed.

CHAPTER 27

Pieces of the Whole

Everything remained still for just a moment.

Not one of those long moments where everyone contemplated their day, how all this could've possibly taken place or what would happen in the days to come. It was just a moment where relief lived for all of Riesenstadt, nothing more, nothing less.

The knight-lord was dead. He sat there on display for everyone to see, slain by his own son. The word *murder* lingered in the minds of some, along with the notion that the bastard had it coming for others. Mostly it seemed to signify the end of an era, good or bad, that it was over, and for most, all thoughts were erased by the relief . . . for just a moment.

All except for one man, who was now living in a moment he wasn't sure would ever end.

As people began to shuffle their feet, an answer to stomp out the dead quiet, Edwin let his eyes wander about. The rest of his body stayed still, in shock, worn out by everything one could imagine and more. They took in the sight of his father, a man who had confused Edwin as far back as he could remember. The lessons of being cold and calculating would stick with him until his last breath. The same coldness Renton had always aimed at his younger son, Alain, and yet Edwin had always felt warmth in his father's eyes when they looked toward him. There had been the fire of admiration when Edwin joined the Brotherhood and the fire of rage when Edwin had betrayed him. Fires that burned at the core of a man who perceived the world in endless winter.

Edwin felt no sorrow for his father or what he had done to him. The great knight-lord was slain, just as he would've wanted it. To die an old man shitting himself and not remembering the world as anything but a confusing attack of mental pictures that others would insist were memories was not an ideal way to go. Despite the insanity of it all, Edwin felt some pride at that moment. He gave his father what he wanted—a good death, a warrior's death. Slain on the field of combat.

His eyes moved from the morbid monument of his father to his brothers standing in victory, amid the gore and the carnage. They were tired from battle but they weighed themselves down further with the exhaustion of war. For too many years, they had lived in a world of trepidation and uncertainty. For so long, they had not known which day would be their last. Edwin stared out at a group of old men with taut muscles and young faces but aged beyond recognition all the same. Where and how they would rebuild, Edwin could not fathom at this very instant, but rebuild was what they needed to do.

Lastly, he let himself look upon his daughter. A heap of black on the cold stones of the courtyard. Her dress lay over her body like a funeral sheath, her dark hair over her face a death veil. Edwin knew he had felt life in her as he let her go. Life at that moment, but perhaps no further. Like her favorite doll so many years ago, she lay there in a pool of blood, surrounded by her enemy. Stared at by a man who wasn't sure if he could have done more while knowing that he could have done better. A coldness like his father's was upon him in this moment, as if the knight-lord was having the last laugh, something that gave Edwin a shiver throughout his body.

***

Mela lay there with her eyes closed, unsure as to whether she could open them or not. Stars of all colors danced about on the dark backside of her eyelids. She could hear people around her shifting this way and that. Men in their armor, clicking and creaking. Citizens rolling their toes in their boots. Children doing their little dance of impatience as they sensed everyone's tensions. She could feel the dead bodies all around, laying in the deepest quiet there ever was, the kind of quiet that brought about the sense of peace one found in a graveyard. She knew her sister was around. She could feel that Acacia was awake, probably already opening her eyes and assessing the situation. Mela stayed quiet and hidden in her own darkness and continued to listen.

***

The men of the Brotherhood took the scene before them in stride. Many were eager to help Edwin up, but were unsure how to go about it. He was victorious but sat on the ground looking defeated. The smell of the dead began to rise as the storm started to weaken. The moist bodies sat in heaps all around them and the entire Untoten army still lay in wait just outside their walls. The Gravewalkers were defeated, yet their minions continued to haunt the people of Riesenstadt.

George looked down from his perch over the gate. Thousands of Untoten lined the road to Riesenstadt, stretched out past the forest. The witches were poised, ready, and had Edwin not been able to close the gate, all would've been doomed. He couldn't stand the sight any longer and instead turned his attention to the stillness of the courtyard. There, Edwin stayed put, everyone staring at him. They wanted answers. They had questions, and they weren't even sure where else to look.

Someone finally took a step to break the silence. Luther set down his great shield and hobbled over to Edwin. His arm was slack at his side and his gait was slow and tedious. The battle had robbed him of nearly everything else, but he had kept his wits and sanity. To look upon Edwin in such a state wasn't bearable; he had to do something.

He knelt gently at Edwin's side and spoke. "Where are you, brother?"

Edwin's face twitched as his ears took in the question. *Where am I indeed?* He curled his fingers into a ball and then stretched them out again.

"I am here," Edwin answered slowly. His head turned away from his daughter and faced Luther. "I am here." Luther held out his good arm and clasped his brother's forearm. They pulled against each other and brought themselves to their feet. Edwin walked over to Mela's limp body, Luther close behind him.

Mela could hear her father approaching. She wasn't sure why everything was so still, so she kept her eyes shut and counted her breaths. Each step toward her made her breathe harder. Then she lost count and opened her eyes in defeat. Mela rolled over to face the sky and heard Edwin's footsteps quicken. He was running to her now, his pain a thing of the past. Luther followed at his own pace, unable to keep a grin from growing upon his face. He watched Edwin fall to the side of his daughter and embrace her as best he could.

The Brotherhood took a collective step toward them, but Luther waved them off. *Let them have this piece of it.* Wherever this was going, good or bad, this moment was something that had to happen one way or another and Luther wasn't about to let it be brought down out of fear.

George glanced once more over the wall to make sure the Untoten were still standing in their mindless inertia and began to make his way down into the courtyard. Where everything had gotten to in this day, he wasn't quite sure, but he was happy for a moment of peace. *Edwin, that poor bastard.* There wasn't anything in his mind that would let him think that any father should have to go through any of this. Glad to not have children of his own, George took a second to take in the sight of Renton's corpse. *A warning to all.* Between a father and his child, there was no stronger love, no stronger anger. Mercy was always given, even if there was some explaining to do afterward. *How to explain this, though?* A dead brother, a father slain by Edwin's own hands, George sat down on the stone and thought upon the tragedy before them all. *Where to go from here?*

Edwin held his daughter beneath her shoulders. The tears wouldn't come for either of them as they simply stared into one another. Both of them knew what they had done to each other, unaware of where it was taking them, but it had brought them here. There were no sounds except for the shallow breaths of the crowd around them. Everyone had taken the hint and followed Luther's example to let the moment be.

George continued to watch the scene in front of him as he heard a stirring to his side. He ignored it at first, but as it grew louder, he was forced to give it his attention. The blonde witch was struggling to raise herself from the ground, her blood-matted hair trapped beneath one of her hands. She didn't seem to be aware of her predicament as she fought to ineffectually push against the stone with bruised hands. George cocked his head to the side and raised himself up slowly. He strode softly toward the struggling witch, counting his steps as he walked. Just as he had reached a rhythm, George struck out with his steel foot and caught Acacia in the ribcage. She collapsed and tore her hair out as her arms flung forward.

Mela gasped and sat up from Edwin's arms. The crowd couldn't help but take a collected worrisome step back from the alarmed witch.

Luther stared on, as if he were studying Mela, some momentous decision he was ruminating upon.

"What is it?" Edwin asked, until he saw George throw another heavy kick into Acacia's side.

"Stay down, you murderous bitch!" George yelled, grabbing at his knife as he circled around her. The gathered knights and citizens, they all watched on in silence, no one daring to intervene. George eventually grasped his dagger and pulled it out in a fit of rage. He nearly lost his balance as his arm flung upward, out of control. The exhaustion had caught him and his wits were running away from him. He threw one more kick into her before he reached down and pulled her up by the hair. Acacia continued to cough and sputter as George put his blade to her throat.

"I'm going to put you down for good now," he growled, as each word seemed to chatter along every tooth.

As the steel touched Acacia's skin, her breathing immediately stopped and her arm struck out toward George's face. His dagger nicked the witch's skin as he pulled back from the strike. Then Acacia was suddenly on her feet and her face was blank, as if she couldn't remember where she was.

"Stand and fight or lay down and accept the blade. It doesn't really matter to me!" George spat, angry at himself for being caught off guard by his temper that continued to rise even now.

Then, Renton's body began to rattle against the sword in his throat, as George approached Acacia. With every step, it rattled harder and harder until George looked away from Acacia to the shaking corpse.

"Stop!" Mela yelled, now on her feet, Edwin standing as tall as he could behind her. Acacia's head snapped in Mela's direction, a look of anger across her face, but Renton's body slowed to an easy clatter, and then settled into silence. George made his way toward Acacia again, his intent clear for all to see.

"I said *stop*!" Mela shouted again.

"Easy, George," Luther said calmly.

At Luther's entreaty, George slowed to a halt. A moment later, he slid his dagger back into its sheath.

Mela began to walk toward them. Edwin reached out to her shoulder, but she waved him off. She could've used her abilities to teleport across the length of the courtyard, but instead, she nimbly stepped over each corpse, her eyes never leaving Acacia's. She covered the courtyard's span in a few blinks and stood a breath away from her sister's face. They stared at each other for several long moments, taking one another's measure, assessing each other's nature, intentions, and future. Mela was the first to break the trance as she looked toward George, who had finally slid his hand away from its grip on his dagger. She gave him a calming nod and turned aside from Acacia.

"Walk, sister," Mela said.

Acacia took an unsteady breath and let her foot hesitate in midair before finally stepping forward. Just as Mela had, Acacia glided gracefully as she stepped over each body and across the courtyard.

Mela followed behind her, but called out to Luther as she went. "The gate, please."

As she spoke, cries of outrage rose up around them, the people of Riesenstadt angrily gesturing toward the Untoten horde waiting just outside, that to open the gate was to spell doom for them all.

Luther raised an eyebrow, but still gave the order for the gate to rise. Without rope, it took four knights to muster up enough strength to hold the gate up high and long enough for the Gravewalkers to pass beneath. The second they were through, the knights let the gate fall down with a crash. Breathing heavier than they had all day, hands on their knees, trying not to retch.

The Untoten had not budged, nor had they taken a step toward Riesenstadt as the gate was raised. Instead, as the two sisters walked past, they fell into military formation, shuffling obediently behind.

"What if she comes back?" Luther asked aloud.

"She won't," Edwin answered back. He watched through the gate just as everyone else did, curious as to where they would go.

George ran back up the stone steps to the top of the wall and watched the two witches suddenly face each other, surrounded by their grotesque legion of pale limbs and fleshless faces. A blot on the land, an unsettling reminder of just how close they all came to utter ruin.

***

Just outside the gate, Mela circled around to face her sister. Behind them, the legion of walking corpses came to a grinding halt.

Mela paused for a moment, as her eyes burned white-hot—

And the entire horde of Untoten crumpled to the ground, the weight of their collapse rumbling the very castle walls. Amid the startled cries of the citizens within, Acacia's eyes opened wide with horror, for Mela had just destroyed the very thing that promised to keep them safe.

"You will leave, Acacia. You will not join us, no matter where our future may take us."

Already in shock, Acacia's face grew pale as she reached out and grasped Mela's shoulder. Mela reached up and slapped Acacia hard across the face. Acacia drew back her hand and let her anger show, her face red-hot as she opened her mouth to protest. "I don't understand."

"You can't," Mela answered. "You have never been able to understand; it is beyond your grasp, and for that, you need to leave."

"But, sister . . ."

"You're no sister of mine, Acacia. You're no one's sister. You are on your own," Mela said firmly. "Now be gone."

Acacia took a step backward, still unwilling to accept what she'd been told. "I won't forget this."

"Of course you won't."

Acacia closed her eyes, her eyelids pressed tightly in concentration as her mind reached out to the castle grounds. There were still corpses to be raised, to wreak havoc once more . . . but she thought better of it. The paranoia, the rage, the bloodlust, it all left her.

Instead, her sense of clarity returned, and along with it, her will to live. For she had no doubt that to engage Mela here and now would result in much more than just a scar or wounded pride.

With that, a pillar of fog rose up around her and she was gone.

Mela turned toward the castle gate, then let herself be engulfed as well.

***

No one in Riesenstadt heard what the two Gravewalkers said to each other that day, not even George's excellent hunting ears. Stories stirred about the castle walls for months and years after but never with any certainty in the voices.

For the second time that day, a moment arose among those people in the courtyard. A moment of collective thoughts all arriving to the same conclusion, the hope that they would know what to do when this moment was over and the next one had arrived.

CHAPTER 28

To Be a Farmer

The first order of business was to clear the grounds of the fallen. The once-strange tradition of burning bodies was abandoned for the now-strange tradition of burying the dead. As each loved one was collected from the battlefield, a new-found kindness was given to each. There was a tender care toward each corpse as it was carried from the cobblestones to a wagon. Each wagon trundled along at an easy pace up the roads and toward the cemetery. Like children frightened in their beds, each body was spoken to softly as it was laid to rest. The rains had stopped and allowed the sun to come out, only to raise the temperature. Everyone in Riesenstadt became reacquainted with the aroma of death as it hung in the thick air and lived in their noses and skin.

All of them, including members of the Brotherhood, found themselves avoiding the knight-lord's corpse. As if he were still alive, Renton's body oversaw all of the preparations as the bodies around him were collected. Steam rose from his body as the temperature did. A morbid geyser in the middle of the courtyard, spewing out the last remnants of their leader. The stink hardened in their nostrils stronger than that of any of the other bodies. Propped up by his own sword, Renton continued to stand as a decaying statue of the dying past, but perhaps also a marker of things to come.

The members of the Brotherhood were having a rougher time of it than most. The steam collecting in their armor cooked their skin and kept the sweat pouring from their brows. They kept the armor on as a matter of pride and so that any citizen with a question could easily find them. They stood brightly among the dull clothes of their people—like beacons, bits of light among the darkness of death. Their minds remained heavy throughout the day with thoughts of the future, where they were to go and what they were to do. Without Renton, there was a lack of focus beyond the day's work. Their war was won, but their numbers had been reduced considerably.

Edwin and Luther worked side by side in silence, keeping each other company as they each bore the heaviest of weights. Leadership was needed for the future of the Brotherhood, and most expected Edwin to take charge as Renton's heir. It had always been spoken in certainty, even when Edwin had been rotting in his cell. The assumption had always been that he would repent and find his place back in their ranks. Edwin spent a great deal of time glancing back to his father for advice he couldn't ask for.

The knight-lord's son also felt that as changes had already started—with him dispatching his own father—they needed to continue. He and Luther eased the body of a young blacksmith into a wagon, gently sliding him on his back to the very edge of the bed. Edwin watched as Luther's eyes glanced at each of the men every chance he got. But he seemed to be ignoring Renton's corpse altogether. He caught Edwin staring and offered a shallow nod. It was obvious they both had a lot on their minds and enjoyed the fact that they had work at hand, despite its emotional toll. The life of a farmer was envied by both, as a farmer always had work to do, always a distraction from anything else he had to do besides the job at hand. Most knights had no such pleasure in things. There was always the next thing to consider: duties, enemies, practice, and the training of others.

All things considered, Riesenstadt was in better shape than its people could see at the moment. Over the course of many years, it had always shown the ability to change and grow and overcome. Despite the trepidation that such abilities could bring about, there was always the pleasure in the notion that it was for the best. Despite the struggles and fears of it all going wrong, the opening minds of the people and their protectors were realizing that once again, it could be taken back and reworked. All forward movement required stumbles and backtracking.

Edwin watched a family carry their son over to the wagon he and Luther leaned against. As they approached, both men reached out and assisted them, carefully placing him in the back of the wagon's hold.

Now full, the driver looked back for approval, to which Luther and Edwin both nodded. As the wagon pulled away, Edwin suddenly had a change of mind, as he clapped Luther on the shoulder and called out to the driver. "Wait up there!"

He jogged to the side of the wagon and looked up. "Mind some company?" he asked. The driver nodded back and let Edwin climb aboard.

"A reason for ridin' with me, sire?" the driver asked.

"What's your name?" Edwin asked in return.

"Hartmut."

"Well, Hartmut, I figured it was time for a change of scenery, a change of pace. Luther there is quite the talker, you see," Edwin said.

"I don't see, sire," the driver answered in confusion. "That there Luther is probably the quietest knight there is, probably the quietest man I've ever known, to be honest."

Edwin sighed at his poor attempt at humor. Apparently Cass had not rubbed off on him as much as she had hoped.

"Yes, he is that," Edwin said. "Too quiet, don't you think?"

"No, sire," the driver answered. "Quiet is dutiful, they say, but I know that quiet is the sign of a thinking man. That there Luther thinks a lot, I reckon."

"Not a bad trait," Edwin said plainly.

"No, sire, not a bad trait at all, I should think."

"You know there isn't any need for the 'sire,' good Hartmut," Edwin added as a way of being polite.

"Any Knight Proper deserves respect," Hartmut answered. "And you'll always be a proper knight, sire."

Not wanting to travel to the cemetery just yet, Edwin bade Hartmut to take him up a ways, riding along the road in silence. More thinking was not what he had in mind when he had climbed aboard the wagon, but he seemed to be incapable of escaping it today. As they reached the outskirts of Riesenstadt, Hartmut pulled back on the reins and called the horses to a stop. Edwin held on to the bench as they came to a halt.

"Here we are, sire."

Edwin swung himself down and then offered his hand to Hartmut. "Thank you for the lift, friend."

"Oi, sire, it was no trouble."

"Then I thank you for the conversation," Edwin said with a wink.

Hartmut chuckled and, with a tug on the reins, made his way toward the distant cemetery, where a group of young men stood awaiting his arrival.

***

Luther had watched the wagon with Edwin roll away and felt a small relief. The burden of leadership always felt heavier with the knight-lord's son around, and for the time being, Luther was happy to be free of it.

As Luther looked around, he saw that some of the citizens were working on washing away the rest of the blood trapped between the cobblestones. The rains had helped spread it all over the courtyard, although the body count had done more than its fair share to increase the problem. Some were down on their hands and knees with rags, washing each individual cobblestone. Luther's splintered arm had been useless since the fight, but his good arm had helped lift more than a hundred bodies, even though the situations had usually been awkward. He knelt down beside a worker and grabbed a rag for himself.

"Milord, there's no need for that," the citizen said.

"There's no lord here," Luther replied. "And everyone can use help at some point. Let a soldier make use of his one good arm and lend you some assistance."

"My thanks," the man said, unsure of what else to say.

It felt good to have a simple and straightforward focus. Luther spent the rest of the afternoon shuffling from one cobblestone to the next, washing and buffing. By nightfall the only remaining sign of the battle was Renton's stiff, unwavering body. Nobody stepped near it, everyone believing it was Edwin's decision on how to proceed with his father's body. Alain's body, or bits thereof, had already been sent up to the cemetery.

***

Individuals began to find their way toward their nighttime destinations. Some made their way to the Pig for a quiet drink; most made their way home to spend time with what was left of their families. The knights made their way to the grand chamber. The last of the wagons made its way through the front gate.

Having returned from his walk some time ago, Edwin stood next to George as they watched the gate creak down to a close.

"Suppose it's time, then," George said aloud to the air. Edwin caught it heavily in his ear. The moment that he'd hoped would never come was closing in upon them. The grand chamber awaited, as did the rest of the Brotherhood.

***

As George and Edwin entered the grand chamber, all of the knights stood in greeting before their seats at the table. George shuffled off to his seat not far from the back, a suitable seat for that of a castle guard. He laid his hands upon the backrest and let his fingers dance a bit on the wood while he joined the rest of the men in watching Edwin's approach.

Edwin walked toward the head of the table, his eyes never leaving his father's chair, sitting there in silence. Armor creaked lightly as each brother turned, their gazes following Edwin across the hall. There was no doubt in their minds that tonight a new knight-lord would soon be leading them down a new path. The path that had started that afternoon would be advanced by tonight's vote. Edwin would call for a show of hands in favor of his leadership and each man would raise his own in confidence. He would sit at his father's place, he would lay out his plan for a new era in the Protectorate, and they would agree and continue to follow suit.

As Edwin neared his appointed seat, he rested a hand on Luther's shoulder.

"Follow me, brother," he said, his quiet voice carrying out and about the massive hall for all to hear. Without question, Luther fell in step with Edwin and followed him to the head of the table. Each man stood on opposite sides of the knight-lord's chair. Edwin cast a glance at the empty chair to his left. His father's sergeant, a ghost, just as the knight-lord was himself, along with so many other empty seats, a stark reminder of why they were gathered here at this very moment.

He took a deep, cleansing breath. "Tonight, we are gathered in mourning for our fallen brothers," Edwin began. The Brotherhood gave a unified pound on the table in agreement. "And to those of our people who fell at our brothers' sides." The Brotherhood pounded in agreement again. "We have also gathered here for a vote. A most important vote that will determine where we go from here."

The knights looked around a bit, sensing a lull in Edwin's speech.

"I know all of you expect me to take up this chair," he continued, his right hand resting upon its wooden frame. He let his gaze wander to each individual knight as each of them nodded to him in approval. Edwin then dropped his posture and grabbed the chair with both hands. He heaved and pulled the great chair toward the gigantic fireplace below their flag. He stood back to look at it one last time and then kicked it over into the flame. He turned and strode back to the head of the table and slammed his fists down into the wood.

"We will no longer sit by!" he yelled out. "We will no longer look at things the same!" He lifted his right arm and pointed up to their crest, his hand shaking. "We are pieces of the whole! We do not overpower, we do not control, and we certainly do not judge those who walk a different path!" His eyes scanned the room again. There were no nods this time, but every man stared in complete concentration, hanging on every one of Edwin's words. "Shall we and should we protect our ways? Certainly. But it is not our way to crush all of those who do not think the same. My father sought power as the head of this order and lost his way. He lost the vision of this Brotherhood. He forgot that we are above those things. He forgot that brotherhood is spread through honor and charity, not held captive by a few select individuals."

No one was moving. The men had now forgotten to even blink as they listened intently to this angry man speak his peace.

"Tonight I am calling for a vote, but it will not be a vote to take my father's place. I am calling to vote my resignation from this Brotherhood."

The men could not help it as they let out low murmurs of confusion.

"Even while I sat in my cell, you men referred to me as his heir, just as you did before my incarceration and after my release. If it were for that reason alone that I left, it would be enough. We are not a monarchy—we came about because of monarchy, and the only blood that matters is the blood we shed out on the battlefield and in the service of others, not to one man. But more than this weighs on my mind. I can call out the errors of my father's ways. I can accuse us of our follies. I cannot, however, lead you away from them. I know this in my heart, and all have suffered for it, including my own family."

He gave a glance to Luther, who stood in silence, just as the other knights did.

"Next to me is a man that has the strength you need. A man that has never faltered in his support of the Brotherhood. A brother who sees our faults and has the stamina and wisdom to bring it back to its true purpose. And a man who has lost just as much as anyone else has."

Luther didn't move, frozen in surprise. Edwin was a man he would follow anywhere, faults and all. But here he stood, at his side, declaring his leave, and pronouncing Luther's right to lead. For all of his pondering and watching, Luther wasn't sure if he was ready for this.

Then again, Edwin is probably aware of that. Maybe that's what he wants.

"So I put it to you, brothers. Will you let me take my leave and will you embrace Luther as your leader, your teacher, and your brother?"

There was no wait as each knight raised his hand and pounded the table in thunderous assent.

Luther took a moment to take in their faces, accepting the mantle that had been given to him. "It is done, then," he said.

He turned to face Edwin and embraced him as a brother one last time. "Good luck," he said as they separated.

Edwin simply nodded and began to walk toward the chamber's exit. Before he had reached the door, he heard the splintering of wood engulf the grand chamber as each knight smashed their own chairs, no longer willing to sit by, but to stand up. Wood cracked loudly, echoing all about, bouncing off of the walls.

Edwin allowed himself a wide grin, then made his way through the door and out of the grand chamber forever.

CHAPTER 29

The Witch, the Knight, and the Dearly Departed Bard

As always, the memories were still fresh in Edwin's mind as he trudged up the winding cemetery road. Meeting Evelina. The birth of their daughter. Their hopeless flight. The endless span of days and nights that he spent in his father's dungeon, revisiting those same turns of events, over and over again.

Thus, in the faint light of early morning, he saw the same furrows in the mud, the same wilted vegetation, all of it just as it was so many winters ago. He saw Evelina as well, running right beside him, her anxious smile hoping for the best, hoping they could still live together in peace.

Peace.

Edwin wondered if it would ever be possible. If the knights, even under Luther's new leadership, would forgive what the Gravewalkers had done . . . defiling their homes, raising their brothers to fight against them. It was an offense of the most treacherous sort, and Edwin couldn't honestly blame them if they chose to once again take up arms, especially knowing that their adversaries were in possession of a fortress only a day or two's march away.

Even now, as he looked down at the churned-up soil, he could see the imprints of charging stallions, his brother's frenzied pursuit of Cass up this very road, the rusty stains of the bard's blood across the mud and grass. And he despaired for a moment, wondering if all the sacrifices that were made had been worth it . . . or whether everything would just inevitably collapse into all-out warfare once again.

Yet, here he was, strolling toward his destination, wearing his traveling leathers instead of his usual suit of armor. His great broadsword had been left behind and his step was much lighter, perhaps for more reasons than just one. A gentle breeze swayed the occasional tree branches overhead and the morning mist felt cool on his skin, which still bore the bruises and cuts from his standoff at the castle.

That was, until a loud snort brought him out of his reverie. Still a good distance away from the cemetery gates, he was surprised to see a lone horse to the side of the road, pawing about with a slight limp in its step. But it wasn't just any horse.

Edwin took a step closer, but Cass's steed warned him off with another snort. The beast had indeed seen better days, scrapes and bruises along its flank, but that didn't seem to change its demeanor any. It lowered its weathered head to chew a patch of stringy grass, all the while keeping one ornery eye on Edwin.

Edwin looked around to see if someone had reclaimed the beast in Cass's stead, but he quickly dismissed the thought. Better that one would charge off a cliff and hope to be carried aloft by the wind than to think they could tame such a creature.

No, despite everything that Cass may have said, the beast was loyal through and through, even after its master's death, a worthy companion to any knight's stallion.

As if knowing that Edwin was thinking such thoughts, the horse gave a loud snuffle. It lifted its head, locking its eyes directly with his. He wanted to say something, some word of consolation for the creature, but the moment escaped him.

With a toss of its head, Cass's horse slowly trotted away.

Incredulous at what he'd just witnessed, Edwin turned to watch the horse go for a long time before turning back to the cemetery road and to the large gates looming before him.

***

The rosy-pink glow of the dawning sun washed over the cemetery gates and its grounds. Instead of being locked shut with heavy iron chains, however, the gates were now open. The headstones and grave markers, once forlorn of any remembrances or keepsakes, were now littered with flowers and small items of affection.

The biggest change in Edwin's eyes was the freshly dug burial plots . . . the graves of the knights who had fallen in the battle at Castle Riesenstadt. Edwin nodded his respect in silent affirmation, thanking them for the role they played in keeping the people of Riesenstadt safe. Thinking back to the farmer who had been forced to burn his wife atop a funeral pyre, Edwin was also grateful to see that people were returning to their customary practices of burying the dead, that things were returning to some semblance of life as it was before.

One grave in particular drew Edwin's interest, the broken shard of a rapier planted into the ground, right next to the headstone. Nearby lay a lute as well, warped and twisted by impact, its strings jutting out like a cat's whiskers. Edwin took a few moments to consider the markings on the stone, freshly inscribed . . . marking the grave as the final resting place of the bard whose sacrifice had ultimately saved them all. Without Cass's heroics, Mela would've surely been killed and Edwin held no doubts whatsoever that her vengeful sisters would've wreaked a terrible vengeance.

Edwin waited a moment more, then reached into the sack at his side. Taking out a gilded bottle, he pulled the cork out and poured a measure of wine over Cass's grave. "To your good deeds, bard. To your good deeds," he solemnly intoned.

With that, he put the cork back in and gently set it next to Cass's rapier. He stood there a few more moments, until a telltale *whoosh* suddenly erupted from behind him.

"Mela," Edwin softly called out before slowly turning around.

Mela pulled the hood of her heavy robes back and regarded her father with a subtle nod. They stood there in silence until Edwin remembered what else he'd brought in his sack. Reaching in once more, he pulled it out and approached her with the greatest care in the world.

Mela had to look twice, for she could scarcely believe what she was looking at. There, in her father's hands, was her long-lost doll. Its tattered black robes were threadbare and worn after all of the years gone by.

She hesitated for a moment but then finally took it from Edwin. She remembered the last time she had held it, all those years ago . . . and now, here she was. A beginning? An end? She couldn't be sure. There was still much work to be done, but for now, the moment itself would suffice.

Still looking at the doll, she suddenly caught movement from the corner of her eye.

Just a few paces to Edwin's rear, she watched, curious, as a pale hand reached out from behind the headstone and plucked a bottle of wine away.

Mela shook her head and try as she might, she couldn't help herself from smiling. *Perhaps a beginning after all,* she thought.

She glanced once more at her long-lost doll, then looked up at Edwin and nodded her appreciation. "Thank you."

Oblivious to what Mela had just seen, Edwin silently nodded in return, the faint traces of a smile on his face as well. The sun was rising to its full glory, sparkling in the crisp morning air, lifting the pallor from the land. The cemetery still carried its ever-present air of solemnity, but there was something else now . . . and it washed over the both of them with startling clarity. It was the promise of renewal, the possibility of a new life.

Edwin had a sudden thought, an understanding, that even though he couldn't choose when he would die, he could always choose when to live. Looking into Mela's eyes, he hoped that she felt the same as they stood there, father and daughter once more.

EPILOGUE

Seated in the shadows of a towering mausoleum, Cassandra Lethellon considered the bottle of wine before her. It was certainly worthy of consumption, of that there was no doubt. She took the cork out and gave it a sniff—until she remembered that she was no longer capable of smelling, tasting, or even breathing. Air was this strange foreign thing to her now. It was just . . . there. She still needed to make use of it to speak, but the process felt otherworldly. Faced with such dire revelations, Cass reasoned that if there was ever a time that she could've enjoyed a quality vintage like this one, it was now.

She glanced down at her chalk-white skin, her veins a faint blue from the absence of her breathing. Even her hair had changed from russet brown to silvery white. It was rather drastic, even for this bard. Then again, she was alive. Well, not really alive, but nearly the same.

Edwin's daughter had done something to her . . . cursed her? Or blessed her? She wasn't exactly sure. She just remembered awakening in the cemetery grounds, her wounds replaced by a dull ache that never seemed to go away. Thankfully, she still had her wits about her, and she wasn't beset with some unholy thirst for virgin blood. Unfortunately, not even virgins themselves seemed desirable anymore, but alas.

She also foresaw an expeditious investment into garments that would protect her from the harsh sunlight. Once a thing of joy, it now set her skin tingling, as if scores upon scores of needlepoints were pressing down upon her. Was she some crypt-thing? Some unholy experiment brought to unnatural life? Cass shrugged and looked down to the open book in her lap, considering the one thing she could still do. The previous pages already full of ink, Cass flipped toward the end of the book, where the blank pages of parchment beckoned her attention.

Dipping her quill into the inkpot by her side, Cass began to sketch line after line into the book's remaining pages, a certain mechanical efficiency about her strokes as she moved from the inkpot, then from page to page. After some time, Cass finally came to rest and considered the words before her. Satisfied, she waved the newly inked letters dry with her hand, then turned to the inside cover of the book.

"What to say, what to say . . ." Moving her head from side to side, she softly mumbled her thoughts aloud as she held the quill poised just above the bleached backboard.

"To my dear friend, Lord Codsack . . ."

No, no. That won't do. Might not appreciate the humor.

"Sir knight, if you ever doubted my theatrical prowess, well, do I have a surprise for you . . ."

Bah.

"Behold, I write this to you now from the cold clutches of the grave and the even colder clutches of my nether regions . . ."

Now this shows some real promise.

"Dedicated to the man with all the temperament and disposition of a gentle flowerpot . . ."

That might go a bit over his steel-plated head.

"Dear milord, if you just would've grabbed your pole when I'd asked you to . . ."

Ha! That joke never gets old, even when you're dead. Or undead?

Cass thought on it some more, and then . . . she had it.

Smiling, she gave the inkpot one last dab and deftly inscribed the words she was thinking of. She set the book down and looked longingly at the bottle of wine like a dog eyeing a side of mutton on his master's plate. A moment more, before she impulsively reached out and grabbed it. She reckoned that damned as she was, an even worse fate awaited her if she let such a fine vintage go to waste.

She peeked around the corner to see that Mela had already disappeared and Edwin was starting to make his way down the hill. While she had many questions for the Gravewalker, for now, she was strangely content. The possibilities were endless, and for once in her life, Cassandra Lethellon cared more about the adventure than she did the spoils. With a flash of her usual lusty grin, she grabbed her inkpot and quill and made ready to leave.

***

Edwin was nearly past the gate when something struck him in the back. Instantly regretting not bringing his blade, he wheeled around, only to find a small rock lying at his feet.

Narrowing his eyes, he looked out over the cemetery, certain that this was the work of some child or a prankster. A few moments passed, but he didn't hear the telltale signs of laughter, nor did he see a tousled head peeking out from behind a headstone. Shaking his head, he turned to leave—until he noticed that the bottle of wine that he'd left in remembrance for Cass was now missing.

He stalked toward the bard's grave, keeping his eyes peeled for anything or anyone that might suddenly dart out from behind a headstone or a mausoleum. Certain that the offender was perhaps hiding nearby, perhaps even behind Cass's grave, Edwin peered over the headstone . . . and saw a book.

Still convinced this was the work of some troublemaker, Edwin kept his gaze on the stones around him, waiting for the first signs of movement.

But nothing happened.

After some time, he finally accepted that his tormentor's interest had waned, either from boredom or from a healthy fear of what Edwin would do to them. He looked back down toward the book and reached to pick it up . . . only to draw in a sharp breath when he read what was on the cover.

Unable to reconcile what he was seeing, Edwin forced himself to say the words out loud.

"The Knight Proper," he breathed out.

Looking up from the book, he cast his eyes across the cemetery. "Cass?"

But there was nothing to see or hear.

Then Edwin opened up the book cover and there, in wildly cursive script, was a message.

Thanks for the inspiration . . .

As he read it, a sudden laugh escaped his lips. Four simple words that for Edwin, as he closed the book and looked out into the full bloom of the rising sun, told him that perhaps this story wasn't over just yet.

ACKNOWLEDGMENTS

Our steadfast and loyal beta readers, to whom we owe a tremendous debt of appreciation: Heatherlynn Pomeroy, Ryan Martinez, Josh Fresquez, Paul Greven, Keith C. Blackmore, Matt O'Reilly, and Ian Greven.

Brian Garabrant, our incredibly talented cover artist. You can find more of his work at briangarabrant.com.

Sinisa Poznanovic, our graphic designer extraordinaire.

Our friend and boon companion Rick Monge for the song lyrics featured in Chapter 6, "Not Whither, but Whether."

The Epicenter Literary Management team, starring Jarrod Murray, Allard Cantor, and Sarah Batista-Pereira.

The lawyers most proper, Nick Reder and Jennifer Levy at Behr, Abramson, and Levy, LLP.

The Inkshares team, for their incredible support and good cheer in seeing our book into production.

To our friends, our families, and everyone who picked up a copy of this book, we raise our cups to your good name.

ABOUT THE AUTHORS

Photo © 2015 Lizzy Valdivia, cameranoirphoto.com

We're Matt and Adam: one part screenwriter, one part writer.

Adam wrote the forthcoming novel *Grey Bargains*, as well as enough short stories to choke a horse (we have nothing against horses, we promise).

Matt worked on the Dungeons & Dragons–licensed video game *Neverwinter Nights 2* and also wrote the upcoming feature movie *Manhattan Undying* from Paramount Pictures, starring Luke Grimes and Sarah Roemer.

And if you're into good old-fashioned human interest stories, we first met seventeen years ago when Adam competed for a high school wrestling team that Matt coached.

Yes, our team won a league championship.

Yes, we shaved Matt's head.

No, it wasn't pretty.

If you'd like to say hello, we'd love to hear from you. You can reach us at theknightproper@gmail.com, or you can stop by Adam's fancy-pancy Facebook page at www.facebook.com/adamwritespages.

Quill

Quill is an imprint of Inkshares, a crowdfunded book publisher. We democratize publishing by having readers select the books we publish—we edit, design, print, distribute, and market any book that meets a pre-order threshold.

Interested in making a book idea come to life? Visit inkshares.com to find new book projects or to start your own.